THE REBEL

REDEMPTION RANCH

LENA HENDRIX

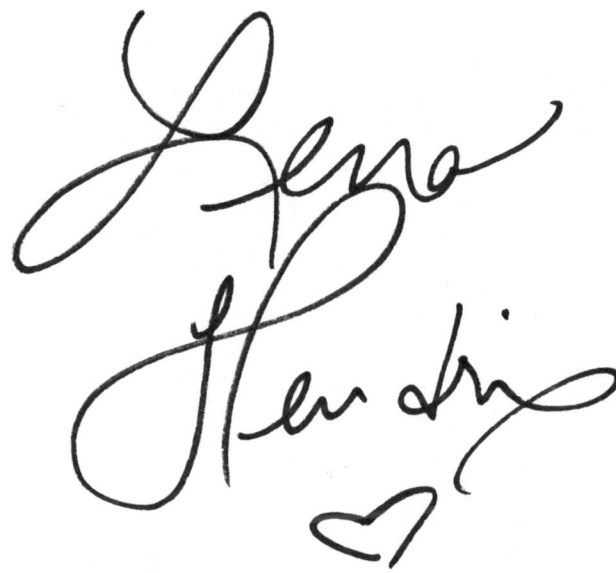

LENA HENDRIX, LLC

Copyright © 2022 by Lena Hendrix

All rights reserved.

No part of this book may be reproduced in any form or by any electronic or mechanical means, including information storage and retrieval systems, without written permission from the author, except for the use of brief quotations in a book review.

This is a work of fiction. Any names, characters, places, or incidents are products of the author's imagination and used in a fictitious manner. Any resemblance to actual people, places, or events is purely coincidental or fictional.

Copy editing by James Gallagher, Evident Ink

Proofreading by Laetitia Treseng, Little Tweaks

Cover by Sommer Stein, Perfect Pear Creative Covers

For anyone who's ever been afraid to be themselves—I see you.

LET'S CONNECT!

When you sign up for my newsletter, you'll stay up to date with new releases, book news, giveaways, and new book recommendations! I promise not to spam you and only email when I have something fun & exciting to share!

Also, When you sign up, you'll also get a FREE copy of Choosing You (a very steamy Chikalu Falls novella)!

Sign up at my website at www.lenahendrix.com

ABOUT THIS BOOK

I was supposed to lie low while my Hollywood drama blew over. **Not fall for a man with golden retriever energy who isn't afraid to take what he wants.**

When I find myself back in the odd little town of Tipp, Montana, the last person I expect to fall for is an Army vet turned cowboy.

Let alone discover he was my first kiss all those years ago. Back then, I never even knew his name.

Josh Laredo is smart, successful, and sexy as hell.

When my efforts to sneak onto his federally protected ranch don't go as planned, he covers for me.

Bit by bit he breaks down the walls I've created to protect my heart. **And there's a filthy mouth buried beneath all that good-guy bravado.**

He's determined to peel back every one of my layers and give us the second chance he thinks we deserve. All he wants is to see the real woman beneath the Hollywood smile.

Now I'm searching for answers from my past, and as more secrets are revealed, I'm learning that things aren't always what they seem in Tipp, Montana.

1

EFFIE

"GIVE IT TO ME STRAIGHT. How bad is it?"

My agent glared at me over the tabloids littered across the smooth Lucite of her office desk. "You're fucked."

She stood behind her desk and leaned toward me, then pushed off, her nails tapering to sharp points and her long, dark legs eating up the empty space in her office as she paced across the immaculate floor. Muted tones of gray and white provided a stark contrast to the riot of black curls and the pop of red on Desiree's lips.

Desiree Spice. With a name like that, she could have starred in porn, but instead she'd chosen to *run* LA rather than simply work there. She grabbed unsuspecting Hollywood heartthrobs by the balls and shaped their floundering attempts at stage acting into multimillion-dollar movie careers. It was a gift.

Desiree probably wasn't even her real name. Hell, I even had to remind myself that *Madison Colt* wasn't mine either.

"Des. Sit down." I steadied my breathing and tried to stay calm by crossing and uncrossing my legs. My feet fucking hurt in heels, but they were a required part of *the look*. My fingers absently toyed with the strands of auburn hair at my shoulders. I had recently departed from *the look*, and Desiree was still not happy about it.

"Sit down?" She looked incredulous and her voice ratcheted higher. "Sit down!" The screech in her throat had office assistants scurrying past the wall of glass that separated her office from the main floor of the agency she owned. "Did you even see the headlines?"

Desiree pointed at the stack of tabloids littering her desk.

"They're all trash," I said dismissively and dropped my hand to my lap.

Desiree stormed toward her desk and picked up one of the tabloids. "Princess Pushy." She slammed the magazine down and grabbed another. "Colt the Coquette." Slam. "Madison Colt Claws Her Way Up the Social Ladder." Slam. "Hollywood Besties Line Up to Spill the Breakup Tea."

I grunted in disgust.

Some besties.

"And the worst one! 'Madison Colt: The Hollywood Racist.'"

I shot to my feet and yanked the glossy magazine from her hand. "Racist? What the hell?"

Des folded her toned arms in front of herself and cocked a hip. "Yep. Benjamin took an internet DNA test and now claims his ancestry is six percent Scandinavian, three percent Iberian Peninsula, and one percent Cherokee—and that's why you broke up with him."

Jesus Christ.

I pinched the bridge of my nose. "There's no way anyone is going to believe that. It's utterly ridiculous."

"It doesn't matter what people think is ridiculous. It's printed. For half of the blue-haired shoppers at the local grocery store, it's *fact*."

It was my turn to pace her office. I gnawed at the dry skin around my thumb until my mother's disapproving scowl popped into my head, and I clutched my thumb in my fist instead. My free hand slipped into my pocket, my fingers quickly finding what they were looking for.

I worried the small, subtly concave object between my fingers. Without even seeing it, I could picture it perfectly—dainty and round with a little dip in the middle. One side was bumpy and white with brown flecks, while the other had a slight divot that was iridescent and smooth. When I first saw it, I thought it could be a seashell, save for the fact it was perfectly round. My fingertip ran around the uniform edge.

It used to live in a little dish on my nightstand, but the further I got from the girl I was born—Effie Pierce—the more I found I needed it. Somehow it had become the only thing to keep the razor's edge of a panic attack at bay. Running my fingers over the planes and edges was a gentle reminder to hold on to whatever pieces of the real me remained. To remember the little girl who craved her mother's love and to meet the father who left her nothing but that small token of his affection.

I took a breath. "So we spin it. The breakup was mutual. We're parting as friends. No harm, no foul." I beamed at her with my most practiced, calm smile.

My agent shot me a bland look. "In three months, you're expected to go on a PR tour with him for one of the biggest action-comedy movies to come out of the studio in nearly a decade." She held up three long fingers to make her point. "Literally *everyone* was invested in your relationship when it came out you two were bumping uglies on set."

A small laugh shot out of me. Desiree was a lot to handle, but she was smart and funny as hell sometimes.

"Okay, I admit: dating a costar was a mistake, if you could even call it dating." I smoothed my palms down the sides of my black leather skirt. "We went out to eat and slept together a few times." After the paparazzi caught Benjamin leaning into me for a kiss in a secluded Italian bistro, they'd gone wild. People had been speculating about us for months, and when it happened, reports were everywhere. Everyone assumed we were dating. I exhaled a deep breath. "It was everywhere before we could stop it. You know how that shit blows up."

"Of course I know it. It's my *job* to know it. But it's also my job right now to make sure that you're not cast as the evil seductress who's going around Hollywood breaking the hearts of their favorite heroes. The next time you decide to break up with someone, clear it with me first."

I lifted my chin in defiance. "If roles were reversed, they'd be patting him on the back and congratulating him on another notch on his bedpost."

"Men get leeway. Women do not." I knew she was right. She held up a photograph of Benjamin looking sufficiently morose, with the headline 'How Could She?' splashed below it. "Look at this face." Des pushed out her lower lip. "How *could* you?"

I rolled my eyes at his near-perfect bone structure and ripped the paper from her hands before tossing it into the tiny trash bin next to her desk. "We had nothing in common. Also, he was far more into my stylist Tomàs than he was into me."

In all honesty, Benjamin Cross was a leading man in

Hollywood, and keeping it a closely guarded secret that he liked men just as much as women wasn't the reason I had broken up with him. The real reason was because he pissed all over the back of the toilet seat and never cleaned it up.

Fucking. Gross.

"Look." Desiree sighed. "We were notified today that you've been dropped from the studio's next project."

Fury rose in my chest, and my jaw clenched. One silly breakup and the studio replaced me. "How is that possible?"

"You're an actress on the wrong side of twenty-five, not Taylor Swift. You do not come out of this breakup on top. Unless . . ." She tapped one long finger against her lower lip. "Can you sing?"

I sighed and looked at the ceiling. Even Des didn't know I actually turned thirty last month. I was smart enough to lie about my age the day I arrived in LA. "Just tell me what to do."

"The team is already taking care of it."

I paused. Desiree is known for cleaning up messes, but she's also ruthless. Unyielding. There was no guarantee that *cleaning it up* was going to be any less pleasant for me than dealing with a few shitty tabloids.

Fine. It's more than a few, but I can handle it.

A wolf's smile spread across Desiree's face.

"You're going to disappear." I cocked my head as she continued. "You're going away between now and the premiere." She moved behind me as I sank back into the plush slate chair. Her hands kneaded my shoulders as I stared ahead, soaking in what she was saying. "You're heartbroken. Healing. You need space to grieve the relationship."

"I live here. My house is on a fucking map of the stars. Where am I supposed to go?"

A wry chuckle had goose bumps prickling at my spine. "I was looking through your phone's search history when the idea came to me."

"You were looking through my phone? What the fuck, Des?"

"I had to be sure that there wasn't going to be any other bombs dropped. And you need to stop listening to so many true crime podcasts, then googling it. You're fucked in the head."

Desiree moved in front of me and leaned back against her desk. I laughed. "I'm still pissed you went through my phone."

"Please." Des swatted the air between us. "It's for your own good. Besides, it gave me the answer to all of our problems. For whatever reason, you've been searching a tiny little town in the middle of nowhere, so I figured it would be the perfect time for you to make a visit."

Oh fuck.

I tried to swallow past the gravel in my throat. "I'm not going anywhere."

She shrugged. "Nonrefundable ticket."

"And if I don't go?"

"Your contract stipulates what you can and cannot do and say. If we don't handle this, consider your career over." Desiree's voice softened as panic coursed through me. She reached out and grabbed my arm in an unusual show of tenderness. "I will not let that happen."

It wasn't often she let anyone see behind the tough-as-nails facade, but I'd been lucky enough to get a glimpse a time or two. I suspected that, deep down, she wasn't quite as battle hard as she put on.

"I booked you a flight, a rental car, and a few nights in town, but I figured we'll talk and decide where you go after that. You can travel to one of the nearby cities if the town is that bad. You'll have the company card—*nothing* with your name on it. You fly out tomorrow night."

I moved my fingertips over my eyes and pressed. "Madison Colt cannot just fly *commercial* and then prance around some Podunk town. The media will swarm twenty minutes after I land."

"I'm pretty sure there's very little 'media' in Tipp, Montana. I'll be the only one who knows where you are. You will disappear. Be someone else for a while." With a delicate flick of her wrist, the conversation was as good as over.

Be someone else for a while.

I had been someone else for most of my life. Madison Colt was miles away from the awkward teen my mother had spent years shaping and polishing. After pageants and classes and casting calls, her hard work had finally paid off. My modeling career had skyrocketed, and almost overnight our lives had changed.

I stared, silently fuming instead of digging my heels deeper and demanding a different outcome. My mother would have been pleased at my ability to maintain a modicum of composure while my insides turned to slush.

Was I really doing this? Was I really going to hide in the place I'd spent the majority of my life wondering about?

"Besides"—Desiree gestured toward me—"after that disaster with your hair, no one will even recognize you."

2

JOSH

"IF I GIVE you the signal, what are you going to do?" Malcolm asked, his soft brown eyes pinning me in place with a seriousness beyond his eight years.

I tried to hide my smile. "We haul ass."

A devious grin stretched across his face as he adjusted his crouch and inched forward. When he turned back, his finger pressed against his lips, willing me to stay quiet as we stalked our prey. I nodded.

My back ached, but I stayed down and followed the orders of my tiny commander.

Slowly we made our way around the barn, hugging the corners of the aged wood. If the passing ranch hands noticed us, they didn't pay us any mind.

Up ahead, Malcolm caught my attention as he pointed two fingers at his eyes and then up ahead at our target.

Ray is not gonna like this.

Malcolm used the series of hand signals I had taught him from my days in the Army. The kid was a quick study and could put a few of my former commanding officers to shame. I followed his orders, as I'd been trained, and we made our silent approach.

The ranch was busy, cattle rustling in and out as we prepared to move a herd to a new pasture. It was the perfect opportunity to get eyes on each cow, visually inspecting them for signs of illness or stress. But today was the first Saturday of May, one of my days with Malcolm, and it was an appointment I never missed.

Ray was hunched over a stall, wearing his signature scowl like a badge of honor. Once, when he thought no one was looking, he may have actually smiled, but it was too quick to be certain. As other workers bustled around him, Ray moved at his own pace. He'd lived, and worked, at Laurel Canyon Ranch since I was a kid, long before it became the local legend everyone called *Redemption Ranch*. He kept most people at a distance with his gruff exterior and general indifference, but I suspected he always had a soft spot for me. I figured it was because I'd come to the ranch as a child when my father had worked as a US marshal and the ranch had opened as a guarded location for federal witnesses under the government's protection.

Malcolm slithered closer, his eyes gleaming with even more mischief the nearer we got to his target. He was fighting a fit of laughter, and I narrowed my eyebrows to urge him to keep it together. We were on a mission. As we got into position behind the low wall of a horse stall, I held up my hand.

Grabbing a bundle of hay at my feet, I rustled it against the concrete ground.

Nothing.

Trying again, I swished the hay back and forth, scraping the dry bundle against the ground. Ray's head cocked to one side. Malcolm lightly tapped a finger against the horse stall. I twitched the hay again.

Clutching the broom in one hand, Ray took a jerky step forward, keeping his eyes narrowed. I steadied my breathing to keep from laughing. I moved the hay again, and Ray stepped closer.

I lifted my fingers to Malcolm.

Three.

Two.

One.

"RAH!" Malcolm jumped and screamed, making his hands into talons and scratching at the air.

Ray jumped, and his broom clattered to the floor. For a split second, I worried we had given the poor guy an actual heart attack.

"Goddamn, rat bastard, son of a bitch."

"Whoa, Ray." I gestured toward the kid, stifling my laugh. "C'mon, man. Language."

His face twisted into a scowl. "I'll start watching my mouth when you start doing your job instead of messing around." He moved slowly and mumbled as he bent to pick up the broom he'd been pushing. "Nothin' better to do than waste my time. Letting kids just run amok like a herd of wild animals . . ."

I laughed along with Malcolm's giggles and swiped my hand across his hair. "We should probably let him cool off. You ready for some grub?"

"Can we eat with the cows?"

"Sure, bud. We'll pack it up and head out."

∽

WITH HALF A PEANUT-BUTTER-AND-JELLY sandwich smeared across his cheek, Malcolm peered out over the expanse of the pasture. His big brown eyes seemed to soak in and catalog everything he saw. We sat in companionable silence, my legs outstretched and my arms propped behind me, bracing my weight.

Out of nowhere, Malcolm cocked his head at me. "Were you really a soldier?"

"Wouldn't lie to you, kid. I sure was."

His eyes moved over my face, something he did when he wanted to ask something.

"You can ask it," I said.

He paused, his little black eyebrows pinched forward. "Did you kill anyone?"

A tightness squeezed in my chest. I knew he'd get the guts to ask eventually. "I did."

Around a mouthful of potato chips, he asked, "But only bad guys though, right?"

I considered his question, unsure of how much an eight-year-old should know about right and wrong in the world and the very complicated shades of gray the military tended to operate in.

"I followed orders. Did what I was trained to do." The rote response gnawed at me. Malcolm was impressionable, and I cared about him, so I added to my answer. "I thought they were the bad guys, just like they thought I was the bad guy. It's hard to say."

Malcolm looked back out across the field, and I squinted against the bright, late-spring sunshine.

He leaned back, using his hands as a pillow as he stretched in the sun. "I know you're a good guy."

I looked at our picnic mess and stuffed the discarded baggies and wrappers into the empty cooler. For everything he'd been through, Malcolm was a great kid. The best days of my month were spent with him. The sun was high, and I knew our time was nearly up before his foster mom came to get him. I planned to ask her for some extra hours this month. Tapping his sneaker with my boot, I angled my head toward the barn.

He propped himself on his elbows as I asked, "Think you can beat me this time?"

"Can I get a head start?"

I grinned. "Not a chance."

"Hmm," he contemplated. "Then ... GO!"

Malcolm scrambled to his feet and ran with abandon through the field toward the barn. I barreled after him, ditching the cooler and growling like a monster as I made my approach. He squealed as I scooped him up and launched him over my shoulder.

His feet kicked in the air, and our laughter had the horses in the distance whipping their heads and scurrying in the opposite direction. I felt lighter than I had in days, all thanks to that kid.

∾

"HEY, BOSS, YOU HEADED OUT THERE?"

I whipped a rag playfully in Chris's direction. "Finishing up, but yeah. I'll meet you up there."

"I'll save ya a seat. Ladies' night tonight." He winked. Chris was no more than twenty-two and fresh out of school.

I laughed to myself as he walked away. Ladies' night at The Rasa in Tipp, Montana, meant all the women you grew up with, and their mothers, got dressed up and took to the dance floor. Every once in a blue moon, a passer-through spiced things up, but it had been months since someone new had caught my eye. While a dry spell wasn't the worst thing in the world, lately it felt like I was walking straight past dry spell and headfirst into a full-on drought.

After I'd finally talked myself into making an appearance at The Rasa, most of the tables were full. Al, the owner and resident bartender, lifted his tattooed arm at me in greeting and gestured toward a table in the back. As I wove through the crowd, I shook hands and exchanged back slaps. Having grown up in Tipp, I knew nearly everyone in the place.

The old jukebox in the corner was playing while the Grundy Folkerts Band was setting up. With the local band playing, the bar was sure to draw a bigger crowd tonight, as everyone around here loved the old country classics and line dancing across the battered bar floor.

My head hurt, and sore muscles from a day's work ached. The buzzing in my ears hounded me—an incessant reminder—but as I approached the table, I took a deep breath.

The happiest guy in the room.

My easy, rehearsed smile slid into place. "Who let these jackasses in here?"

"Hey, you made it!" A round of whoops and hollers mingled with handshakes as I found a seat, just as a server dropped a beer in front of me.

I caught her eye and nodded. "Thank you, ma'am."

She swatted at my shoulder and laughed, the fine lines around her eyes deepening. "Oh, Joshua Laredo. You use that devilish charm on someone your own age."

I lifted my smirk for her. "Now what's the fun in that?"

Janine blushed, and I enjoyed our playful banter, knowing it made her feel good. "You and your *fun*. That face will get you into trouble."

"God willing." I lifted my glass as she laughed and sauntered away. After my attention moved over her shoulder, I paused.

Oh. Well, she's new.

The woman's long legs covered the distance between the door and the bar with strong, confident strides. Her manicured hands smoothed over the dented and worn oak of the bar as she waited to catch Al's attention. Clearly, she didn't know how things worked around here. Most newcomers gave up after a few minutes of Al's cold shoulder, but she stood undaunted, lightly tapping her manicured finger and drilling the back of Al's skull with a hard stare.

I laughed to myself and shook my head. She was in for a rude awakening.

Easy conversation flowed around me. I was sure to throw in a laugh or a head nod, but my focus was squarely on the stunner who'd breezed into The Tabula Rasa. Long auburn hair hung in waves around her shoulders. Her casual white tank top was tucked into a pair of high-waisted jeans that seemed painted onto the swell of her hips. They ran down impossibly long legs before flaring out. Her feet poked from beneath the wide bottoms. From where I was standing, I could see her toenails were electric pink to match her fingernails. Even in casual clothes, the air about her screamed *elegant*. I scoffed at myself and took a deep pull from my beer.

A floor lamp could look elegant in The Rasa.

Still, my eyes wandered back to the woman as she continued to try in vain to get Al's attention.

"Damn." Chris bumped my arm and tipped his chin toward her. "Dibs."

I shoved him back and laughed. "Fat chance. That woman could run circles around your sorry ass."

My stomach pitched at the thought of Tipp's finest throwing themselves at her for a chance to buy her a beer. If she were into dirty cowboys and calloused hands, she'd have her pick in this town. Just then she turned to scan the crowd. Her blue eyes were electric as she huffed a frustrated breath and leaned back against the old bar.

"Well," I said, draining the last of my beer, "better go help the poor girl out."

"Attaboy," Chris teased. "Go get her, old man."

I turned in a circle to flip him off, smiling before making my way across the crowded dance floor toward the bar. He whistled loud above the crowd, and the table laughed around him.

I shook my head and set my shoulders.

Dicks.

With my eyes trained on the stranger, I watched. A local regular walked right up to the bar and signaled Al with two fingers. With a nod and a smile, Al dug two cold beers from the cooler and slid them across the bar. The woman turned back to Al and lifted her arm higher. She raised her voice to say, "Excuse me?"

Al continued to actively ignore her.

Another patron was served by the time I slowly made my way across the crowded barroom floor. I sidled up to her, then straddled the stool and rested my elbows on the old wooden top.

She spared me a lift of her eyebrow, but her eyes stayed keen on Al's back. The woman was stunning. Absolutely gorgeous. From the sharpness of her nose to her full lower lip, she was damn perfect. For half a second, I couldn't breathe. An odd familiarity bloomed under my breastbone.

Something about her tugged at me, and I couldn't quite place it.

The woman waved toward Al again.

"That won't work."

She let loose a quiet, frustrated grunt in my direction, but she barely spared me a glance.

"Can I help?"

Her eyes moved down me like a schoolteacher assessing how much mischief I could cause.

A lot.

When she leaned farther over the bar to get in Al's space, I let my eyes wander over the lush curve of her ass. Heat poured through me. My smile pulled at the corner of my mouth. "Have you tried an air horn? Maybe a flare gun?"

Her soft laugh melted the hot ball that had formed in my chest.

The beautiful woman's face softened. "I'm not even sure if that would help. He has got to be the worst bartender in the world."

"Nah. Al's all right. Just a bit wary of new faces. Here, let me help." I cleared my throat and gently tapped a rhythm on the bar top and leaned toward Al, catching his eye. I lifted my chin, and he immediately turned, the deep lines of his face curving into a smile for me.

"What'll it be, son?"

A little disgusted sound escaped the woman, and my smile widened.

"Another beer for me." I gestured toward her. "And whatever the lady likes."

"Sazerac." It rolled off her tongue, and the single word sounded like a challenge.

Al paused, and his steely eyes flicked down and up

before he gave a curt nod and turned his back to make the drinks.

After he slid my bottle toward me, I scooped it up and couldn't help the smile that spread across my face as I watched her shoot daggers from her eyes toward our town's beloved bartender.

She muttered "unbelievable" under her breath, and as she moved her hair to one side, I appreciated the long line of her neck. The urge to lean closer and take a bite was staggering.

"I see you're enjoying Tipp's warm welcome."

She looked at me again, the corner of her mouth turning up and revealing the tiniest dimple. "It could use some work."

"Next time we'll be sure to roll out the red carpet."

Her eyes flashed and her mouth dropped open.

"Don't let Al hear you," I continued. "You'll hurt his feelings."

She seemed to recover and leaned closer to prevent Al from overhearing. "I'd be shocked to learn he has any feelings at all."

"Ah," I teased. "Don't let his tough exterior fool you. He's a big baby. Like I said"—I gestured toward her with my beer—"he's wary of new faces."

A skeptical little smirk teased the corner of her lips as she held her palms up, gesturing to herself. "Ah, yes. I'm clearly up to trouble."

I cracked a smile. "The tall, mysterious stranger who rides into town."

"Hide the womenfolk."

A genuine laugh rumbled from my chest. "I'm not too worried about it." I glanced down. "You wouldn't get too far in those shoes."

The woman kicked out a foot to examine the shoes, and I couldn't help but notice how fucking tall they were. They added at least four inches to her height. Without them, she'd come up only to my shoulder, and a protective swell bloomed in my chest.

"If we're not going to be strangers, shouldn't we at least know each other's names?"

Flirting with this gorgeous woman was the most fun I'd had in months, so I only shrugged and feigned indifference. "Eh, not really."

Shock flashed across her face, flaming her cheeks, and the spark behind her eyes was the sexiest thing I'd seen in a very, very long time. I couldn't help but laugh at the flare in her temper.

I held out my hand. "Josh."

She eyed it, then slipped her hand into mine and shook it with confidence. "Effie."

Interesting. "That short for something?"

"Euphemia." Her cool blue eyes pinned me in place. "Don't call me that."

My smile widened. "It's pretty."

She lifted a slim shoulder. "It's Greek, I think. But I only go by Effie."

"Well, maybe Greek Effie. What brings you to Tipp, Montana?"

Al delivered her drink with a smile. "On the house, darlin'. Didn't realize you knew our Josh here."

She tried to argue, but before the words could come out, he was gone. She looked at me with confusion. I shrugged. "It's good to know someone."

She smiled, lighting up her whole face as it reached her eyes. "Apparently." She raised her glass in salute. "Thank you."

"My pleasure." That was the thing with Tipp. If you knew someone, you were *in*. You were one of us. So while Al still didn't know Effie, the fact that I was sitting and chatting with her was enough to earn her the credibility to get a drink.

The tug of familiarity pulled at me again. There was just *something* about that woman that I couldn't quite place.

"New in town?" I asked.

Her dimples deepened, and heat ran up my back. *Goddamn was she pretty.*

"What gave it away?" she asked. A playfulness laced in her voice, and I vowed to keep it there.

"Lucky guess." The jukebox transitioned to the live band, and the hoots and hollers from the crowd warmed my blood. This town knew how to have a good time. As the band launched into an upbeat country classic, I stood from the stool. One hand out, I asked, "Take you for a spin?"

Effie glanced from the dance floor to me and back again. "Uh . . ."

"C'mon. You can't walk in here looking this good and not let a man show you off a little."

3

EFFIE

"ONE DANCE." Even as the words left my mouth, I knew it was probably a lie. From his scuffed boots to the way his shirt strained against the muscles of his shoulders, everything about him was my type. Carefree. Charming. Dangerous. A mixture of small-town boy and wild, roguish charm. There was just something that told me if he asked for a second dance, I'd say yes.

My heels pinched my toes, but it was a familiar feeling, so I stuffed the discomfort down and concentrated on the ruggedly handsome man in front of me. God was he beautiful. His dark hair was long around his ears, curling the tiniest amount at the ends. I couldn't tell if the stubble on his cheeks was intentional or if he'd just not bothered with a shave, and I could see how easily the local girls must moon over him. His movements were slow. Languid. Even the casual way he moved across the room screamed, *Big Dick Energy*.

But it was his smile that did me in. It was all white teeth and earnest charm.

As the music pumped from the speakers, his solid arms

pulled me around the dance floor. Despite not knowing the steps, he led with confidence, his hand at my lower back, pushing and pulling me into the correct position. From the outside, it may have even looked like we knew what we were doing.

I let myself smile at him. Not the polished, demure smile that had been drilled into me since I was young, but my real, too-wide smile that rarely appeared.

He didn't have a clue.

When he'd made the comment about rolling out the red carpet, I thought maybe he knew, but the flash of recognition never came—that dawn of realization when someone discovers I am *the* Madison Colt. It wasn't there.

Maybe Des was right about my hair after all. Dyeing my typically platinum-blonde hair back to my natural auburn was an act of defiance and a night of one-too-many glasses of red wine, but it did a damn fine job hiding the fact that a celebrity was drinking watered-down cocktails and dancing with the sexiest man in the bar.

For the briefest moment, I was free of her.

As the song died down, Josh kept his strong hands planted at my lower back, our hips pressed together. We'd laughed and stood, breathing in each other's air, as the room continued to dance around us.

His hand stroked up my back as he leaned toward a table of people staring in our direction. "Come hang out for a minute."

I wanted to. More than anything I wanted to be Effie Pierce, normal girl passing through town. A thousand reasons to stay flipped through my mind. I could enjoy a night out, free of the expectations and schedules and rigidity of my life. I could be a different version of me.

Until someone recognized me.

They always did.

I smiled up at him. "I should go." I pulled away and took measured strides toward the door.

"Wait a second," he called at my back. "Can I see you again? Get your number?"

I closed my eyes as the pang of *what-ifs* shot through me. But I knew how this ended. If I left now, I'd be saving myself from the uncomfortable conversation later. "Thank you for the dance."

"Effie."

My name was liquid over gravel in his throat. I flushed with heat as he leaned over me.

Kiss me. Kiss me and I'll stay.

We stayed locked.

Waiting.

"It was a pleasure. Thank you for the dance."

THE BRIGHT MID-MAY sun blinded me as I stared up at the large wooden sign—LAUREL CANYON RANCH. On the flight to Montana, I decided if I had no choice but to be there, I'd use my time in Tipp to look into my father. On the airplane, I had done my research. Laurel Canyon Ranch was a working cattle business, but besides a meager website listing prices for things I didn't really understand, and the local farmers' market schedule, there was nothing.

No pretty pictures.

No contact information.

No social media.

It appeared that Laurel Canyon Ranch solely operated locally, and the need for a larger online presence was unnecessary. But it still didn't add up. From what I remembered and the sparse information my mother had let slip over the years, there was no way in hell my father worked on a *ranch*.

Why had my mother come here?

My stomach was in knots. It had been over twenty years since I had crossed the small creek under that sign and onto the expansive grounds of Laurel Canyon Ranch. A lifetime ago. I was so careful to read the words aloud and try to commit them to memory after my mother's clipped tone warned, *"Never speak that name again."* I never did, but I also never forgot my mother's one attempt at finding my father. When gravel sprayed from beneath her tires as we left, it had been the last time I'd seen her shed real tears.

What the hell are you doing, Eff?

I cleared my throat, and my mind, and eased the car forward. I was here. I had to know. Armed with determination and confidence, I wound the rental car up the tree-lined path toward the large lodge at the end of the road. Before I got very far, a large man stepped into the road to block my path. The car sputtered to a stop as he stood, legs wide, arm out.

I popped my head out of the window, *What the actual fuck?* painted all over my face.

"Can I help you, ma'am?"

"You can try to not get run over."

He was not amused. "Do you have an appointment?"

"I'm sorry. Who are you?"

"Security, ma'am."

Shit.

Dressed in jeans and a black T-shirt, he didn't look like security, but his size alone indicated he was probably telling the truth. I needed a new tactic if this guy was going to let me pass.

"Yes." I drew the word out, buying time and lacing sweetness into my voice. "I *do* have an appointment." If I could act against a green screen and convince millions of people that I kicked ass in an alien invasion, I could lie my ass off to *one* security guard on a power trip. It was a cattle ranch, for fuck's sake.

"Visitors and vehicles are documented at the lodge. Park around back, and the main office is just inside. Ma Brown should be in."

"I will do just that, honey." I smiled through the fact I had slipped into a gentle Southern drawl like a moron. I blinked rapidly, but his bland expression never wavered. Stepping aside, he let me pass, and a deep exhale filled the car.

As I got closer to the lodge, I realized the beauty in its high glass windows and weathered wood exterior. It was stately but blended seamlessly into the rugged terrain of the nature surrounding it. Wire fences stretched across the earth, and in the distance, men on horses rounded up cattle.

The way the flat pasture butted up against the mountain in the distance looked straight out of Yellowstone. It still chapped my ass that I had let my then-boyfriend talk me out of that role. *"You're a movie star, not a made-for-TV special."*

What a fucking idiot.

But the show could never do justice to the scene before me. The land was vast. Powerful. I stared in awe at the mountain. If you stood at the peak and screamed at the top of your lungs, I wondered how long the wind would carry it. The mountains of Northern California were impressive, but the way the flats of Montana worked in harmony with the river and the range before me was breathtaking.

It was as if you could get lost and found all at the same time.

I rolled my eyes at myself and let out a little laugh. I rounded the hood of my car and found my way into the massive lodge. Around me, wary eyes flicked in my direction, but still no flash of recognition. My steps were tentative, unsure of where to find what or who I needed.

From inside the impressive kitchen, a young man leaned into the open refrigerator.

"Excuse me? Hi."

The young man bolted upright, and his eyes went wide.

"Can you please tell me who's in charge here? Someone I can speak to," I said.

After a moment of him staring, I raised my eyebrows.

"Yes!" His voice cracked a bit as he shouted. "That would be Ma Brown. She's just down that hallway."

I smiled at him and headed down the wide hall without another word, leaving him staring behind me. As I passed each doorway, I peeked inside, searching for someone who looked like a *Ma*.

I came up short just as the hot cowboy from the bar exited a doorway. My head reared back to look at him, and my mind went blank. What the heck was he doing here?

"Effie?"

I recovered quickly enough to smile at him. "Yeah. Hi. Josh, right?"

He cocked his head. "Are you stalking me?" His playful tone had a bubble of laughter catching in my throat.

My smile widened. "That would be something. Unfortunately for us both, I am not."

"Hmm, yeah. Too bad." The deep scratch of his voice sent unexpected warmth racing through me.

"I'm actually looking for someone named *Ma Brown*. Do you work—? Can you help me?"

He crinkled his eyes. "Sure. I'm headed there now. She's this way." He gestured to the large office and shook his head in disbelief. When we reached the open door, he rapped a knuckle on the frame.

From behind a large wooden desk, an older woman hunched over stacks of paperwork. "Door's open."

"Hey, Ma. Someone's here to see you."

The woman lifted her mossy green eyes and studied me. The way her jaw ticced and she held me in her stare sent prickling up my back.

"What can I do for you, miss?"

"Um."

Blank.

Nothing.

I hadn't even rehearsed a cold opener and had no idea how to approach this woman. Her hard stare immediately told me I wasn't going to be able to charm her and pump her for information. Panic danced at the base of my neck. I needed more time. "Josh, you needed something first, right?"

Ma looked at him. She was clearly annoyed at the interruption. "What is it, son?"

He paused, rubbing his large palms together before letting out his breath. "Dennis is out. Skipped town."

The woman tossed her pen on the stack of papers with a sigh. "Damn it. Thought this time he'd stick. Can you hire an outsider to cover it?"

I looked between them, trying to decipher the code they were speaking. *Outsider?*

He dragged a hand through his hair, and I could appreciate the way his corded forearm flexed. "I can try. Seems lately everyone's short-staffed. It's possible the Devneys have some extra hands." I watched his handsome smile spread and settle into place but not quite reach his eyes. "We'll figure it out."

My eyes whipped up. "I can do it."

"Do what?" I didn't miss the light scoff in his voice.

I screwed my face up in his direction. "The job."

Amusement danced in his eyes, and he looked over my polished outfit. "You? You're looking for a job on a cattle ranch?"

I lifted my chin. "You don't think I can do it?"

Ma looked between us. "You two know each other?"

Josh laughed as he sighed. "Uh." His smile really was arresting. "We've met."

"Can you vouch for her?"

My eyes flicked between the woman and the handsome stranger I'd met only the night before.

Yes. Please say yes.

His cool gray-blue eyes held mine for a beat, and tension crackled between us.

His throat bobbed once. "I can."

Relief flooded over me, but I stood rigid. Waiting.

Her lips flattened as she openly assessed me. "Absolutely not." Ma Brown peered over the glasses perched on her nose. My ears rang, and my throat got thick as her words settled over me. Panic skittered through me.

"I'm sorry, but I . . ." My voice cracked, and I clutched the strap of my purse, knowing the iridescent talisman was tucked inside but also that I wouldn't be caught *dead* reaching for it in front of anyone.

The woman sighed gently but looked at me directly. "I know nothing about you. You walk onto my property, attempting to insert yourself on my ranch. The answer is no."

I quelled the rising panic in my belly.

This cannot be over. Think, Effie.

I aimed my calm, practiced smile directly at her. "My apologies, Mrs. Brown." She raised a skeptical eyebrow at the smooth tone of my voice. "I thought going about this in the most authentic way would work, but I was wrong. You see, I am an actor, preparing for an upcoming role." The lie rolled off my tongue, the bitter taste snagging in my mouth.

Out of the corner of my eye, Josh stared at me, unmoving.

I raised one manicured hand. "My name is Effie, but you may know me as Madison Colt."

A sudden, though not entirely surprised, smirk crossed the woman's face. Her hand clasped mine, and we shook.

"Oh, I am aware of who you are."

I pressed my tongue to the roof of my mouth and took a breath. "You knew who I was." I smiled at her again, letting genuine affection seep into it. "I admit, your poker face is better than mine. Impressive."

"My husband is a big fan. It's a shame about Benjamin Cross." She shook her head, lost in thoughts of his handsome face, no doubt. I had to actively keep my eyes from rolling toward the ceiling. "You have a very recognizable face, Ms. Colt. Despite the new hair."

I smoothed a hand over my natural color and tried to ignore her comment and the way Josh's rigid posture consumed the energy in the room.

"It suits you, by the way," she added.

"You are too kind. I was hoping that in preparation for the role I might be able to spend some time at your ranch. I am a Method actor by trade, so fully immersing myself is the only way to truly connect with my character."

Her eyes roamed over me again. "Why Tipp?"

This woman could sniff a lie from a mile away. I knew the truth—at least, as close to the truth as I was willing to admit—was my only option. "It's remote. You don't have a social media presence to worry about. Plus, as a child, my mother and I had visited the area. It left an impression."

Ma Brown assessed me as I waited. "I do not want your presence to turn this ranch into a circus."

"No, ma'am. I assure you it would be in everyone's best interest—especially mine—if we could keep this between the two of us." I glanced at Josh, whose jaw was clenched, his eyes never leaving my face. "Well, three of us, I suppose."

"Darlin', this ranch hides federally protected witnesses. I think we can handle one misplaced starlet." Ma Brown folded her arms across her chest. "And there's no better place to hide than here. Welcome to Redemption Ranch."

After a brief handshake, I turned on my heels and scurried out of her office before anyone, especially Josh, had a chance to ask more questions.

I had done it.

Sure, I'd completely blown my cover while an intensely sexy man stared at the side of my face, but I'd done it. I could use my time to see if anyone remembered my father.

I wasn't two steps toward my car when a firm but gentle grip closed over my arm. "So you came to Montana for a job?"

I pressed my lips together. "Not exactly, but here we are."

He squinted across the pasture and raised a hand to someone who called out a greeting. "Here we are." Several seconds of silence passed as I calmed my internal freak-out. He knew as well as I did that I had no idea what I was doing.

Josh pulled his wallet from his back pocket and a pen from his shirt. On the back of an old receipt, he scrawled his phone number. "The day starts at sunup." He glanced down at my leather high-heeled booties, and I followed his gaze. As he strode away, he called over his shoulder, "You're gonna need better boots."

4

JOSH

I WAS equal parts annoyed and intrigued that Effie had shown up at Redemption Ranch. I spent the better part of the evening beating myself up over not getting her number after our flirty exchanges at The Rasa. A sick part of me liked the magic and mystery of not knowing what became of her. I told myself if I ran into her again, all that would change.

Madison fucking Colt.

She looked different from how she'd appeared in the movies I'd watched, but there was no denying it was her. A strange wave of disappointment caught me off guard. Most men would relish the fact they had flirted and danced with a movie superstar, but I was more bummed that it meant nothing would ever come of the sexy banter back at the bar.

I watched the first bursts of crimson peek over the horizon as I leaned against the bed of my truck. She wouldn't have known where to go, so I opted to meet her outside of the lodge—if she bothered to show. Something about her presence gnawed at me. I suspected Ma knew more than she was letting on. It wasn't like her to so quickly agree to allow access to the ranch. Effie was fully vetted by sundown, I have no doubt.

As if I'd summoned her from my thoughts, Effie's small sedan crept through the gate. She parked the car next to mine and hopped out with a smile.

"Morning!" she chirped. Her soft denim shirt rippled in the morning breeze. The cropped pants hugged her curves and stopped short of a pair of white canvas sneakers. She watched me assess her outfit but didn't wilt under my stare.

Her arms stretched out. "Short notice. It's all I had."

I pressed my lips together. "It'll have to do, but I can't promise that outfit won't get trashed."

Her sunny smile hit me right in the chest. "I'll live."

I slapped the bed of my truck before moving toward the driver's side. "Let's get on then."

Effie hopped into the truck, and I pulled onto the main dirt road that wound around the ranch. It was hard to see much in the soft light, but I pointed out what I could on the way to the barn.

The main barn was where I spent most of my time when I wasn't checking on animals in the pastures.

"My office is in the main barn, but I rarely use it. We've got the cattle but also horses that we tend to. It's our job to make sure they're taken care of—fed, watered, healthy."

Effie's eyes stared out the window as I spoke. "We take care of any minor issues. Watch out for stress or disease. Pregnancies."

"Aren't you awfully young to be in charge around here?"

My hands tightened on the steering wheel as I kept driving. "Yeah."

We wound around the path, driving past outbuildings that I pointed out to her and past the main pasture. "Ahead is the stable and the tack room. There's a riding area for the horses."

Her eyes flicked to me. "Horses aren't really my thing." I studied her face and wondered why something akin to worry passed over it.

"We have ATVs, but most check on the herd by horseback. You won't be checking the animals. You need a trained eye to spot issues."

Relief settled in, and she relaxed against the seat. "So what's the job?"

I tipped my head toward her. "Mucking stalls. General chores. Feeding the animals." I let a wry laugh escape. "Generally all the work no one wants to do."

"Ah, so the new girl gets it."

"Pretty much."

Her practiced smile irritated me more than it should. It was so far from the one she'd given me at the bar, and I hated how plastic it looked. "Perfect. I can really get into the role if I experience it firsthand."

I glanced down at her. I hated that she was still lying to me about what brought her to Montana. I swallowed down the irritation and hoped it wouldn't show in my voice. "Speaking of hands. We need to get you a decent pair of gloves. And work clothes. There's a shop in town that can get you what you need." I fought against the protective swell that came from being in the confines of the truck with her. The smell of her skin, earthy and floral and altogether feminine, filled the cab, and I knew it was the kind of intoxicating scent that would linger long after she was gone.

There would be no getting work done this morning. She

was dressed like a socialite greeting starving children in some third-world country—casual but put together and ready for whatever photo opportunity would make her look the most sympathetic. Five minutes on the ranch and she'd be covered in dust and cow shit.

Instead, I pulled the truck over a far ridge. The slope of the mountain allowed for my favorite view of the sunrise, and I wasn't quite sure why I felt compelled to show it to her. When the truck's brakes squealed and the vehicle came to a stop, she let out a sigh.

"Come on, then." I exited the truck and waited for her at the front. The air was crisp and she shivered. I pretended to not notice how her nipples peeked through the front of her shirt. Working next to this woman for god knows how long was going to fucking kill me.

Be the man everyone wants you to be.

"I think you'll like it here." My positive, upbeat tone was my armor against the hammering against my ribs and the ringing in my ears. "It's hard work, but most people are surprised to find Montana is exactly what they'd been looking for."

Her only response was a soft *Mmm* in acknowledgment. As the sun slowly crested the hills in the distance, her soft gasp sent heat down my spine.

"Josh." The stunned awe was exactly what I was going for.

"I know. There's nothing like it."

After a few moments of silently watching the sunrise together, the chill had become noticeable, even to me, and I wanted to make sure she wasn't getting too cold. "Let's head in. You can explore the grounds if you want, but we won't start work until tomorrow. It'll give you time to get some decent gear. What do you say we call it a day, Madison?"

"Please." Her strained words cut me off. "Please don't—call me that."

Her electric-blue eyes held me, stripped me bare. I managed a rocky grunt before nodding. "Let's go."

5

EFFIE

THE MAIN STRIP of downtown could have been plucked from a movie set—equal parts Hallmark rom-com and sprawling Western saga. With the commanding mountains as the backdrop, that cozy town was humming with energy. In the daylight, I could see various storefronts advertising everything from fresh-baked pies to hardware and paint. The Tabula Rasa was even open, serving lunch from eleven to four. For the briefest moment, I wondered if the frosty welcome I'd received was due to the surly, heavily tattooed owner or if that was common in Tipp.

I tugged the small black ball cap lower on my head. Ma Brown had recognized me so easily, and the confidence I'd garnered at the bar had withered. Ready to work with Josh, I'd forgone makeup, but I still worried someone on the street could recognize me and draw unwanted attention. Ma was explicit in that I needed to fly under the radar, and that was exactly what I intended to do.

Once I found an open space, I parked my rental car and walked along the sidewalk. Testing my friendliness theory, I offered a small smile to a woman passing me and received only a terse, tight-lipped smile in return.

Well that answers that question.

Before I left, Josh had claimed that on Main Street I would find a Harding's Supply Store that sold the work clothes I would need to pull this off. I chuckled at myself.

When was the last time you bought something off the rack?

It was a new day, and if I was stuck hiding out in some rural godforsaken town, I was determined to dig as deeply as I could to get the information I wanted. If somewhere down the road I could use this experience for an acting gig, then that would be a bonus.

When I pushed open the door to Harding's, the earthy smell of dirt and gasoline hit me. Past the two cashiers, aisles and aisles of animal feed were stacked in long rows that were at least fifteen feet tall. On the right, round carousels of clothing hung limply on cheap plastic hangers.

This is a means to an end.

My hand dipped into my pocket and found my good luck charm. After a determined little nod, I moved to the racks.

Denim.

So. Much. Denim.

And something called duck cloth.

I moved from one rack to another with no idea what I needed to purchase.

"Something in particular you're looking for?" A friendly, though slightly accusatory, voice had me turning. The young woman wore a blue cotton vest with *Shanna* stitched on the front.

I wanted her help. I *needed* her help, but I also had no clue what I was looking for. "Just browsing. Thanks."

"Fine. Your sizes are going to be on the rack over there." She pointed to a rack of clothing to my left.

"Thanks." I turned, cheeks flaming.

What the hell size am I?

Ashamed to admit I didn't even know how standard clothing sizes worked, I moved to the other rack. Finally, after aimlessly flipping through canvas pants, jeans, long-sleeved shirts, vests, and a bin labeled *breathable underwear* (no, thank you), I took a step back.

Overwhelmed, I dug my phone out of my purse.

Me: *Hi. It's Effie. HELP ME.*

My phone rang immediately. *Fuck.*

I hated talking on the phone. Everyone hated talking on the phone. My finger hesitated over the button until I finally gave in.

"Where are you?" Josh was hurried and slightly breathless.

Was that his truck starting in the background?

"Hey, sorry. Yes. I'm fine. I'm standing in Harding's Supply Store. What do I need, exactly?"

He let out a deep sigh, and I swore I heard him mutter something akin to *Jesus* under his breath. "Jeans. Long-sleeved shirts. Leather work gloves. A hat. Definitely boots. Ones that will cover your ankles. Ask them for mid-rise boots. They'll know what you're asking for."

I committed the list to memory, nodding as I glanced around the store and spotted nearly everything he mentioned.

"Also," he continued after a slight clearing of his throat. "Some good underwear. Breathable."

My stomach sank to my shoes. "The bin." I stared down at the sad bin of rumpled underwear. "Really? The underwear bin?"

Josh's soft laughter spread warmth across my chest. "Yup. The bin. I imagine a woman like you doesn't have practical undergarments, and you're going to need them."

"Sir!" I laughed and enjoyed the playfulness that danced through me. "Have you been thinking about my undergarments?"

"A gentleman never tells."

I couldn't help my smile from growing wider. "Some gentleman," I teased.

"Make sure whatever you buy is practical and sturdy."

I looked around and enjoyed the fact no one was staring or could overhear my teasing. "Well that's not very sexy."

"If you're that worried about it, go across the street to the boutique, The Rebellious Rose. The owner, Johnny, is a town favorite among the ladies. But you better show up tomorrow in proper working attire."

"Yes, boss." I ended the call and basked in the glow of flirting so openly with Josh. Sure, he knew who I really was, but we both understood my time here was fleeting. There's nothing wrong with a little harmless flirting, and with him I didn't have to worry that he was some douchey playboy hoping I can give him a leg up in the industry.

I ended up with far too many clothes, a pair of heavy boots, three hats, and a pair of leather gloves in obnoxious pink camo. I smiled to myself, thinking about Josh's possible reaction when he saw such a frivolous touch. When the total was less than I would normally spend on a single outfit, I stepped out into the sunshine and inhaled a deep, satisfied breath of mountain air.

The Rebellious Rose sat across the street, and while the large sign sported an ornate floral design around a white skull that should have been out of place in such a quaint town, it appeared to fit in seamlessly. Excitement bubbled in my belly. I couldn't remember the last time I had gone shopping by myself. It was one of those things that was *handled* by someone on my team. Convenient, sure, but I'd be lying if I didn't admit that a part of me missed digging through racks and hunting down the perfect outfit.

When I pushed through the glass door, soothing smells of patchouli and ginger pulled me inside. I inhaled deeply as I took in the tables stacked with neatly folded items. A man in a black sweater was assisting a customer, never looking up as he gave her his undivided attention. The other patrons simply glanced in my direction and went back to shopping. I scanned, in awe. Along each side wall, an array of dresses hung in a way that highlighted their structure and beauty.

The Rebellious Rose was a gem hidden in a tiny Montana town.

I immediately moved toward the dresses in the back corner. Luxurious fabrics draped elegantly from the wooden hangers. There were several statement pieces I was itching to try on, but they were tucked among dresses with more traditional cuts and fabrics. Somehow the curator had managed to mix elegance and functionality for the women of Tipp.

It was masterful.

"That piece is a particular favorite of mine." The man who'd been helping the customer leaned his hip on a table and smiled at me. His lips curled in, like he knew a secret.

I laughed uncomfortably and ran a hand across the ball cap on my head, pulling it down just a bit.

"Oh, please. You don't need that. No one will bother you here."

Damn it.

I offered him a tight smile. "You have a gorgeous collection."

"Isn't it luxurious?" His friendly smile and casual attitude was arresting. I suspected he knew my identity, or at the very least had some vague recognition, but he also made no move to ask for an autograph or a selfie. Instead, he watched me carefully as I thumbed through the hangers.

"Heard we had a new face in town." A stunning blonde with piercing blue eyes approached us, and the store owner wrapped her in an embrace. When she shifted, the scoop of her shirt revealed several pale-pink scars that crept up her chest and neck.

Her eyes caught my gaze, and I immediately looked away, embarrassed to have been staring.

The store owner cleared his throat. "We were just doing introductions. I'm Johnny Porter. I own The Rebellious Rose, as you likely guessed. This is Gemma Walker. Gem, this is . . ." He trailed off, dark eyebrows raised, waiting for me to fill in the answer.

"Effie." My own name was still uncomfortable on my tongue. "Pierce. I'm Effie Pierce."

His smile widened with a soft laugh, and he nodded as if to say, *Okay, sure it is.*

Gemma reached out her hand. "It's nice to meet you. I heard you'll be working with us up at the ranch. Welcome."

At that news, Johnny slowly looked toward her with wide, knowing eyes. One silent exchange and they had left me feeling completely out of the loop.

How the hell are they communicating without speaking actual words?

His head moved toward me as he spoke. "Well, that is . . . interesting."

Trapped between them like the last, forbidden cookie

between two starving models, I sidestepped to remove myself from the conversation.

"It was nice to meet you." There was a comforting kindness in the blonde woman's eyes. "You are very welcome here. I hope I'll be seeing you."

A soft ache, like pushing on a fresh bruise, bloomed under my skin. "Thanks, you too."

"Now"—Johnny took a step closer—"let's find you something fabulous."

An hour later, my car was loaded down with bags. I hadn't thought about how I was supposed to fly my new wardrobe home, but that was a problem Desiree could figure out. In addition to my sturdy, unsexy work clothes, I'd splurged on several outfits that Johnny recommended. His taste was truly flawless. I was surprised to see, tucked into the back corner of the shop, a stunning collection of lingerie that would rival La Perla any day. I couldn't resist picking out a few pairs with delicate lace and told myself the only reason Josh's stupidly handsome face flipped through my mind was because of the bargain underwear bin.

By the time I made my way back to the rental, my arms were aching from carrying the bags from the car, but my heart was soaring. A buzz of frenetic energy shot little pings of hope through my system. Something about Tipp felt so right. Connected.

I hopped down the last step on my final trip to the car and halted when I saw Ma Brown leaning against the sedan, arms and ankles crossed. Dark sunglasses hid her expression, but I could tell she wasn't here to tell me anything good.

Her head tipped toward the last bunch of bags thrown haphazardly in the back seat. "Settling in, I see."

A little breathless, I huffed out a laugh and gestured

toward myself. "I was told my attire wasn't up to snuff. I got some work clothes and wandered around town a bit. I got a little carried away at The Rebellious Rose."

Her features softened. "Yeah, Johnny'll do that to you."

Still wary of her visit, I let my practiced smile ease its way onto my face as I squinted against the fading afternoon sun. "Something I can help you with?"

"I think it's best we go somewhere private to talk."

I nodded, but my heart sagged in my chest, falling nearly to my feet as I led her to the side entrance of the duplex.

Once inside, Ma Brown stood in the kitchen, her rigid posture unmoving.

"Can I get you something to drink?"

"There are things you don't know about Redemption Ranch. It is a very private facility. I have agreed to allow you to work, but I can't risk an outsider recognizing you and having a media circus."

Panic skittered beneath my skin. I'd spent all afternoon shopping and hadn't asked a single question about my father to anyone. I was no closer to getting answers than I was in LA. "I can lie low. I promise no one will recognize me."

Ma's lips pinched to a hard line. "They already have."

"No. That's impossible. No one knows I'm here. You've been the only one to recognize me so far." I ignored the image of Johnny's knowing assessment at the boutique.

Ma sighed. "The residents of Tipp are very discreet, but it's a risk. An out-of-towner thought they recognized you at the bar. Started asking around."

Damn it. I recalled the way dancing with Josh at the bar had drawn the attention of nearly every woman in the place. Someone must have had an inkling they recognized me from somewhere. This couldn't be over. Not yet.

I took a controlled breath and clasped my hands in front of me. "There must be something we can do. I know it's unusual, but this research is very important to me." I paused. "To the research for my role," I corrected. "I could make a sizable donation to the ranch if that would make any difference at all."

As her eyes roamed over me, I knew I had a chance. Throwing money at a problem was my favorite way to find a solution, and it hadn't failed me yet. She glanced around the small space.

"You can't stay in town. It's too big of a risk that someone would see you and draw too much attention. We need some time for information to circulate through town that you're on the ranch—one of us."

My eyes narrowed slightly. "Is this like a cult thing? Am I going to find out that you're all worshipping an intergalactic vacuum that will bring the end of days or something?"

A sharp, crisp laugh erupted from Ma Brown. "No. Definitely not. Tipp just has a different way of doing things. We take care of our own."

I shared a smile, though the concept of a town taking care of a stranger like me was as ludicrous as the space vacuum.

Ma considered for a moment. "Normally I would have a cottage at the ranch for you, but they're either occupied or under renovation."

"There isn't a Hotel Bel-Air just outside of town, is there?"

She shot me a bland look a parent might give their spoiled child, and my eyes sank to the floor. "The only person with additional space that I trust implicitly is Josh, and that won't work."

My head whipped up. "I can stay with him—if he's got the space." Desperation clung to my voice. I had no other choice. "I can use that opportunity to learn as much as I can. He'll hardly know I'm there."

She glanced at the very large pile of shopping bags and paused. "It goes against my better judgment, but my dear husband Robbie would be so disappointed if I sent you away without even giving him the chance to fawn over you."

"It would be an honor to meet him. Besides, my research should be very brief." I squeezed my hands together to keep from bouncing.

"You stay out of trouble." Ma gazed past me and out the large bay window that overlooked the historic section of downtown. "I suppose staying with Joshua is a better option than here. His house is on the outskirts of town, and there's less of a chance someone will recognize you." She paused to lift a finger. "If he agrees."

6

JOSH

MY PHONE DINGED, and I couldn't help but grin when I saw her name.

Effie: *Can I move in?*

The fuck?

I immediately hit "Dial," and my insides flopped at her exasperated sigh. "Do you have something against texting? Are you a bad speller or something?"

I laughed and continued to toe off my work boots. "Maybe I just like hearing your voice."

The sharp intake of her breath was satisfaction enough.

"So can I? Move in?"

"I think it's a little early in our relationship, but I'm listening."

"Apparently, I was recognized last night at the bar, and someone already started asking around about me. Ma is worried that if I stay somewhere in town, it'll be more likely people will figure it out."

"So you want to stay here?" I looked around my house. There was no denying I had plenty of space to accommodate her—hell, I'd done it for others on more than one occasion, but the thought of Effie and me sharing this space was all-consuming. I had a hard enough time focusing at work without my thoughts drifting to her and whether she was lost or recognized or being treated kindly. There was no way I'd be able to keep it together if we were spending our after-work hours here too.

I pinched the bridge of my nose while Effie continued to try to convince me by listing her many domestic assets, which included picking the best movies and dishing dirt on the celebrities in them.

I thought, as I did in any situation where I wasn't sure what to do, about what Dad would have done. It ached a whole lot less now to think of him, but the fact I had to imagine what his advice would be rather than have the ability to call him up and ask still shot a sharp pain between my ribs. I recalled what he would tell me any time his job would take him out of town.

It's your job to take care of them. Make me proud, son.

"Yeah." I expelled a resigned sigh.

"Yeah?" The giddiness in her voice eased the tension in my jaw. "Great! This is great. Thank you! Text me your address and I'll come right over."

She hung up before I could get in another word. I sent my address and finished peeling off my socks before leaning back against the kitchen chair. With my head tipped toward the ceiling, I closed my eyes and imagined Effie sweeping into my home like a hurricane and knocking everything off center.

Dropping my hands against my thighs with a slap, I pushed up to find fresh sheets for the spare bedroom. "Fuck."

Despite her proclamation that she'd *be right over*, it was

nearly two hours before she knocked on the front door. At least ten times I almost called her but thought better of it.

When I pulled open the front door, I was slammed with her gorgeous, bright smile, and it winded me.

Effie pushed past me into the foyer. "Thank you so much. I cannot tell you how much this means to me. I know this is unexpected but—" Effie cut herself off mid sentence as she turned in a circle. "You live here?"

I raised my eyebrows. "I do."

She quirked her head and narrowed her eyes at me. "This doesn't look like somewhere a bachelor lives. Are you sure you're not married?"

I furrowed my brow and stepped closer. "I wouldn't have danced with you the way I did if I had a wife waiting for me at home."

She swallowed thickly, and I watched the movement of her throat. Her only response was a throaty hum. I had to step away before my thoughts ran away from me and I made her uncomfortable. She was in a tight spot, and I was helping her out. Nothing more.

"I'll show you around."

Effie got the two-dollar tour as I walked her through my home. She remarked at the open concept and bright countertops. She noticed the balance between modern and rustic, and a swell of pride coursed through me.

"People in LA would lose their minds over a house like this." As Effie looked up at the thick wood beams of the vaulted ceiling in the living room, I couldn't take my eyes off her.

"It was a lot of work, but I like it." I tucked my hands into the front pocket of my jeans to keep from reaching out and twirling a strand of her auburn hair between my fingers.

"You did all this?" She didn't bother to hide the shock in her voice.

I grinned. "I had help. My brother owns a construction company, but, yeah, we built it. Start to finish."

I kept moving in the direction of the bedrooms upstairs. I gestured down the main hallway. "Down that way is my room." She was so close I could smell the fresh floral scent of her soap. I shifted my stance. "Over here is a bedroom with an en suite bathroom. You can take that one."

Effie turned and tipped her head so her eyes could meet mine. In the dim hallway, we were close enough that if I moved one finger, I could brush the back of her hand. "Josh."

I clenched it into a fist instead.

"Thank you for this."

I pressed my lips together and nodded, taking a step toward my room. Toward safety from the snares she was setting by simply existing.

"There's dinner downstairs. I waited because I wasn't sure if you'd eaten yet."

Her blue eyes went wide. "You waited for me?" You'd think I'd saved a puppy or cured some disease and not just waited to eat until she arrived.

"Thought you might be hungry." A slight blush stained her cheeks, and I flexed my hand. "It's down there when you're ready."

∽

SOMEHOW GETTING the rap as the nice guy in town also meant that you were the one people thought to call when they were in a jam. I was pretty sure it also meant you didn't walk around sporting morning wood when you had a houseguest. Even if that houseguest was irresistible and you couldn't stop thinking about the way her bottom lip was slightly puffier than the top and wonder what it might be like to bite down on it.

I adjusted myself and tucked my work shirt in before buttoning my jeans. I looked down at the bulge created by my semihard cock and quickly untucked my shirt. "Jesus Christ." I exhaled.

Last night I had made every effort to help Effie feel comfortable. She refused my offer to bring her luggage in from her car, claiming she was exhausted and would bring everything inside in the morning. Based on the rolling clatter and low grumbles, she was attempting to drag a bag up the stairs.

The soft, throaty grunts did nothing to help the ache that was taking up residence between my legs.

Sure enough, Effie had her back to me, and I could appreciate her for a moment. Her auburn hair was pulled into a loose but high ponytail. The long column of her neck led to a formfitting black T-shirt and denim work pants. Though they were a far cry from the designer outfits I had seen her in, a smile tugged at my mouth to see her wearing rugged work clothes. Up the stairs, she was gripping an enormous piece of luggage and dragging it up each step.

Grunt. Drag, thump. Grunt. Drag, thump.

I shook my head and stomped toward her. She really needed to stop making those noises. Effie startled when I came up behind her and grabbed the suitcase with one hand. I walked it to the top of the landing and set it next to the overflowing shopping bags.

"How did all this fit in an airplane?"

Effie had the sense to look sheepish. "Some of it was acquired from Johnny." When I rolled my eyes, she pointed an accusatory finger in my direction. "Something *you* suggested, I might add."

I grunted, then glanced at my watch. "Time to go."

The energizing buzz of the ranch was something I'd still not grown tired of. The air was cool and the sun was warm. We drove together in my truck, and I'd managed to keep the conversation on strictly friendly and informational subjects. I was successful in avoiding more dangerous topics like *You're so beautiful it hurts to look at you,* or *I like when you give me shit,* or *I'm learning the difference between your real smile and your fake smile.*

"What's on the agenda, boss?"

I pulled up to the main barn to park. "Basic chores while I work in the office, then I'll show you around, introduce you to some people."

Effie scanned the faces of everyone who walked by, and she rubbed her palms together before plastering on a cheery smile. "I'm ready!"

I laughed to myself. She was going to be a lot less chipper when she realized mucking cow shit from stalls was far less glamorous than she was expecting.

To her credit, when I handed her the shovel and pointed her in the direction of the stalls, the flare of her nostrils was the only flash of emotion she let slip. Rather than show how she really felt about it, she simply let her plastic smile slip into place.

I watched her as she worked and navigated the ranch. People were curious about her, but whenever she met someone new, her shoulders would bunch as if she was waiting for them to call her out. It was unlikely at Redemption. She was simply welcomed with a warm smile, which she inevitably returned with her artificial one.

Effie wore that smile often, and I wondered if it was just

habit or a kind of armor. Something to keep people at a comfortable distance.

I hated that smile. I wanted the one she'd given me at the bar—cheeks pinched, dimples deepened, every one of her straight white teeth on display. It was big and full of life and *her*. I got it once, and I was hell-bent on getting it again, but not until she learned she couldn't fake it with me. So I gave her another task. Then another. And another. By the end of the day, we'd both worked and walked the land and circled back to the barn a thousand times. Each trip she held the hopeful gleam in her eyes that I would call it a day.

Finally, as the sun was sinking lower in the sky, I handed her a broom, and she let it clank to the ground. "That's it." She planted her hands on the swell of her hips and lifted her chin. "I'm done."

I let out a breath. "About damn time. I'm fucking beat."

Her eyes widened. "Are you kid—" She grunted in frustration. "Unbelievable."

I smirked in her direction. "You're the one acting like you had something to prove. I've been waiting for you to call it for over an hour now."

Effie stomped past me, but I caught the way she was suppressing a smile. "You are the worst."

I turned but didn't move. Instead, I folded my arms over my chest. "You're the one who said this was research about actual ranch work. What did you think about your first day?"

Effie rolled her neck and kept her glare focused on me. "This is horrible." Her hand reached up to knead the predictably aching muscles at the base of her neck. "One day and I'm more sore than a week with my trainer, Sergei."

"More fun, though." She looked at me and I winked. "Better company."

She looked me up and down. "I don't know. Sergei's pretty great," she teased.

"Okay. Okay. I'll keep that in mind for tomorrow. But let's call it a night." I reached down to grab the discarded broom and tuck it away.

Effie stifled a groan behind me as she plodded toward the truck. "I vote tomorrow is spent soaking in the hot springs."

I paused to watch her hips sway as she walked to the truck, and that was when it hit me.

Effie had been to Tipp before.

7

EFFIE

ONLY MY FIRST day at Redemption Ranch and everything from my shoulders to my feet were screaming. Even my hair hurt as I fanned it out beneath the surface of the claw-foot bathtub.

If there ever was a time running your mouth got you into deeper shit, I can't name it.

Following Josh around all day was only slightly more agreeable than I was expecting. I had worked with the fittest men in Hollywood, but they didn't hold a candle to the way Josh's shoulders strained his shirt or the way his muscular thighs moved beneath his denim jeans. Muscles that were formed from hard days working the ranch. He wasn't just the lead stockman. He got in there, working beside his men without missing a beat.

The way his hair moved in the breeze and that vein pulsed in his forearm was downright distracting. Had I actually been researching for a role, Josh would be the perfect teacher—charming, informative, patient. That stunt he'd pulled at the end of the day was highly annoying, but he wasn't wrong. I had been so accustomed to stuffing down my true feelings that sometimes it was hard to give voice to what it was I really wanted or needed. The reality was people didn't want Effie Pierce. They sought polished, fierce starlet Madison Colt. That is, until they decided she was no longer what they wanted and trashed her all over the world in social media.

Irritated, I sighed and sank lower into the hot bathwater. I let the warm water soothe my aching body. Josh also didn't seem to notice my slip about the local hot springs. If he asked, I would play it off as though my knowledge of them came from Google.

Water flowed around my ears, deadening the world around me. Even the incessant hum of the critical voices in my head, namely my mother's, had calmed in a way I hadn't felt in far too long. The soothing quiet left space for my mind to wander to my absent father.

Who was he? Why had he come to Redemption Ranch? Why did everyone call it that?

I scanned every face, hoping to feel some semblance of recognition or a spark of . . . *something*.

I felt nothing.

I inhaled through my nose, allowing my lungs to expand, and I held it there. Brief, faded memories of my father's face in a photograph were all I had to go on. But I was certain my mother had met him here. They'd argued. I'd run like hell toward the tree line, and by the time she'd found me and grabbed me by the arm, we'd left so quickly it almost didn't feel real.

But it was.

I could still feel the way her hand wrapped around my upper arm as she dragged me toward the car. I had screamed that I wanted to meet him. *"Your father doesn't exist."* Tears stung the back of my eyelids at the memory.

My limbs swayed in the deep water of the tub as I pushed past the painful, buried memories and let my mind go back to the more pleasant thoughts of my very accommodating host. He definitely scored extra points for having such a luxurious soaker tub. Steam rose and curled around me.

As my breasts floated on the water, my nipples hardened at the thought of Josh moving with such capable strides. How he spoke to everyone with care and confidence.

A low groan escaped me as my hands skated over the hard peaks. It had been months since I'd been with someone, and spending the day with Josh had every nerve ending sizzling and paying attention. Heat bloomed, heavy and low in my belly. I blew out a firm but steady breath.

I relaxed more as one minute bled into the next, and then a flicker of movement caught my eye. I jerked and thrashed in surprise, and water sloshed up my nose. I swiped furiously at my eyes, smearing thick black mascara down my face as the bathroom door swung open.

"Damn it! I'm sorry. Shit." Josh's irritated voice shot electricity racing down my arms as they covered my nakedness. He pulled the door closed but left it open an inch. "I'm so sorry. I realized you didn't have fresh towels."

Still wiping the sting from my eyes, I processed what he'd said.

"I swear to god I knocked, Effie." He muttered, "Damn door. I am so sorry. I'll leave them right outside."

His obvious embarrassment and remorse caused a bubble of laughter to fizzle out of me. He really was a good guy. "Can you just bring them in? I don't want to track water all over the floor. Maybe set them on the sink?"

Silence.

I could almost hear the gears working in his head and

his jaw grinding. I hid a smile beneath my hand. The door creaked open, and I sank low beneath the thick layer of bubbles. Keeping his back to me, he took three steps inside.

"Thank you." My voice was breathier than I'd intended, and he paused, turning his head to the side but still averting his gaze.

He looked like he might apologize again. Instead, the muscle popped in his jaw, and he offered only a curt nod before exiting the bathroom. I listened intently to his heavy footfalls down the stairs.

As I finished my bath, my overworked muscles felt marginally better, but my body was humming. I wasn't ashamed or embarrassed that Josh likely saw me naked. Hell, any man over the age of sixteen had already seen my tits if they watched mainstream cinema.

No, it was the fact he saw me so relaxed, so undone, that was unnerving. It couldn't happen again.

∽

"JUST SLIP your boot here and fling yourself over the top." Marcus, the young ranch hand, smiled at me like this was the easiest thing in the world, but I swallowed thickly.

My feet were planted to the ground, lead boots sinking deeper into the earth. I felt the subtle, early signs of panic creeping up my spine, one vertebra at a time, like fingers of a skeleton walking between my shoulder blades. Higher and higher still.

My heart clunked as the beast in front of me blew steam from his nostrils.

Even he knows this is a terrible idea.

"Here, I can help you." The man stood behind me, and before I could prevent it, Marcus gripped my waist and hoisted me on top of the animal. I clutched the reins until my knuckles strained and turned white. He slipped the tips of my boots into the stirrups, unaware of the pounding between my ears.

"Mar—" I tried to squeak out his name, but my voice was rough and quiet.

In one quick movement, he was atop his horse and maneuvering closer to me. "We'll ride along that ridge and check on the cattle in the northwest pasture, then circle back." With a click of his tongue and a tap of his heel, his animal was moving him forward. Mine loped after him, and a gasp had me clutching the horn in front of me.

I squeezed my eyes shut, willing my breath to calm. I had been working on the ranch for only a week, but apparently Marcus thought it would be a great idea to throw me up on a horse. Behind my lids, I envisioned my limp body being trampled beneath angry hooves, and tears pricked at my eyes. Marcus looked over his shoulder but only smiled and continued moving forward out of the riding area and into the neighboring pasture.

"You coming?" he teased as he shifted his horse in a small circle to wait while I caught up. I could muster only a small nod as my breathing became erratic and shallow. My horse knew the routine, because without any help from me, he began trotting behind Marcus, and all I could do was hold on for dear life and hope I didn't pass out.

My lungs constricted, and I couldn't quell my rising panic.

Please don't do this here.

I adjusted in my seat and attempted to look out into the field and not focus on how much the beast underneath me must weigh. As I shifted, my boot tapped against the horse, signaling him to lurch forward. I lunged for the reins but managed to pull on only one, jerking the horse's head to the side.

The horse took off. Pissed to be lugging me around. Tight lungs stifled my scream. The horse bolted toward the tree line at the base of the buttes, galloping along the winding path and giving zero fucks about me holding on for dear life.

My overactive imagination could see my lifeless, crumpled body dumped in the middle of the forest. It would take days, weeks, for someone to find me. Thanks to the last psychological thriller I'd starred in, I knew by that time I'd be nearly bones.

Would anyone come for me at all?

As my hair whipped my face, the tears came freely. I clung to the horse and flattened my cheek against the rough hair of his mane. My stomach bottomed out, and I pressed my tongue to the roof of my mouth to brace myself. I barely registered the gruff yell behind me.

Opening my eyes, I saw a horse and rider barreling toward me. Too afraid to loosen my grip, I squeezed my thighs tighter and willed the rider to be faster.

The horse never slowed. Faster and faster he pushed toward the trees. The harsh afternoon sun was muted by the canopy, and slices of light flickered in my eyes. Behind me, hooves pounded closer. I tried to turn my head without loosening my grip.

In the edge of my view, Josh raced toward me, a hard, determined line between his brows. I couldn't focus on the thick tree trunks whipping dangerously close, so instead I focused on him. He made steady progress as his horse pounded the forest floor. When he was within earshot, his voice boomed over my racing heart.

"I got you. Hold on!"

Josh was next to me, reaching one muscled arm toward the reins that flopped wildly in the wind. My mind was frenzied as I tried to reach for him.

"No!" he boomed. "I need you to hold on."

My eyes widened at the harshness of his voice, but I did as I was told.

He reached again, his fingertips brushing the straps of leather but not gaining purchase.

"Please," I pleaded. My voice shook as I bounced like a rag doll.

"I've got you." Again Josh reached for the reins, this time—finally—clutching them in his broad palm. In one confident movement, Josh dug in his heels and pulled back smoothly on both sets of reins. As if it were nothing at all, my horse slowed and stopped with only a huff of his breath.

Josh dismounted, and I scrambled off my horse, snagging my boot in the stirrup and falling to the ground with an ungraceful thud. My breath sawed in and out of me as I crawled on the forest floor, sticks and leaves clinging to my sweating palms before Josh hauled me up by the shoulders and turned me to face him.

His palms covered the caps of my shoulders as his eyes floated over me, assessing and cataloging.

"I'm fine. I'm fine." My breath was shaky, and I don't know if I was telling him or trying to convince myself.

"Well, I'm glad you're fine, because, Jesus, I'm not." My eyes cut to his and found his cool gray-blue gaze focused on my face. "You scared the hell out of me."

I swallowed thickly, enjoying the way the expanse of his palms soothed and relaxed my rioting pulse.

My jaw clenched, steadying my scattered, swirling emotions.

Do not fall apart in front of this man.

I lifted my chin. "I'm fine," I lied again.

Marcus rode up and pulled on the reins to halt in front of us, his breath coming out in hard pants. I couldn't look him in the eye.

"I'm so sorry, boss. I don't know what happened." Marcus struggled to catch his breath. "Horse must have spooked."

"We're good here, Marcus. Go on back. I've got her."

"I'm real sorry, Effie." He sounded contrite, but I was barely holding back tears, so I only lifted my hand and listened to his horse trot way.

When Josh shifted toward me, I looked up at him. His eyes were soft and kind. He plucked the sticky strands of hair that sweat had plastered to my forehead and tucked the stray pieces behind one ear. I held my breath. Unable to move as my heart hammered against my ribs.

"It's just us." His soothing voice was a cool breeze on a humid day. Wanted. Needed. A comfort you didn't realize you missed. "Just you and me. We're alone. No one can see you."

As his words tumbled out, my resolve broke. We were alone in the forest, and emotions consumed me, racked by broken sobs.

Fear.

Relief.

Shame.

Exhaustion.

It was all just too much.

Josh murmured words of comfort, and while I had no idea what he was saying, it was balm to my frayed nerves. I rested my head against his chest, his strong, firm arms pulling me into him. His heartbeat hammered against my ear, suggesting he wasn't nearly as calm about it as he appeared.

I clutched the back of his shirt, bunching it in my fists. We stood, my breasts flush against the hard planes of his chest and stomach, his warmth seeping into me at every point of contact. I focused on the rustling of the forest floor and the twitter of birds rather than the low tug that pulled below my belly button.

Minutes. Hours. Days. A lifetime passed before my heartbeat slowed, and I realized I hadn't moved from the protective circle of Josh's arms.

I eased back, trying to lower my gaze to hide my embarrassment, and he gently tipped my chin upward. "You okay, baby girl?"

My cheeks flamed with heat, and I cleared the tightness in my throat. "Yeah," I croaked. "I don't know what happened. I—"

"Shh—" he soothed. "You don't have to talk about it."

I blew out a slow breath and fought the fresh wave of emotion that threatened to overwhelm me. "Thanks."

Josh turned and gathered the two sets of reins, clicking his tongue to get the horses' wandering attention. "It'll be a trek back, but we can walk if you're not ready to ride. Otherwise we can ride double."

The thought of getting on a horse again made my stomach pitch and roll, but the crash of adrenaline made my legs feel as though they were filled with sand. "Double."

His lips flattened and he nodded. In silence, he tethered my horse to his so it could trail behind us safely. Then he lifted me onto his saddle before settling himself behind me. The earthy, masculine scent of sweat and aftershave cut through the pine of the forest as his arms circled me to grab hold of the reins. Thank god I was facing forward so he couldn't see me close my eyes and sneak a deep inhale of his scent.

"Did you just breathe me in?"

Fuck.

His playful tone and rumbling chuckle had goose bumps erupting on my forearms, and a cold sweat prickled behind my ears. I scoffed and tried to play off the fact I most certainly *breathed him in* and was totally busted doing it.

"You wish."

Josh bent down and dragged his nose up the shell of my ear. A deep, appreciative hum rumbled from his chest against my back. "I think you smell nice too."

Without waiting for my response, Josh clicked his tongue and maneuvered his heels to set the horses on a calm walk back toward the ranch.

Josh didn't scold me for the incident with the horse or pressure me to talk about what had happened and why I had freaked out. Most of the ride was in companionable silence as I took in the forest and appreciated the way the dirt path opened up toward the rolling pastures at the far edges of the ranch. When he did talk, it was to point out an interesting bird or share how the shape of the buttes in the distance got their names from Native American tribes that had roamed these lands.

Despite his reassuring presence, the entire ride I was hyperaware of every point of contact our bodies created. The way his thick, muscular thighs pushed against the outside of mine. How safe it felt in the cocoon of his arms. The way my ass fit perfectly against the cradle of his hips.

I readjusted once, and his hand found the plush crease of my hip. The tiniest squeeze—a warning—sent sparks crackling toward my center. My stomach swooped at the contact, but he dropped his hand almost as quickly as he'd placed it there.

My mind should not have wondered if he enjoyed the closeness of our ride as much as I did. My body was humming, and he was the sole cause. I risked a glance at his handsome face over my shoulder, and he only glanced down, his signature smirk planted on his face as we made our way across the pasture toward the barn.

Josh is a good man. Protective. He clearly loved the land and the work he did on the ranch. I definitely should not have let my mind wander to thoughts like, *Would that man ask permission, or would he let instinct take over and kiss the fuck out of me?*

Because, while he may be gentle and accommodating, that cowboy also had a hidden hot streak. My gut told me the happy-go-lucky facade he put out there for the world was only a fraction of who he really was. An actor could sniff out another actor in a heartbeat. It was a skill honed over time and used to protect ourselves from each other.

In the short time we'd known each other, he'd found subtle ways to reassure me. Take care of me. Someone in my position was used to having staff and assistants to handle things, but as I rose in fame, my free will had also been strangled. I couldn't go shopping or go out to dinner with a friend or break up with someone without considering some PR angle.

What would it be like to go on a date with a man and not worry that every previous relationship would be unearthed and dissected, only to be splashed all over Page Six?

I wasn't even *me* anymore, and that hard truth was something I hated to even consider but couldn't deny. There may be a primal attraction between us, but *Madison Colt* was who everyone saw when they looked at me. That was who I put out for the world to adore. Without her, Effie Pierce would still be a tragic child beauty queen from Nowhere, USA.

Nothing could ever come of my curiosity about this small-town cowboy, so I lifted my chin and focused on the sole purpose of coming back to Tipp. My father had been here. Someone knew *something*. I believed that in my bones, and I was going to find them.

8

JOSH

THREE DAYS since I lived out my Western fantasy of saving a woman on a runaway horse, Effie still hadn't brought it up. Aside from one last *thank you* when we'd gotten back to my house, she'd also been careful to avoid me, never quite getting close enough for me to smell her heady floral perfume or count the tiny flecks of navy in her blue eyes.

Back at work, I could find odd jobs that kept her close. Watching her bend and move in work pants was an added bonus. Her head swiveled just fast enough to catch me before I could flick my eyes away.

Busted.

"Can I help you?" she teased.

I cleared my throat and moved to the large whiteboard that helped communicate each day's tasks to the hands who worked for me at the ranch. "Once these bays are prepped, we'll be taking in some of the cattle for a quick inspection and vaccines before rotating them out to the northwest pasture. Later today the vet is coming by to look at a few of the horses that have been a cause for concern."

Her eyes flicked outside the large windows to the riding ring just beyond the barn. A crease deepened in her forehead, and her lip curled in a sneer.

"You gonna mean mug that poor horse all day?"

The look she shot me was pure annoyance. "That horse is the devil. Maybe the vet should inspect its head."

"Maxine is a handful, I'll give you that. But the vet is coming by to look at two others. They've developed a cough, and I need to be sure it's not something that's going to spread."

She paused, resting her hands on the top of the broom and balancing her chin on them. "You really care for all of them, don't you?"

I considered her words. "The animals are the lifeblood of this ranch. We take care of them, and they take care of us. Even the cattle who are eventually processed for meat deserve a good life."

"Doesn't that make you sad though? Knowing they're going to die?"

I understood where she was coming from. Most people couldn't stand to be around animals they knew would eventually become food. I blew out a sigh. "I like steak and bacon. I also love animals. It's about respect. I respect their lives and the sacrifice they're making for us. I've been to other operations where the animals are penned. Stuffed in barns and treated like a commodity. I will never accept that. My hope is that the animals here are treated right—respectfully—and only ever have one bad day."

Effie's bright eyes glittered at me as her smile widened. "You're a softy, Joshua Laredo."

I liked when she teased me and used my full name. "Ah. Just don't go telling anyone."

By midafternoon, the cattle were sorted, and the vet was

busy inspecting the quarantined horses. I brushed the dust from my hands. "What do you say we call it a day? I want to show you something."

Mischief danced in her pretty eyes. "Oohhh. Playing hooky?"

I stretched my arms out wide and grinned. "Benefits of being the boss."

Effie's smile, the one from the bar I'd been trying for days to see again, started slow but spread across her face. It was a shot to the chest, knocking the wind from my lungs.

Goddamn she's pretty.

I scrawled a note on the whiteboard in red, letting my crew know I was MIA for the rest of the day and to call me if any emergencies popped up.

Excitement skittered under my skin as I walked Effie toward my truck. "We'll drive a ways and then walk the rest. It's not too far."

I held the door for her, and she shot me a knowing look over her shoulder. I dragged a hand across the stubble on my face to hide my grin. She knew damn well I was planning another peek at her ass.

Once I closed her in and rounded the hood, I settled in my seat and pulled the truck onto the dirt path. I could take the shortcut around the lodge, but as her warm, floral scent filled the cab of my truck, I opted to stretch out our little adventure.

Effie balanced her arm out the open window, feeling the wind against her palm. She rode the wave of air, her long fingers dancing. I did the same, mirroring her movements with my left hand as I navigated through the dusty roads toward our destination.

"So you really hate horses?"

She wrinkled her nose in a gesture that was a departure

from her typically poised demeanor. "Kinda? That's probably shocking for a cowboy like you."

"I'm a stockman, not a cowboy. And it's not shocking so much as intriguing." I let my interest hang in the air, hoping she'd take the bait and open up.

A few moments passed as we rounded the hills, climbing higher toward the buttes in the distance and around a copse of trees.

"My experience with horses is limited." Effie settled her hands in her lap, twisting her fingers. "But once . . . on set? I insisted on doing my own stunts for a job—this small Western action movie that never made it out of postproduction."

I nodded but stayed quiet and hoped she'd continue.

"I played this spitfire barrel racer, and while I couldn't do most of the action sequences, I *really* wanted to do some of the basic horse work. As you can imagine, I got bucked off, nearly trampled, and berated by the director in front of the entire cast and crew."

I winced. "Ouch."

"The worst of my injuries was my pride. Needless to say, it was the last time I insisted that doing my own stunts made the art of acting more authentic. Fuck that noise."

I laughed, but when my right hand found hers and I squeezed, I saw her. The *real* her that Effie tried so hard to keep hidden. Her pride had been wounded, and she'd been kicked when she was down. It was no wonder she worked so hard to protect herself from the real world.

"You could try again," I offered.

She scoffed. "Not happening. My horse days are over, if I have anything to say about it."

"Maybe." I smiled to myself. A new determination bloomed in my mind. I would find a way to help Effie see that she was capable. Brave. She could fuck up but try again.

Effie's attention returned to the landscape outside the window. "We are really out here." The cab of the truck darkened as we found our way under the forest canopy.

"I took the long way. We're actually not all that far from the main hiking trail." I parked the truck and leaned back in my seat. "It's a short walk but it's worth it."

A smile teased her lips. "If you murder me, I'm going to be pissed."

I tugged a strand of her coppery hair. "Not a chance, baby girl. Let's go."

Anticipation built as I walked Effie down a worn dirt path. We hugged the curve at the base of the butte and traveled deeper as the forest closed around us.

Effie stayed quiet, soaking in the views around her. "I'd say this is definitely murdery if it weren't so breathtaking."

From the towering mountains to the trees that opened up to small clearings, it was stunning. Remote and undisturbed. Here nature was free and wild, and we were just lucky to be a part of it.

When I led her around the final curve, she stopped. It was eerily quiet. The forest sounds hushed behind us under the protection of the trees above. Steam rose from a pool of water in front of us, despite the climbing May temperatures.

"Welcome to the best spa on the planet." I watched her face transform from curiosity and wonder to pure excitement.

"A hot spring?" Her hands came together at her chest as if in silent prayer, her eyes widening with hope.

"Sure is. Wanna dip?"

Before I could even get the words out, she was peeling

off her T-shirt. I swallowed the lump in my throat and looked away as she bent to unlace her boots.

With my back turned, she asked, "Aren't you coming?"

My heart thunked.

"Yeah. Just giving you some privacy is all."

"Well, you do know I'm wearing bargain-bin panties, so that has to count for something." My eyes floated over the sensible underwear. Designed for function and comfort, they still had my body reacting—raging—with lust. I would bet my life she didn't own a single pair of *sensible* panties before coming to Tipp. I imagined hers were tiny scraps of material. Delicate laces and silky swaths of fabric that barely covered her pussy. I imagined sliding a finger down the thin edge and twisting my hand until the lace was flush against her.

I swallowed a groan and turned.

At my back, Effie let out a gentle laugh. "Joshua Laredo. Always the gentleman."

Blood pooled, warm and thick between my thighs. I called over my shoulder. "I'm only a gentleman until the lady begs me not to be."

Steam rose between us as her heated stare locked me in place. One sculpted eyebrow twitch was her only reaction.

Damn it, I wish I could read her mind.

My hands found my belt buckle as I moved to undress. In nothing but my black boxer briefs, I adjusted my hardening cock and took a deep breath to settle the desire that was rapidly spiraling out of control. I had brought Effie here to answer my suspicions. I needed a clear head to do that.

I turned to see her standing at the edge of the pool of water, dipping a toe to test the warmth.

"It's hot, but the spring waters from upriver cool it enough to not scald you."

Effie took her first, tentative step into the water, and I captured her hand. "Careful." My voice was rougher and more intense than I'd planned. Effie licked her bottom lip and stepped deeper into the hot spring.

I followed behind her, maneuvering over the smooth stones beneath the surface until I was chest deep in hot, soothing water.

Effie tipped her head back, allowing the water to splash over her shoulders. "Oh," she moaned. "This is ridiculous."

When she closed her eyes, I used the opportunity to soak in her beauty. She'd piled her long hair on top of her head in a wild bun, and her long lashes swooped against her cheek. I traveled the long column of her neck, pausing on the heartbeat that thumped at the base. I wanted to dip my tongue into the hollow and tease her with my teeth. Everything about her was irresistible.

"How long have you worked here?" Effie never opened her eyes as she spoke.

I propped one elbow against the rocks and rested my head against my fist as I let the hot spring ease the ache from my muscles. "I've been around the ranch since I was a kid." I watched her for any semblance of recognition. She stayed quiet, her arms making slow circles in the water. "My dad worked for Ma Brown."

"Was he a stockman too?"

I grumbled in disagreement. "Redemption Ranch isn't a typical cattle ranch. Things are . . ." *Shit. How do I put this so she doesn't freak the fuck out?* "Different."

She peeked out from under one skeptical eyebrow. "How so?"

"Let's just say it isn't *just* a cattle ranch." I had my suspicions, but I needed to know. "But you already knew that, didn't you?"

At my statement, she sat up straighter, her full tits floating in the spring. I sluiced through the water, settling an arm on the rock face above her head. "Tell me you've never been to Tipp, Montana."

She looked up at me, her lush lower lip glistening from the humidity in the air. "I can't do that."

I inched one heartbeat closer. "Tell me you don't remember seeing the hot springs before."

"I can't do that either."

"Effie?"

"Yes," she breathed.

"Tell me you remember meeting a boy. Right here. That you remember crying and him telling you not to worry. Tell me you remember what he said to you."

She swallowed thickly, but as she inhaled, her breasts pressed against my chest. "I don't—I don't know."

"Then tell me you remember this." Effie inhaled as I lowered my mouth to hers, and my mind went blissfully quiet.

9

EFFIE

JOSH'S MOUTH WAS SEARING. Hot and wet. A coil tightened inside me. My kiss swallowed his guttural moan as his wide palms found me. One hand tangled in my hair, gripping it tight to keep my head at the perfect angle. The other splayed across my back as I arched into him.

My nipples pebbled under my bra despite the hot water splashing around us, and his hips drove me into the smooth rocks at my back. I was ravenous for him. My hands ran over the hard muscles at his sides and up the wide expanse of his back. His hard length pushed against my stomach, and my pussy clenched at the thought of him stretching me open.

God I want this man.

His stubble scratched at my cheeks. The deliciously abrasive rasp tickled as he moved his way down my neck to lick and suck and bite.

He fisted my hair tighter as his other hand reached lower into the hot spring. The way he toyed with the waistband of my underwear made the fact that they were granny panties completely irrelevant. His thick finger inched lower, pulling at the elastic and caressing the smooth skin of my inner thigh.

A whimper escaped me.

"Do you like to be teased, Effie?"

I could manage only a soft moan as he continued to dance his fingers over the outside of my underwear. Teasing. Taunting me. My hips moved forward, but he refused to give me the pressure my body craved.

"Tell me," he demanded. "Tell me if you're the kind of girl who likes to have sex or the kind that likes to fuck dirty."

Those deliciously filthy words had me practically crawling up his hard body. My skin was on fire. I wanted him—I wanted every hard inch of him pressed against me.

Josh's hand found my face. His hand cupped my chin and neck, holding me in place so I was forced to look at him.

My mouth hung open. My body, a wire pulled taut. His kind face transformed to a devilish, knowing grin. "You like to fuck dirty, don't you, baby girl?"

"Yes, sir."

I don't know where it even came from. Some deep, needy part of me spewed the words *yes, sir*, and it. Was. Hot.

I stroked the ridge of his cock through his boxer briefs, and he pulsed in my hand.

In the safety of the spring, Josh transformed from happy-go-lucky boy next door to a feral man on the edge of his desire. Somehow I had tapped into an unknown part of myself that *liked* how dirty and demanding and vocal he was. No one had ever treated me with such wanton desire. It was exhilarating.

And frightening.

I *had* been here before. In Tipp. At this exact hot spring.

Clarity bloomed at the edges of my mind, and I couldn't

fight it. Josh's words, just before his mouth consumed me, rang in my ears.

Tell me you remember this.

I had been too consumed by his body and his mouth to fully register the words. As Josh reached back to grip my ass and wrap my legs around his trim waist, my hands found his shoulders.

"Hey," I breathed.

He slowed his assault to look at me. "What is it, baby? Tell me what you need."

I swallowed past the tightening in my throat. "I need a minute." My breaths came out in desperate pants.

The muscles in his jaw worked as he closed his eyes and lowered his forehead to mine. "Of course." I could tell it took effort, but he settled me back on my feet.

Josh dragged a hand through his mussed hair. "I'm sorry. I got—I shouldn't have—fuck."

I moved toward him, pushing an errant strand of hair from his forehead and forcing him to meet my eyes. "I wanted this. I *still* want this. I just need . . ." *What the hell do I need? Answers? Clarity? A cold shower so I can think straight?* "A minute."

Josh moved to the opposite side of the hot spring. He adjusted himself, and I swallowed a groan at the intensely masculine gesture. I wiped warm water across my face and neck in hopes it would clear my head.

I closed my eyes before I spoke again. "It was you? All those years ago, you were the boy I ran into here?"

"'Fraid so."

I risked a peek at him, and he looked as bemused by it as I was. A hand covered my mouth as my mind raced, dissecting the impossibility of it all. "When you mentioned the hot springs, I kind of knew. The eyes. The hair. All together I knew you had to be the girl I remembered."

Embarrassment flamed my cheeks. I had never told anyone, especially my mother, about kissing the cute boy by the hot spring. It was a secret I held closely and remembered fondly.

"It was my first kiss. But it was definitely a lot more innocent than *that*," I mused.

A proud, cocky smirk crossed his gorgeous face. "It was my first kiss too. You were just so pretty and so sad. I wanted to make you feel better."

Heaviness settled over my shoulders. Revisiting old memories was painful, and being in the exact spot where they had happened made it a thousand times worse.

"Will you tell me about it?" Kindness crossed his face, but I wasn't ready. Opening myself up to him would mean that he had access to the parts of me I'd learned to keep hidden. He could poke and prod at the lonely little girl who had changed everything about herself to appease her mother and had been rewarded for it.

But Josh deserved more than the shell of the person I learned to be. He was kind and good. I offered the small part I could. "My mother brought me here looking for my father." I shrugged a heavy shoulder. "It didn't work out."

He nodded slowly, knowing full well there was a hell of a lot more to the story, but he didn't push. His patience only made me want to spill *everything*.

"I was so excited to finally meet him, but something happened. She got into a fight with him and told me we were leaving. I ran. When I met you, I was sad and angry and confused. You were so kind and made me laugh. When you kissed me, I wanted to run away with you. But I knew she'd come looking for me."

"You were afraid of her."

I huffed a humorless laugh. "I still am, to be honest." I shivered despite the heat of the water lapping at my shoulders.

"You're cold." A furrow deepened at Josh's brow. "We should go."

Without waiting for my answer, he hopped out of the hot spring and walked toward our pile of clothing. Water ran in rivulets down his back and over the curve of his ass, and I tamped down the disappointment that I'd stopped what had started between us.

"We'll be mostly dry by the time we walk back, and I have a blanket in the truck." I studied him but couldn't find any traces of annoyance or disappointment in the passing of our heated moment. Affable, kind Josh was securely in place.

"Thanks." I grabbed my clothes and hugged them tightly to my body as I slipped my boots on.

He was right. By the time we made it back to his truck, everything but the ends of my hair was dry. I slipped back into my clothes and ignored the pang of disappointment that he hadn't touched me again as I climbed into the truck. I kept my focus on the passing scenery during our trip back toward the ranch. He was right—the short drive was much closer than the long way he'd taken out there, and in a matter of minutes we were surrounded by the bustle of the ranch.

He pulled next to my car and stopped. "I need to check in on the vet, so I will see you tonight."

"Oh, sounds good." I infused my voice with positivity despite the rock that settled in my stomach. "See you tonight." I climbed out of Josh's truck and had started to walk toward my car before I paused and turned.

"Hey, Josh?" I called. He stilled and lifted his chin. "What's different about this place? What did your father do here?"

He looked around as if to see if anyone was within earshot. A zing of awareness ran down my back as my ears pricked.

"My father was a US marshal protecting people in witness protection."

10

EFFIE

FOR THE THIRD night in a row, I lay awake, staring at the white ceiling of Josh's spare bedroom. My hands were clasped at my chest as one finger tapped out an erratic beat. My thoughts raced, and I tried to make sense of it all.

What if my father was also a US marshal protecting people in witness protection?

The pieces started clicking into place. The overzealous guards at the front entrance. Ma Brown being hyperprotective of the people she allowed to stay here. The reference to hiring *outsiders*. If Josh was telling the truth, then Laurel Canyon Ranch truly was a front for witness protection.

I needed answers.

My mother never spoke of my father, and I damn well couldn't ask her if I wanted clear information. Mentioning him at all was enough to send her into a tailspin of rants and blame and tears. In the end, it would circle back to my many shortcomings, and I'd leave the conversation drained.

The faint glow of the alarm clock stared back at me. Four a.m. Flipping off my bedsheet, I padded out of the bedroom. I tiptoed down the stairs, and as I moved past the chair in the living room, I pulled a quilt off the back of the chair and draped it over my shoulders. Around one corner was an office.

An office with a laptop.

I listened quietly to the sounds of a slumbering house. The whoosh of the overhead fan and the rhythmic tick of a clock were the only sounds filling the darkness as I silently made my way to the office.

Slipping behind Josh's desk, I smoothed my hands over the polished wood top. Even his office exuded masculine confidence—leather and soap. Not a paper clip was out of place. His desk was sparse, but a calendar had reminders like *Ray's birthday* and *Ma and Robbie's anniversary* scrawled in his neat, blocky handwriting. I smiled to myself as I ran a finger over the all-caps writing. He was considerate enough to write down dates that were important to the people in his life. No one in LA had recalled my birthday in years.

Opening the laptop, I shook my head at the fact it wasn't even password protected. I had gotten my hopes up that I might be able to guess it correctly.

JoshHeartsCows

Cattle4Life

RopinStud

I bit back a laugh when I opened the internet browser, and immediately my face flooded the screen. I was posing in a siren-red body-con dress with a matching crimson lip. I looked powerful. Fierce. Like someone else.

Josh Laredo had googled me.

A giddy little zip of excitement danced over me at the thought of Josh being curious enough to type my name into the search bar. Another tab revealed he had tried to search

Effie Pierce and come up with nothing. Not that he would. That person barely existed anymore.

"Find something you like, Columbo?"

My eyes whipped to the doorway where Josh stood, his forearm propped above his head and looking sexier than any man had a right to. As it filled the office space, the deep husk of his voice made my limbs feel heavy. I looked away quickly but not before I got an eyeful of the smattering of hair that trailed below his belly button and dipped into the waistband of his gray sweatpants.

Gray. Freaking. Sweatpants.

I barely stifled a groan. Instead, I cooled my gaze and opened a new tab to begin my search. "You really should have a password for this thing."

"Don't need one. I've got nothing to hide."

I flipped the laptop around, revealing the search of Madison Colt.

He suppressed a smile and shrugged. "Wasn't me."

I stared blankly.

"Fine," he said. "I was just making sure you weren't going to kill me in my sleep."

I playfully rolled my eyes and continued typing. "Find anything interesting?" My heart pounded as I waited for his response.

He shook his head. "Nothing your PR company doesn't want found. I find the girl who sneaks around and snoops on people's laptops much more interesting."

"I'm looking for . . . anything. The reason why my father was here. I wasn't snooping." I held up three fingers. "Girl Scouts honor."

Josh tucked his tongue into his cheek to barely hide his smile. Without another word, he turned his back and walked away. Only moments later, he returned and set down a mug of coffee.

"What's this?"

"I can hear your grumbling from the kitchen. I thought coffee might help."

I stared at his back as he sauntered out of the office without another word, and I smiled into the cup as I took a sip and dove headfirst into my search.

My initial searches included general information about Tipp and its residents. From the simple searches, it was clear the town had been established through hard work, cattle ranches, and cowboys. It was a pass-through town, a stop on the map before travelers headed toward the more populated cities. I tried searching my mother's name. I thought maybe even Dorthea Brown might ping something that would provide a nugget of information.

By 6:00 a.m. the sun was peeking through the slats of the office shutters, and weary exhaustion was settling in. In order to keep up the facade, I still had a full day of ranch work ahead of me, and I stifled a low groan. Clearly, I was not built for manual labor. My tired eyes burned from the harsh light of the laptop, and I pressed my thumbs into them. It did nothing to help the bleary, dry ache.

I stared back at the laptop in disgust.

Nothing.

I had found nothing that helped me identify who my father was or how he was connected to Redemption Ranch.

Frustrated and pissy, I huffed my way toward the kitchen. I eyed the coffee maker and wished I had time for one more cup. As I dragged my hand through the rat's nest of my hair, Josh loped down the stairs and beamed at me.

I scowled.

Even his footsteps were happy.

"Good morning, sunshine!"

I stifled a yawn and swatted in his direction.

"I take it the sleuthing did not go as planned." Josh sat at the table, and I did my best to ignore how my body reacted to him. His fingers moved quickly as he laced his boots, and I could feel the heat crawl up my neck to my cheeks.

I pushed down my feelings. I'd worked hungry, exhausted, and in far worse shape than this. I could rally. "I'm just tired," I lied. "I'll be ready in five minutes. Can I ride with you today?"

"No, ma'am." He stood, his full height towering over me as one step brought him close enough to breathe in his intoxicating mix of leather and laundry. "You're off the clock today."

"It's fine. I promised to do a job, and I'll do it."

He mussed my already tangled hair but let his hand drop to the curve of my neck. When he squeezed, my body leaned into him.

Fuuuuck. It feels good to have his hands on me.

"You're no good to me dead on your feet. Go back to bed."

Far too frustrated and tired from a sleepless night to argue, I turned, and Josh planted a *thwack* right on my ass. My head whipped around to glare at him, but he only beamed a devilish grin at me in return before walking away with only a silent hand raised in goodbye.

∽

BY 10:00 a.m. I was a brand new woman. Rested, showered, and shaved, I felt a renewed sense of certainty that I could get to the bottom of the mystery of my father. I was there in Montana, after all—closer than I had ever been to knowing the truth.

Music played from the Bluetooth speaker on the kitchen counter. It was already set to the Black Keys station, and I kept it there, appreciating Josh's taste in bluesy country with a little rock mixed in. I hummed along to the songs I knew and wrote down a few new-to-me ones that I wanted to add to my own playlist.

A knock at the door had me abandoning my growing list of songs. I stared at the thick wood door.

Do I answer it?

Not entirely sure what to do, I peeked through the side window. The blonde woman from the boutique was standing at the door, her hands planted at her hips.

My movement caught her eye through the window. "Hey! Remember me?" She pointed at herself. "Gemma. We met at Johnny's store."

I quickly unlocked the door and pulled it open. "Hey. Yeah, of course."

Up close the woman was a knockout. Leading-lady material, for sure. Her platinum-blonde hair brushed her shoulders in delicate waves. It was clear the color was natural and suited her stark blue eyes perfectly. The delicate shape of her sharp nose led down to full lips. Models all over the world would be crying over their steamed broccoli if she hit the scene.

"Josh told me you were off today. I am, too, so I'm headed to town for some retail therapy." She hooked a thumb over her shoulder. "Wanna come?"

I was honored. Flattered, even. Friendships were something I wasn't afforded as Madison Colt. No matter how genuine the intentions seemed, there was always something behind it. Some *ask* that was lurking in the shadows. *Can you introduce me to Benjamin Cross? Can you give my audition tape to the director?* It was exhausting to navigate the minefield of friendships in Los Angeles. And the backstabbing? Christ. Not only would anyone throw you under the bus, but they'd back it up over you if they thought it would give them a leg up with the right crowd.

It may have seemed like I was an antisocial bitch, but it was the only way to know I was protected. Gemma was so far from being like those women.

I smiled at her. "Definitely. Give me two minutes!"

She waited while I grabbed my purse and locked up the house. I climbed into the cab of her truck. "Does everyone drive one of these around here?"

Gemma cranked the ignition and it roared to life. "Pretty much."

Before I could secure my belt buckle, Gemma was peeling out of Josh's long driveway and barreling toward the road. A barking laugh escaped me as I scrambled to secure the seat belt.

A wicked grin was planted on her face as we bounced and sped down the highway toward town. By the time she whipped into a parking space, my adrenaline was spiked, and my heart was pounding in my ears.

Gemma didn't seem to be fazed at all. "Coffee or shopping?"

"Shopping. Always. Then coffee."

The tinkling bell to The Rebellious Rose announced our arrival, and as soon as Johnny finished up with a customer, he made his way toward us.

"Gorgeous, gorgeous girls! What gives me the honor?"

Gemma popped her thumb in my direction. "Josh Laredo told me to spoil her today."

My head whipped in her direction, and Gemma had the

sense to look sheepish. She bared her teeth in a sort of *Surprise!* smile, and Johnny's shocked expression transformed into a not-so-quiet *"Ooooh."*

Gemma looked at the shop owner. "He's a smitten kitten."

I rolled my eyes and walked away to look at a rack of summer dresses, but I couldn't help the flutter that erupted in my belly.

Since we weren't pressed for time, I was able to meander through the racks of clothing Johnny had curated. It was an exhilarating challenge to pair outfits, mixing and matching to design a sort of capsule wardrobe that would be pretty *and* functional. Well, maybe not "ranch wear" functional, but it was something I could see myself wearing at dinner or a date night out.

Maybe even a date with Josh.

I allowed myself to revel in the thought of Josh taking me out on a proper date.

"You've got an eye for design." Johnny interrupted my date-night fantasy and took to adding a few more pieces to the rack in front of me.

I smiled at him. "I used to go to the thrift shops and try to find designer pieces. Sometimes it might be an Oscar de la Renta tweed jacket or Gucci shoes. Always random. But I'd find ways to make outfits from the normal clothes I had."

"I usually stick with smaller designers than what you might find in California."

From across a table of clothing, Gemma pinned him with a wide-eyed stare that clearly communicated, *Shut the fuck up.*

Johnny cleared his throat. "What I mean—"

"You knew," I interrupted. I looked between them, confirming my suspicions. "This whole time?"

His hand covered mine. "Oh, honey, we know."

"Wait. What?" My mind spun with that information. "You know? Know what exactly?"

He shrugged. "Who you are, of course."

I shot my attention to Gemma, who nodded and scrunched her nose. "'Fraid so. I think everyone knows."

A thousand thoughts raced through my head. This was bad. Really, really bad. My heart beat wildly against my ribs. "And who is everyone?"

Gemma shrugged. "The whole town, I'm assuming. Word travels fast around here."

"But don't sweat it." Johnny did his best to reassure me with a swat of his hand. "Absolutely no one would say anything. It's just not our way."

I slowly released a breath. "This is the weirdest fucking town."

Gemma and Johnny laughed, and Gemma moved toward another table of artfully folded clothing. "You're not wrong there. Let's finish up, and I'll tell you all about it over coffee."

Four dresses, a pair of stylish boyfriend-style jeans, heeled booties, and two *very* sexy sets of lingerie later, I walked out of The Rebellious Rose. Johnny refused to let me pay for any of it. *Josh is taking care of it—he insisted.* A little zip of excitement ran through me at the thought of Josh paying for the lacy undergarments. My body tensed in anticipation of him seeing it. Despite Josh acting like our kiss at the hot springs never happened, he was going to get an eyeful of me.

And soon.

Gemma sipped her latte as we settled in a booth at Brewed Awakening, the local artisan coffee shop. As I nestled deep into my seat, she hummed along to the song drifting through the café.

"You have a beautiful voice."

She cleared her throat, looking embarrassed, and shook her head in dismissal.

"Do you sing?" I prodded.

"Not in front of anyone." She smiled at me. "Not on purpose, anyway." Changing the subject, she leaned a little closer to me. "So . . . there are things you need to know about this town."

I nodded, enraptured by what morsels of information Gemma might be able to provide.

"The ranch is a cattle ranch, but not *really* a ranch . . ." Gemma continued to provide similar information that Josh had. Laurel Canyon Ranch was a front for witness protection. Locally, it was affectionately known as Redemption Ranch. Ma Brown was the matriarch, and she ran a tight ship. US marshals and witnesses alike worked alongside each other. She provided employment and housing when it was needed. Apparently, I was the first nonmarshal/nonwitness to be granted access to the ranch, and that in itself was curious.

"If you still have questions, definitely talk to Ma. She's a straight shooter. If there is information she can give you, she will."

My fingers found the smooth charm in my pocket. I had so many questions. Every scrap of information I received led to more.

As Gemma spoke, my eyes drifted down to the high collar of her button-up chambray shirt. Peeking just above it, pale-pink marks crept upward on her neck. She caught me looking and continued her story without stopping. Slowly she undid a few buttons.

"I'm sorry. I didn't mean to stare."

She continued to unbutton the top. "It's fine. I'm getting more used to it." She flashed her collar to reveal a mass of thick, tangled scars that spanned her neck and collarbone before disappearing down her shoulder. She lifted the cuff of her sleeve to show that the ends of the scars reached nearly down to her wrist.

Damn.

"I came to Redemption two years ago. My brothers had been mixed up with some pretty bad people in Chicago, where we're from." She paused and laughed to herself. "They *were* some pretty bad people. I got caught up and there was an accident. I was injured. My brother Evan and I came here for a fresh start. Parker and his wife joined us soon after."

I had heard the names *Evan* and *Val* spoken on the ranch. They were respected. Revered, even. I would never have guessed that they were once witnesses under protection, let alone the kind of people who might *need* witness protection.

I swallowed and searched for the right words. "Wow. I'm—"

"It's fine." Gemma quickly buttoned her top back up. "I don't talk about it a lot, and I keep my scars covered because it makes people uncomfortable. It's a reminder for them, you know?"

My heart ached for her. She covered herself for other people. I knew the feeling all too well. My hand found hers, and I offered a gentle squeeze. "Thank you for sharing a part of yourself with me."

She responded with a tight smile, and I knew it was time to change the subject. My lack of awareness had dragged her trauma to the surface, and that wasn't fair when Gemma had been so good to me.

"So what can you tell me about Joshua Laredo? Other than he's my lingerie benefactor, apparently."

Gemma stifled a giggle. "Josh is great. Everyone loves him. He's the kind of guy that makes people feel welcome." She sipped her latte and considered. "There's more to him, though, I think. He reminds me a little of you."

"Me?"

"There's the surface Josh—the nice guy. The happy guy. But I think there's more there he doesn't let people see. Did you know he was in the Army?"

I considered her words. I didn't know but wasn't altogether surprised. He liked structure and order. He was clean and tidy. "He hadn't mentioned it."

"From what Evan's told me, he's lived through some intense experiences. He was in combat and had seen some awful shit. Evan made a comment about how well he carries the load, considering what he saw over there. Everyone at Redemption has had their share of traumatic life experiences. It's no wonder we all stick together."

My heart squeezed for Josh. He carried darkness around with him but only radiated sunshine.

My coffee did nothing to soothe the bubble that expanded in my throat. "I had no idea."

"But good for him, you know? Making the best of things. I know for sure that kid of his helps. He's always lighter after Malcolm visits."

Kid?

Holy shit. Did Josh have a child?

11

JOSH

FLAT ON MY BACK, shoulder to shoulder with Malcolm, I stared at the puffy clouds as they rolled across the Montana sky.

"It's a pirate ship." Malcolm squeezed one eye closed as he pointed.

"Mmm . . ." I considered and tilted my head. "I dunno. I think it's an elephant wearing a top hat."

"Oh! What about that one?" A round blob floated across the early-June sky. "I think it's a butt crack." A peal of laughter burst out of him.

I would have said a beach ball or peach, but the kid had a point. I nodded. "Definitely a butt crack."

His carefree giggles tightened my chest. It was the coolest sound in the world. Months ago we'd go hours, days even, and I couldn't so much as pull a smile out of him. I checked my watch and stifled a sigh. Time with Malcolm always seemed to go by too quickly.

I glanced at my watch again, and my stomach filled with lead. "It's almost four, bud. We should get back for supper."

Malcolm sat up, draping his arms around his knees and

looking much older than an eight-year-old should. "No sleepover tonight?"

"Not tonight, but I did ask about next time. We should be good to go." I had a whole plan for him—camping out, fishing in the river, dinner by the fire. Real manly shit. I was waiting for his foster mom and case manager to approve it, but I hadn't lost hope. A whole slew of new camping gear for Malcolm was neatly organized in my garage, just waiting for the green light. He was going to lose his mind when he saw the new equipment I'd gotten him.

Despite my reassurance, Malcolm's face dropped. He'd learned quickly to not rely on promises. His doubt in me only renewed the fire in my gut to prove to him I was different.

I was always in his corner.

"Can I let you in on a secret?"

"Definitely." His serious face was enough, but when he used his index finger to make an X over his heart, I nearly died. This kid was too much.

"I met a girl." His little face twisted up, and I laughed, throwing my arm around his shoulder and bringing him in for a hug.

"Do you like her?"

Oh, yeah, buddy. Probably a little too much.

"Wanna know something wild? I met her before. A really long time ago."

"You did?"

"Sure did. When I was a kid—maybe four or five years older than you—I was up at the hot springs."

Malcolm whispered. "The secret place?"

I smiled at that. Malcolm had been the only other person I'd brought to that exact spot.

"Yep. I was up there mad that my dad had gone on

another assignment and we didn't know when he'd be back. Hating life and being angry about it when this girl just ran out of the woods and into the clearing."

"Was she lost?"

I shrugged. "I didn't know. She just . . . showed up. She was crying and mad too."

"Weird."

I looked down at him and gave him my best serious expression. "Super weird. But we talked and hung out. She was really cool. Then we heard someone calling for her. Next thing I knew, she got up and was gone."

I left out the part where, after sitting together for a long while, her mother's voice had echoed through the trees. Feeling like our time was fleeting, I had followed my heart, leaned over, and planted one chaste kiss against her lips. My first. I was nearly as shocked as she was. Even so, when she heard the angry voice calling for her, she had hopped to her feet and run off into the woods.

But not before looking back and giving me a wide, toothy grin.

"She was just gone?"

"Never even knew her name."

"And now she's back?"

I let my thoughts return to Effie. She was back in town, but certainly not staying. Her whole existence was wrapped up in LA.

No. That wasn't exactly the truth.

Madison Colt's life was in LA. The real Effie was stuffed down so tightly she barely saw the sun. That gnawed at me more than it probably should have.

"She's here now, anyway. Pretty cool chick too."

Malcolm tapped his forehead. "Does she know about your thing?"

I frowned. "No, bud. Not yet."

"If you like her, you should probably tell her."

Damn this kid.

"How about that supper? You can meet her and see if she passes muster."

~

IF SHOWING up with a kid in tow shocked Effie, she hid it well. Outside of the sidelong glances she kept shooting me, she never let on that this wasn't completely normal behavior.

When we burst through the front door, loaded down with pizza boxes, we both stopped dead in our tracks.

Me because my heart ceased beating at the sight of Effie in my kitchen. She wore a green-and-white sundress with a frilly bottom that showed off her toned, tanned thighs.

Malcolm's eyes went wide for very different reasons as soon as he saw her. "Whoa! You're the girl from *Stardust Guardians!*"

Effie visibly cringed with a crinkle of her nose, but her discomfort was gone so quickly I questioned whether I'd seen it at all. She hid well behind the practiced smile that she projected to the world. "And who are you, friend?"

"I'm Malcolm." I could practically count every small white tooth in his grin.

"It's great to meet you, Malcolm." She pointed to the stack of boxes in my arms. "Is that pizza for me?"

Malcolm, clearly starstruck, beamed up at her. "Breadsticks too!"

Effie motioned toward the large kitchen island. "Well let's go then."

Over Malcolm's head, I mouthed, *Sorry,* but she

discreetly waved it away with a shake of her head and a wink. My heart thunked, and I was relieved she wasn't mad with the sudden whirlwind of a tiny, unexpected dinner guest.

"Did you really battle those aliens? They were fake, right?"

Effie grabbed plates from the cabinet while I started opening boxes. "Well . . ." Effie seemed to consider how best to answer his questions. "Did they seem real?"

Malcolm nodded enthusiastically. "They. Were. Epic!"

Effie's tinkling laugh filled my kitchen. "Well, then, that just means I did my job right. If you can believe I was really in an intergalactic war and you had a great time, then that's real enough for me." She leaned down for a stage whisper. "But between you and me . . . the aliens were stunt guys in makeup, and they had harnesses to help them jump so high."

Malcolm gave her a knowing nod before grabbing two slices of pepperoni pizza.

I watched Effie look over the boxes on the counter. "So what have we got?" She probably didn't eat things like take-out pizza.

Damn it. Maybe I should have gotten a salad.

I scrubbed my hand on the back of my neck. "We got our usual." I pointed to each box. "Pepperoni. Cheese. And trash pizza."

"Trash pizza?"

"Sausage, pepperoni, jalapeño, onion, banana peppers, mushrooms." I rattled off the ingredients from our local pizza joint's claim to fame.

"No olives!" Malcolm added.

"Sign me up." Effie snagged two slices and a significant chunk of my heart in the process. Being this close to her, sharing take-out pizza, and hearing her natural way with Malcolm were doing things to my chest. I couldn't breathe.

Rein it in, man. Nothing can come of this. She's only here for a while. Don't let Malcolm get attached.

Truth is, I was worried about more than Malcolm getting attached. In the short time she'd been my houseguest, I had already found ways she'd carved out her place here, and I wasn't sure how I felt about it.

I plated my dinner and walked around the large island to sit. Effie and Malcolm were already locked in a deep debate about the third installment of the popular movie franchise. Effie's arms flung wide to emphasize her story.

Malcolm grabbed one steaming slice of his pizza. "Wait till it cools down, bud."

Instead of listening, he took one bite and exhaled around the hot slice like a fire-breathing dragon. "Ha—hot."

I rolled my eyes in Effie's direction, and she shot me a knowing smile over his head. The tug in my chest forced me to cough to dislodge the ache.

Effie moved toward the fridge to get some drinks, then turned to me. "Can I get you a beer? Glass of wine?"

"I, uh . . ." I glanced down at Malcolm to see him stone stiff and staring at his plate. His little shoulders were bunched, waiting for my reply.

I rubbed between his shoulders. "Just a Coke for me."

Effie's eyes flitted between Malcolm and me. She didn't miss the way he visibly relaxed at my response. "Yep. Got it."

We ate our pizza and breadsticks. I was an outside observer as Malcolm peppered Effie with questions about stunts and aliens and what it was like to make a movie. She answered thoughtfully, and by the end of their conversation, he was already half in love with her.

That makes two of us, pal.

I shook off the errant thought as I suggested Malcolm burn off some energy in the backyard before it was time for him to leave. As Effie settled next to me on one of the matching Adirondack chairs, I could see the thoughts tumbling in her head.

When Malcolm was out of earshot, she leaned closer. "You've got a great kid."

He's not my son.

The words clogged in my throat, refusing to dislodge. "I'm not his biological father."

Her eyes went wide. "Oh. Oh, I—"

"It's okay. I didn't explain. I met Malcolm through a community outreach program about a year ago. There's a really active women's club in Chikalu Falls. It's a few towns over. It started with a fishing program for veterans and developed into other opportunities for us. They organized a way for disadvantaged kids or ones needing mentorship to pair up with veterans with too much time on their hands. People to rely on. Show them adults can be responsible and . . . safe." My stomach curled in on itself when I recalled the trauma Malcolm had endured.

She lowered her head, and a soft smile played on her lips. I couldn't look away from the way her lashes swooped low across the apples of her cheeks. "How very noble of you."

I looked out at Malcolm doing his best to climb the rope I had tied to a low limb in the backyard. When he made it a little farther than the last time, he jumped down and turned toward the house. His wide eyes, huge smile, and thumbs-up tugged at my heartstrings. "Doing the right thing isn't noble."

"Hmm." Her light laugh had a wistful quality to it, and

I wanted more than anything to be able to read her mind. "I guess."

"It's also why I don't drink in front of the kid."

Her lush mouth popped open before snapping closed. "Right. I'm sorry. I should have—"

"Hey." I gently gripped her forearm to stop her as she turned her face from me. "It's fine. He's just had some unreliable adults in his life, and a lot of times alcohol was involved. I don't ever want him to think he isn't safe with me."

She considered my words as we watched him climb again. "Wouldn't it be better to show him that adults can be responsible *and* live their lives? It's not like you were going to get drunk in front of him or put him in danger."

I immediately bristled and shook my head. I tried to clear the buzzing in my brain despite knowing it was useless. "No. It wouldn't be better." My clipped tone had her eyes widening, but I ignored it. Though her words rang with a bit of truth, I didn't need her telling me what was best for Malcolm. I was already doing my best with him and feeling like it wasn't enough. When I checked the clock and found it was only a few minutes until his foster mom was scheduled to pick him up, my mood soured further. I stood and walked toward Malcolm in the yard.

"Time's almost up."

Malcolm's face melted. "All right." He dropped the rope and his shoulder hung. Then he walked toward the house.

He and Effie said their goodbyes, and when she told him she hoped they could hang out again soon, he perked up. My phone buzzed with a text. His foster mom was right on time.

"Your ride's here."

Malcolm swallowed thickly. Saying goodbye after a

great day was hard on the both of us. His voice was barely above a whisper. "I wish I could stay with you all the time."

Gravel filled my throat. The idea had crossed my mind a hundred times, but we'd never talked about it. I knew he had fun when we were together but had no idea he liked me enough to want more than our current arrangement.

I could barely get any words out. "I'll see you next time, bud. I've got some fun things planned."

Malcolm threw his arms around me, and I squeezed him back. I lifted a hand in goodbye to his foster mom as she loaded him in the car and drove away.

For a minute, I stood on the porch and stretched my arms above my head. There was something coming. I could feel it in my bones. My life was good, comfortable, but I couldn't shake the feeling that changes were looming. Big ones. Big enough to upturn the good and comfortable life I'd built here.

I didn't have a fucking clue what to do about it.

Just do the next right thing.

With the words of my commanding officer ringing in my head, I stomped back into the house and straight toward Effie.

Always doing the right thing was fucking exhausting.

12

EFFIE

THE FRONT DOOR slammed behind me, and I turned from the dishes I was loading into the dishwasher. My stomach swirled as I watched Josh cross the room.

Offering parenting suggestions was off-limits. Noted.

A war waged inside him, clear as day on his face as he stepped into the kitchen.

"I owe you an apology."

I shook my head and turned back to the dishes. "Not at all," I called over my shoulder. "I overstepped. No big deal."

Josh stood with clenched fists. Tension filled the kitchen. "I let my emotions get the best of me. It won't happen again."

A thousand thoughts tumbled through my mind as I wondered what kinds of dark and naughty things might happen if he stopped bottling everything up and really let those feelings free.

He took a measured breath. "I apologize for being short with you."

I barely contained the urge to roll my eyes. I didn't want the even-tempered, composed man that everyone in town loved. I wanted to see the real Josh beneath the polish and good-guy smile. I'd already seen glimmers of complexity, and I wanted more.

I turned and lifted an eyebrow. "Apology not accepted."

He blinked at me like he couldn't believe someone wouldn't accept and forgive him.

I turned back to the dishes but glanced over my shoulder. A furrow deepened in his brow, and I felt a smile tease the corner of my mouth. "You didn't do anything that necessitated an apology; therefore, I will not be accepting your bullshit apology."

He shifted on his feet. "I was short with you."

"I was out of line." I lifted a shoulder in dismissive indifference and clenched my jaw to keep from smiling at the huff from behind me.

"Please forgive me." It sounded as though he spoke through gritted teeth.

I turned to see him take one step that closed the distance between us, darkness swirling in his eyes. His face transformed from the carefree friend to hard lines and bunched shoulders. I leaned back against the cool marble. My hands bit into the hard surface as I gripped it.

I knew I'd hit a nerve when I questioned him about Malcolm. I had no right to insert myself, but despite the kiss at the hot springs, I thought we'd started to develop an understanding. Some semblance of friendship.

There was nothing friendly about the look on Josh's face. As his measured strides ate up the distance between us, a buzz started at my toes and worked its way up. I suspected that the man struggling to get his emotions in check wasn't the person he let just anyone see.

My heart rate spiked to see the muscles beneath his shirt stretch with each measured breath.

My eyes paused on him as realization dawned. "You can't stand it." I took one step forward, erasing the inches that separated us. "You can't stand the fact that someone might be offended by something you did."

He shook his head. "What you see is what you get with me, sweetheart." His words dripped with cowboy charm, but the hammering pulse in his neck gave him away.

There was something fierce and wild beneath the surface, and I couldn't help wanting to peel back those carefully crafted layers. To see the *real* man who stood in front of me.

So I did it. I poked the bear. "I. Do not. Believe you."

His voice lowered in a way that sent a chill down my spine. "You better be careful, Effie. I don't think you want to find out what lurks in the shadows of this house."

My heart spun out of control as the deep timbre of his voice rolled over me.

"Try me." My eyes locked with his.

"I told myself I wouldn't touch you again." His hot breath swept across my neck. The exotic mix of mint and laundry and leather collided.

"Maybe it's time to stop being nice all the time." He studied my face as the words tumbled from me, and I could see a switch flip in him, but I couldn't stop. The calm words of my therapist rattled in my head. "You shrink yourself down to be more digestible for everyone else." For good measure, and dramatic effect, I added, "As far as I'm concerned, they can choke."

Josh stood in front of me as if my words were all the permission he needed. He stared down, and our eyes locked. Heat vibrated between us, the seconds ticking by. His wide, calloused palm found my collarbone and moved to encircle my neck in a gentle but possessive grip. "I have something you can choke on."

I was shocked at his filthy mouth. His other hand found my hip bone through the light fabric of my sundress and squeezed as my traitorous hips bucked forward and felt a hard ridge between us.

I dug deep to level my voice against my unraveling nerves. "You sure about that?" Fire danced in his eyes as I challenged him. "I thought maybe it might just be . . . *nice.*"

His mouth crashed to mine as he pinned me against the counter. Both arms planted on the marble behind me, trapping me between his tanned, corded forearms.

There was nothing nice about the way Josh kissed. He demanded. I could feel his pent-up energy cracking like a rope whipping in the wind of a storm. His mouth devoured mine. I was helpless against it.

My hands grabbed at the front of his shirt, fisting the fabric and pulling him impossibly closer. With my eyes squeezed shut, I reveled in the way his tongue tangled over mine.

Powerful.

Possessive.

So sure of himself.

A hot, needy ball tightened in my belly as I moved my hands over his broad shoulders and into the locks of hair. His hips rocked forward, and his words flashed through my mind.

I have something you can choke on.

Liquid heat pooled between my legs, and I could tell my panties were already soaked through at the image of me on my knees in front of him, trying to take him to the back of my throat.

Who is this dirty, delicious man, and why the hell has he been hiding this part of himself?

His hands found my back and pulled me closer, smashing my breasts against the hard planes of his front. Unlike the fake men in Hollywood who relied on sparse diets and movie magic to give them the appearance of strength, every part of him was firm, delicious muscle that had been formed by hard work and tanned in the sun.

I tore his shirt from his waistband and fumbled with his belt buckle. His muscles flexed as my fingers danced across the thin skin above the top of his jeans, pausing on the thick vein that disappeared into his waistband. His mouth assaulted my neck, nipping and biting the sensitive skin. I moaned, and it seemed to make him only hungrier.

Just as I slipped the button free and yanked his zipper down, Josh swiveled behind me, moving me forward and pressing my hips into the center island. His hard erection pressed into me as his hands moved up my back, bunching the short sundress at my hips.

"Did you wear this for me?" he growled. I could only nod, my throat coated in sandpaper. "Tell me. Tell me you wore this dress knowing I could slide my hands up your thighs and feel how wet I make you."

My knees trembled at the boldness of his words. All my life I'd been delicately handled. Treated with care as if I were porcelain. His rough hands dulled the incessant voices that told me I wasn't perfect enough. Talented enough. Polished enough.

I swallowed past the ache in my throat. "I wore it for you."

One hand found the center of my back as Josh bent me forward onto the island. Searing heat pooled between my legs, and I squirmed to ease the building pressure. Behind me, he dropped to his knees, his face inches from the hemline that barely covered my upturned ass. He raked his short nails down the backs of my thighs, and I cried out.

"That's my girl." His fingers slipped beneath my skirt, moving over my curves with purpose. He hooked his fingers into the top band of my underwear and slowly stretched it over my backside and down my thighs. "Shit. I can smell how much you like this. Your pussy is so fucking sweet."

His breath moved over my heat and sent tingles racing through me. One hand moved over my inner thigh, slipping between my legs, dragging the side of his forefinger along my slit. Teasing me.

"You're probably used to being cherished. Adored."

"I like—" I fought against my hammering heartbeat to even speak. "I like the way you handle me."

"What if I told you I could cherish you too. But that I could worship you with tender strokes and rough dick." His fingers worked against me, spreading my wetness and slipping across my sensitive skin.

"Yes. God, yes." I wanted him. All of him. I wanted to know what it felt like to be stroked and handled and filled by him.

A guttural moan streamed out of me as my breath hitched when he slid one finger inside me. From behind, he lowered his mouth to me as he dragged the finger in and out.

"So fucking wet for me." His voice was quiet and hungry.

"More. I need more."

"I'll give you more, baby girl." He slipped a second finger inside me, pumping harder and moving his mouth against me. After slipping his tongue inside me along with his fingers, he then dragged his tongue back over my ass. I clenched in surprised delight at the sensation of him devouring every inch of me.

I cried out at how bold and assertive he was. I had been craving him ever since our moment at the hot springs, but that—*that*—was nothing compared to how he was breaking me down as he moaned into my pussy and plied me with firm, demanding strokes.

My knees began to shake as he ran a line from my ass to my clit. My hands scraped against the cold marble, begging to gain purchase.

He fucking owned me with that tongue. As I was about to let go, he pulled away, leaving my body screaming for more.

"Hearing you moan while I eat your pussy is the most intoxicating sound in the world." My inner muscles clenched at his words, but I could only pant and squeeze my thighs together as he grabbed a condom from his wallet.

I was desperate to have him between my legs. Over my shoulder I watched him grip his cock as he dragged it over my entrance. Gentle, teasing strokes. My body screamed for more.

I cast a defiant look over my shoulder. "I thought you said rough?"

His eyes smoldered as one hand reached forward and laced into my hair, pulling my head back. In one stroke, he slammed into me. A cry ripped from my chest. Without a moment to get used to his size, Josh filled me with every solid inch.

Heat rushed down my spine and pooled between my legs, and his deep moan was nearly enough to send me tumbling over the edge into bliss.

"I can hear how wet I make you. Your tight little pussy is like a goddamn vise."

With my hair still firmly fisted, he changed his tempo. Pleasure and pain danced as he fucked me. Long, deep strokes of his cock hit every pleasure zone inside my body.

My nipples pinched tight as I got closer to the edge. With a deep, smooth stroke, I finally—*finally*—came around him, squeezing and releasing uncontrollably. My legs turned to lava as the flood of my orgasm flowed over me. He released his hold on my hair to wrap one arm under me and around my hips. With a few more languid pumps, his impossibly big cock thickened as he filled me with long pulses of his own orgasm.

Josh's body folded over mine on a moan, his weight pressing me into the cool marble countertop. After a shaky breath, he lifted and pressed soft kisses down my spine, leaving a cool, tingling sensation in their wake.

"How was that for nice?"

"Mmm," I moaned. "I stand corrected. It was a lot of things, but I definitely would never call it *nice*."

He laughed as he pulled away, leaving my body already missing the full feeling of him inside me.

"You have wickedness behind that good-boy charm." I smoothed the skirt of my dress down my backside as I straightened. Josh moved to me, pressing his lips against mine. His arms wrapped me in a warm embrace as his tongue moved over mine, and it was the best kind of aftercare. Roughed up, then gently cherished.

Safe.

"Don't go telling anybody." His gruff voice was low and sexy as he lowered his forehead to mine. "I've got a reputation to maintain. Mothers love me."

"If word got out you fucked like *that*, I guarantee the women of this town would be beating down your door. The mothers included." I tried to make light of the moment, but my stomach curled at the thought of Josh being with other women. I had no real claim to him, but I suspected very few had ever seen the wolf behind the smile.

The air was thick with silence as Josh's eyes continued to rove over me. To cut through the tension, I ran a hand over the smooth marble. "Well, I'll tell you one thing . . . I'm never going to look at this counter the same again."

Josh laughed, big and full, and I quietly sighed in relief. "That makes two of us. When you're gone, I'll still be able to picture how gorgeous you looked splayed out in front of me."

When I'm gone.

My throat burned. I reached down and bunched my discarded panties in my fist. My legs wobbled and felt completely useless after Josh had fucked me so thoroughly. So unexpectedly.

What now? I looked around the half-cleaned kitchen. *Do I just keep doing the dishes? What. The. Actual. Fuck.*

At a total loss for how to salvage the rest of the evening, I pressed an open hand to my fluttering belly. Josh had alluded to my leaving, and he wasn't wrong. My time in Montana was limited. Sleeping with the man you're staying with didn't have to be awkward. It could be . . . fun.

But definitely not serious.

I turned to leave the kitchen as Josh adjusted himself back into his jeans. "Where are you going?"

My mouth popped open. *I have no freaking clue. I can't escape you in your own house.* I popped my thumb over my shoulder. "Cleaning up."

With my back to him, he huffed out a frustrated breath. "Effie, wait."

My heart bounced around my chest as I turned to see him drag a hand through his thick hair. Standing in the dim lighting of the kitchen, all his roguish charm was on full display, from the smirk on his lips to the way his hand rested on his hip. I was used to being around attractive men, but the intrigue and the mystery tied up in that cowboy had my cheeks flaming.

Keep it light. Casual. Indifferent. I smiled but could tell it didn't reach my eyes. Josh's frown deepened.

"Let me take you out."

My eyes flitted back to his. "Out?"

"Something simple. A drive, maybe."

The thought of a night country drive with Josh formed an excited bubble in my chest. I couldn't help the smile that lit up my whole face. *So much for indifferent.* "I'd love that."

Relief washed over him. Gone was the intense, feral wolf who'd fucked me against the counter. In his place was the warm, affable man who remembered people's birthdays and helped little old ladies cross the street.

Not that I'd seen him do that, but it's definitely in his wheelhouse.

The question was, Which version would be taking me out tonight, and would I even see it coming when the wolf came out to play?

13

JOSH

THE WARM EARLY-JUNE air filled the cab of my truck as I drove down a quiet country highway. The curve of the road hugged the mountain on one side, and the flat prairie sped by in flashes on the other. The constant image of Effie bent over the counter while I devoured her from behind was seared into my brain and had me shifting in my seat.

When I risked a glance in her direction, I was hit once again with just how stunning she truly was. She'd changed out of the little green sundress and swapped it for expensive-looking jean shorts. The faded band T-shirt she wore looked vintage, with an old rock band logo stretched across her full chest.

Her face was turned toward the open window, and I could openly appreciate the way her straight nose tipped up just a little at the end and how her time in the Montana sun had a few light freckles dotting the bridge. The sun had even pulled out a few more strands of copper in her long hair. Dressed down with her hair floating through the cab of my truck, she looked like every country boy's dream of the girl next door.

And I was too rough with her. Downright feral.

I risked a hand on her smooth knee, and warmth spread through me when she didn't pull away. "You okay?"

She smiled up at me, and it practically cracked open my chest. "Never better."

More relaxed, I fiddled with the radio in my old truck. I still hadn't gotten around to paying for satellite, so our options were limited to the honky-tonk stations and talk radio relaying USDA daily crop prices and agriculture news.

I gestured toward her shirt. "Favorite band?"

She looked down and frowned. "They're all right. I haven't actually seen them in concert yet. I found this at a consignment shop my very first week in LA."

"So it's good luck then."

She smiled. "It was cheap and it's comfy. I didn't have the heart to ever get rid of it."

I flipped through a few more stations on the radio without much luck. "Not much of a selection out here. Why don't you take my phone? I should have decent enough service to play something."

I handed her my phone from the console between us. She tapped the screen, and it opened immediately.

"You and your lack of passwords is astounding." When I just grinned, she continued. "Any requests?"

I thought for a moment. My taste in music was steeped in old country classics, but there were some eclectic favorites mixed in. I was more interested in learning about Effie's favorites.

"How 'bout this? Play me a song that reminds you of Montana."

I could feel her eyes on me as she considered. Before

long, a smirk teased her soft lips. After a few taps on the phone, twangy dueling banjos filled the cab.

I could barely hide my grin. "Har-har."

Her bubble of amusement pulled my own full laughter from me, and I reveled in the shared moment. "Fine," I added, "how about your hype song?"

"Hype song?" she asked.

"Yeah. The one song that no matter what mood you're in or where you're at, you can't help but rock out to. Sing from the top of your lungs. Everyone's got a hype song."

Color rose in her cheeks, making them the prettiest shade, and I wanted to run my thumb across them.

Her fingers flew across the screen. When she was about to press play, her finger froze. "No laughing."

I laid my hand across my heart. "Scout's honor."

As she pressed play, the familiar, hammering opening beat of "Eye of the Tiger" flowed through the small phone speaker.

I began slapping my hand against the steering wheel and singing with the beat. "Bum. Bum bum bum. Bum bum bum. Bum bum bummm—it really is a good one!"

Her knee bounced as we both drummed out the opening beats. As the song started, I belted out the lyrics I knew, mostly making them up where I didn't and giving the performance of my life.

"You're ridiculous!" Effie shouted, but soon she was singing just as loudly out her window, the cords of her neck straining as she belted the power ballad into the night air. We flew down the dark roads, singing and yelling the song. I pumped one fist out the driver's-side window.

As the final notes faded, I pulled down a quiet stretch of road and eased the truck into a familiar, secluded clearing. From here, I backed the truck up and turned so the bed faced a steep drop-off. The view was spectacular, and a million stars exploded across the inky sky. I doubted she'd seen a view like that in LA, and a part of me was driven to show her the hidden gems of my home.

She looked at me quizzically as I parked.

"Hop in back with me."

I helped her onto the tailgate, doing my best to keep a respectable distance, but not so much that I didn't let my palms drag down the curve of her hips before hauling myself into the bed of the truck. She shot me a heated look, and my blood ran hot.

Settled beside her with our backs against the cab of the truck, I took out my phone and handed it to her. "Okay. Next one."

She shook her head. "No way. It's your turn."

"All right. What am I looking for?"

She tapped a long finger along her full bottom lip. I couldn't help but notice her pink manicure was slightly chipped from working at the ranch, and the fact she didn't seem to give a fuck amused me. "Play me a song that makes you think of your ex."

Fuck.

It had been a long while since I'd attached myself to someone. My dates were primarily casual and served a singular purpose. One lighthearted song came to mind, so instead of revealing the total lack of depth of my recent relationships, I opted to play "Pray for You" by Jaron Lowenstein.

As the ridiculous lyrics registered, her face lit up. She laughed so hard that little glimmers of tears shone at the corners of her eyes. "Really?" she admonished. "Praying for a tire blowout?" She could barely contain her giggles, and I committed the sound to memory. "Savage."

"Nah. I'm teasing. Any past girlfriends and I have kept it pretty friendly."

"I bet. Always the gentleman."

I winked at her as my focus dropped back to her lips and my voice got thick. "Not always."

"No," she breathed through her shy smile as the tension between us built. "Not always."

I lowered my mouth to hers and teased the seam of her lips with mine. A bolt of heat shot through me as she sighed into the gentle kiss. The soft sound fueled a hunger inside me. One that was dangerous and all-consuming. I'd let that part of me go untethered earlier, and I couldn't do it again. She deserved more than a man who was more than willing to maul her in the back of a pickup. Instead, I eased back and smoothed her jawline with my fingers.

She smiled up at me, and we settled back, side by side—something clunky and important feeling dislodged in my chest. "Okay," I said. "Something that reminds you of your mother."

A little barking laugh erupted from her. "That's easy." She swiped the phone, and soon "Bitch" by Meredith Brooks played under her barely contained giggles.

"Harsh." I laughed along with her but felt a tug at my heart when she just shrugged.

"You probably adore your mother. I bet she makes homemade pies and knits and calls to pester you about grandchildren."

I laughed and nodded. "Yeah. That's about right," I conceded.

"What about your dad?" She looked up from under her long lashes. "A song that reminds you of him?"

I'd admitted to her that my father was a marshal working on the ranch, but I hadn't mentioned him since. I clenched my jaw and swallowed hard. Our fun game had turned serious somewhere, and one request flayed me open. With one song choice I could reveal more to Effie than I had in any actual relationship.

I picked up the phone and began typing. Clearing my throat, I said, "Uh. This is one that always reminds me of my dad."

Soon the haunting, sorrowful words of "Fire and Rain" by James Taylor ebbed into the darkness. We sat in silence.

When her small hand linked with mine and squeezed, I nearly lost it. My voice was thick with emotion. "Usually when this song comes on the radio, I change it after the opening notes."

"Yeah," she said. Effie's voice was heavy with sadness.

She pulled me closer, leaning her head on my bicep and hugging my arm against her body. We sat through the entire song. When the final notes ended, I stared into the night sky.

She moved slightly, and the soft piano intro of "Home" by Michael Bublé wafted over us. I nodded quietly as I listened to the sad lyrics.

When I found my voice, I looked down at her. "I bet you're feeling pretty homesick right about now."

She thought for a moment. "It's funny . . . I think I feel homesick for a place I don't even know." I tilted my head toward her, willing her to continue. "We moved around a lot when I was younger. New Orleans, Vegas, New York, California. I don't really miss LA—not like I thought I would. It's more . . ." In the low light of evening, Effie looked more vulnerable than I'd ever seen her. "I miss the *feeling* of home. Of belonging. I haven't felt it in a while."

I tucked my arm around her and pulled her close. My

chin dropped to the top of her head. She didn't need my words of comfort, so instead we sat in silence.

Finally her soft voice floated on the night air as she looked out into the vast wilderness. "This place suits you. It's captivating—like it calls to you and draws you in. But underneath it's still rugged and wild. There's something dangerous about it."

I hummed in acknowledgment. "It could suit you too." The words were out there. I was interested to see what she'd make of them, and part of me wanted to draw the attention away from the way she described this place, my home, so acutely befitting.

"Maybe." Her warm breath curled over my chest as she let out a small laugh. "I would live in a little house tucked into the side of a mountain. I would have a woodstove and a rocking chair on the front porch where I could drink my coffee in peace. I would have chickens." She paused. "Flowers. Honeybees. And a garden. I've always wanted a garden."

I squeezed her in my arms. That life struck me as pretty fucking great. "Sounds like a peaceful life."

"The best part?" Effie shifted her head to look up at me, her blue eyes sparkling with mischief. "All of the neighborhood kids would think I was a witch."

Together we laughed, and I pulled her closer and kissed the top of her head. Our conversation was easy and relaxed, but the rest of the night, I willed the words to stop running on a loop in my head.

I want that life too.

14

EFFIE

I WAS SHOCKED at how easy talking with Josh was. On the drive home, we bounced from favorite movies to childhood friendships to my experiences in child beauty pageants.

He will never ever see the photographic evidence of that particular disaster.

Whenever things got heavy or he asked a personal question about something that I typically kept to myself, I expected the familiar feeling of panic to creep up. My fight-or-flight response to facing uncomfortable emotions had kept people at a safe distance my entire life. Instead of those feelings of dread, Josh held my hand, and when he stroked his thumb across my knuckles, I felt centered.

When we got back to his house, he held open the front door, and I stepped in. My eyes immediately flew to the kitchen island, and I swallowed thickly and tried to ignore the flutter below my belly button.

When I turned, his eyes were focused on the island too, and I knew immediately he was thinking about how completely he'd wrecked me earlier. I took a steadying breath. "Thanks for the drive."

He moved one step closer to me, crowding my space in the dimly lit hall. "Any time."

My hand reached out to his hip, smoothing my fingertips along the leather of his belt. An unrestrained image of him swatting my bare backside with it flashed through my mind, and I gently gripped the belt to steady myself.

"Good night, Josh."

His calloused hand reached up to smooth my brow and trail a line down my face. I eased up on my toes and raised my chin. He cupped the back of my neck and squeezed. My mouth dropped open, and he inhaled one quick breath before crushing his mouth to mine. His kiss had changed from the demanding pressure of earlier to something hungrier. Needier. Like he wanted to consume me whole.

I pressed my body into his as he wrapped me in his arms. My leg hitched up over his thigh, and sparks radiated from my scalp to my toes. I braced myself against his broad shoulders and reveled in the feel of his powerful, muscular frame.

I wasn't shy when it came to sex, but the way he had me lowering my defenses so easily was frightening. I pushed away the errant thought that I was giving him too much of myself. Crossing into dangerous territory.

I could only think: *More. More of this.*

Breaking the kiss, Josh pressed his forehead to mine as we breathed in the electrified air between us. "Good night, Effie."

My throat was raw. My body was humming. I pulled myself away from him and straightened my shoulders as I walked toward my bedroom without looking back.

In the safety of my room, I leaned against the closed door and tried to catch my breath. Something about the way he kissed me—*the real me*—was troubling. If he knew all the ways in which Effie Pierce was lacking, he would be like everyone else. In the blinding light of Madison Colt, Effie Pierce was a poor consolation prize. A duller, less-fantastic version.

Through the walls of the house, I could hear the muted sounds of the shower. My body hummed as I thought of Josh's hands running over the planes of his hard stomach. Lower until he reached his thick cock. I groaned and rapped the back of my head against the wood door. I glanced at the thick white comforter and array of pillows on the bed.

Madison Colt wouldn't have walked away.

A devilish glint sparked inside me. I dashed to my bathroom to fluff my hair and apply a fresh coat of matte-red lipstick. Stripping down to nothing, I pulled open my door and went directly to Josh's bedroom. There I paused.

Do I knock?

The door wasn't latched, so I harnessed my inner badass and eased it open. Josh's bedroom was a large rectangle with huge, tall-paned windows that gave a breathtaking view of his backyard and the mountain beyond it. His bed was made, and the dark-gray comforter was plush enough you could sink into it and get lost. On the bedside table, a small sound machine and a handful of loose change were the only signs an actual human male occupied the space. His time in the Army must have trained any messiness right out of him.

Listening in the darkness, I could tell he was already in the shower. I stifled a smile and stilled the giddiness that danced through me.

Josh's bathroom was massive and masculine. Dark-gray

walls contrasted the brilliant-white marble countertop. His-and-hers sinks gleamed as steam rose from the shower, already fogging the mirrors.

It was then I heard the soft, low moan.

My ears pricked. He was half-turned away, and the steam curled around his muscular body. For the first time, I had unfettered viewing access to every inch of him. His feet were planted wide. His thick thighs gave way to a round, muscular bubble butt. I couldn't wait to get my hands on *that*. His trim waist moved up in a V to the expanse of his chest and shoulders. There was nothing but a beast of a man hiding under his denim and plaid work clothes.

When he groaned again, low and needy, I realized exactly what he was doing. With one arm braced against the hexagon tile, his right hand was fisted around his very long and very erect dick.

"Effie."

Oh shit. Oh shit!

Stroking his cock, Josh was getting himself off to my name, and it was the most erotic thing I had ever seen. Confidence coursed through me. He may not have said *Madison*, but I knew what he meant.

I infused my voice with a lusty confidence I had perfected over the years. "Yes, cowboy?"

His head whipped in my direction as his ragged breathing huffed out of him. I was standing in the bright light of his bathroom, naked with my feet wide and my hands planted on my hips.

His eyes dragged down my body once before a growl practically tore through him. "Get your ass in here."

Without hesitation, I pulled open the shower door. Before it was closed again, he was all over me. We fumbled with soapy hands and messy kisses. His moan vibrated into my mouth as his hard cock pressed against me. I raked my nails across his shoulders and down his back. He sucked a breath in through his teeth with an *"Ah"* that ignited my insides.

When I pulled away, I could finally appreciate his naked form. Sinewy muscles flexed and moved as he breathed. My eyes danced lower and snagged on where he fisted his length. I knew it was big—had felt the way it stretched and filled me before—but seeing it was something else entirely. In his grip, it was long and thick with a slight upward curve that had me understanding exactly how it had hit the deepest angles inside me.

That dick was pure magic.

I turned, showing him my ass and rubbing it along the head of his cock. He slipped it between my cheeks and teased along my backside. Hot water flowed over my shoulders, but it was nothing compared to the heat building inside me. I glanced at him over my shoulder, sinking my teeth into my bottom lip and throwing him my best come-hither look.

His hand moved over my hip and up my stomach. His soapy touch slipped over my breasts until his hand rested on my throat. "What is this?"

"What?" I pouted my lips and turned.

His brow furrowed, and his indigo eyes went darker. "This act."

I rubbed myself against him and hummed. "This isn't an act."

It is, but it's what men want. Let me be this for you.

His hands continued to caress my neck and shoulders, but seriousness lowered the timbre of his voice. "I don't want it." His hands wove into my wet hair as he tipped my head, forcing my eyes to his. "I want *you*."

Emotion crashed over me. I cried out and threw my arms around his shoulders, pulling him down into a sloppy kiss. Our teeth clashed.

Too much. It's too much.

The need for that man was overwhelming. He could have fucked Madison Colt senseless, but instead he refused. He'd rather have unpolished, kind-of-a-train-wreck Effie Pierce.

Me.

When we broke the kiss, a smirk spread across his face. "There's my girl."

Fireworks exploded beneath my skin. Desire hummed through me as the steam of the shower enclosed us in a hidden sanctuary. Emboldened to give him a piece of myself and take everything I wanted from him, I dropped to my knees.

As I moved my hands over him, Josh pivoted the shower head to allow the hot water to run over my shoulders without blinding me.

"I heard you moan my name. Were you thinking of me?" I took his length in both hands and stroked.

He moaned. "Yes, baby. I was stroking this cock, thinking about all the ways I wanted to take you."

I laved my tongue over his tip as he spoke. "And I've wanted to feel my mouth around you."

I teased him with my hands and my tongue before sucking him deep. His appreciative groans fueled my desire. My body clenched as his hips flexed and he pushed himself deeper into my throat.

I used my mouth and my hands to suck and stroke and taste every delicious inch of him. I liked that he let me set the pace and was a vocal lover. As I changed the pace or direction of my strokes, I knew exactly what was working for him. He let me take the lead, but memories of him taking control assaulted me. I loved how he was the perfect combination of tender and rough.

I craved it.

As my pussy clenched, aching to be filled, I pulled him as far back as I could. When his tip teased the soft palate at the back of my throat, I gagged around his cock.

"Oh fuck." He moaned and tried to pull back.

I eased off him only long enough to pant, "No. I like it. Again."

"I'm gonna come."

I smiled up at him. "Good."

Josh braced himself against the opposite wall as I slowly licked and sucked him. Deeper and deeper every time. One hand wrapped around the back of my head as he got closer to the back of my throat. I hummed my approval and permission. One slow, languid pump and I gagged again, loving the way my body reacted to this newly undiscovered erotic side of me.

I was powerful.

Primed and ready.

I reached between my legs and slipped my fingers across my pulsing clit. My hand moved in tandem with my mouth on him, stoking my own need as he filled my mouth. Feeling my nipples tighten, I released a high-pitched moan.

As my orgasm pumped through me, I sucked him deeper and felt his cock pulse in response. Hot liquid ran down my throat as I swallowed around him and struggled to maintain my balance against the quake of my own release.

As my mind went blank, Josh reached down. He

gripped my elbows and bundled me into his protective embrace.

"Jesus, Effie."

Effie.

Not Madison Colt but Effie.

Me.

15
———

EFFIE

HOURS LATER, my limbs were leaden, and I sighed deeply, fully enjoying the postorgasmic bliss. After the shower, we barely made it to the bedroom and spent hours tangled in each other. It still blew my mind how Josh could go from feral wolf to tender, attentive lover with the flip of a switch. I was quickly becoming addicted to the man Josh became in bed with me. One burning look transformed him from the charming all-American boy next door to a dominant, unrelenting lover with a filthy mouth. The tender throb between my legs was clear evidence of how much I had enjoyed that newly discovered side of him.

Josh ran a hand up my back as his knees tucked up around mine. "Morning."

I groaned and buried my face deeper in the pillow, inhaling his laundry-and-leather scent that clung to the sheets. "Ten more minutes."

Josh dragged his nose against the shell of my ear. "I like waking up with you in my bed."

My stomach tingled as his rough morning voice floated across my ear. When I rolled toward him, he shifted to his back and tucked me under his arm. My limbs sprawled across his body. My fingers raked across the light smattering of hair on his chest. His heart thunked under my fingertips, and I gently pressed a hand into it.

I like waking up here too. Probably a little too much.

I tilted my head to look at him, and a laugh hummed through my pressed lips.

"What?"

"You're different."

"Is that a good thing?"

That's a dangerous thing.

"Yeah. On the outside you're all charm and rugged good looks and everyone's hero. But here you're . . ." *Mine.* "Different."

He considered a moment, staring into the white ceiling. "Everyone likes the nice guy."

I nodded. He wasn't wrong. If anyone knew what it meant to meet the demands of others' expectations, it was me. "Kind of tiring though. Always being *on*."

He ran his hand down my hair and dropped a kiss on the top of my head. "Yeah."

Josh's fingers tangled with mine. Soft, gentle strokes. He moved his fingertips over the back of my hand and across my palm. The delicate touch had goose bumps tightening on my arm.

For a moment, I closed my eyes and enjoyed lying in the quiet, early hours of day, wrapped in Josh's arms.

I turned to my stomach, my arm still draped possessively across his chest, and propped my chin on the back of my hand.

"Do we need to talk about . . ." I motioned my hand between us. "This?"

A small furrow deepened on his forehead. "How long are you here?"

Until I'm no longer a pariah. Until I get answers about my father. Not nearly long enough. "Probably another couple of months. The premiere and press junket for *Terminal Justice* kicks off in about two months."

Josh was quiet for slightly longer than was comfortable. "I'd like to keep doing this. With you. Casual until it's time for you to go back to your life."

It made sense. Casual, mind-blowing, toe-curling fun until my time was up. My stomach pitched and rolled, but I infused confidence in my voice anyway and forced a smile. "That's perfect."

Besides, whatever was happening between us would inevitably come to an end.

Unease rolled through me. I needed space. Time to think. Dropping a light kiss to his pec, I stretched and peeled myself from his side. I plodded across the bedroom and scooped up his discarded T-shirt. After I'd pulled it over my naked body, it hugged my chest and landed just shy of covering my ass. Josh sat up, his back against the headboard and his arms folded behind his head.

Damn, he looks good all mussed up.

"Day's wasting, lazy bones." I shot him a sultry look. "Let's get to work."

On a growl, he clawed over the covers toward me. I squealed and tried to run, but he was quicker and scooped me up.

"You're such a shit," he said. His fingertips tickled at my rib cage.

I laughed and shouted. "Stop! We have to get ready!"

He laughed and dropped me on my toes before placing

a gentle kiss on my lips. As I turned toward the doorway, he swatted my ass. "Be ready in ten."

Exactly thirteen minutes later, I was nearly ready to go and thoroughly impressed with myself that I'd managed to whittle my morning routine down to the essentials: eye cream, sunscreen, mascara.

I was surprised I enjoyed the light freckles that bloomed across my nose from Montana's early summer sun, but I also knew any more fine lines meant career suicide and a lifetime of roles as *the mother*. No thank you.

I gathered the last of my things and slipped the smooth, circular stone into the front pocket of my jeans.

"What's that?"

I turned toward Josh's voice. He leaned against my doorframe, two to-go cups of coffee in his hands and an endearing smile across his face. My heart squeezed.

I hesitated a moment, feeling silly under his watchful gaze. I had never told anyone about it or how much the small, flat object meant to me. "It's nothing. Just sort of a talisman, I guess."

If he was curious, he didn't let it show. Instead, he extended a cup to me with a wink and left me to follow. As I walked out the door, I traced the outline of the stone with my fingertip.

I needed all the luck I could get if I was ever going to get anyone at Redemption Ranch to open up about my father. I took a steady breath and studied the way Josh's muscles bunched and moved beneath his shirt.

If I wasn't careful, I was going to fall for that rugged, irresistible charm.

Hard.

AS THE WEEKS ROLLED BY, life on the ranch was unsurprisingly predictable. What was a surprise, however, was the peacefulness I found in the simple routines. It was disarming how easy it was to be around Josh, both on the ranch and in his home.

Too many times I caught myself smiling at his back or laughing to myself as a previous conversation came to mind. He was a fascinating dichotomy of charismatic yet confident, accommodating yet assertive.

And we'd managed to keep it mostly professional while we worked, only sneaking off a handful of times to fuck like horny teenagers in a cramped storage closet. It was easy to convince myself I was playing a role, diving into this new life like a true Method actor. Any time my mind wandered toward thoughts of a real romantic relationship with Josh, I squashed them immediately. We hadn't talked again about the expiration date of our arrangement, and I wasn't about to be the one to bring it up.

Ignorance is bliss.

Despite his agreement to *keep it casual*, Josh operated like a seasoned relationship professional. Morning coffee, cuddles on the couch, devouring my pussy after a picnic under an enormous oak tree. When I ignored several calls from Desiree, I knew my grip on the situation was slipping. I texted her back, checking in and letting her know I hadn't fallen into a ravine or snapped an ankle on the rugged terrain. *Yet.*

I refused to check social media to see if the drama with Benjamin had blown over, but Des assured me that our plan of keeping me out of the spotlight was working. If anything, the sharks were frenzied with new theories, and we'd turned the tide of *soulless heartbreaker* to crestfallen damsel on the verge of a comeback.

Desiree: *Your return is going to be EPIC. You'll be bigger than before. There's even talks of a sequel.*

I stared down at the text.

Sequel.

I clicked my phone off with more aggression than necessary and buried it in my back pocket. How I'd ever considered being with a man as artificial and smarmy as Benjamin left a sour tang on the back of my tongue.

Annoyance darkened my mood as I attacked my next task. Stacking hay bales was sweaty, messy work, but my personal trainer, Sergei, would be pleased with the strong, toned muscles I was developing in my arms. Maybe it would counteract the few extra pounds he would gripe at me about. As I stacked one last bale, I grunted and struggled against the weight. Before it could topple onto me, the flat end of a square shovel pushed against the bale, moving it into place.

I turned to see Ray's signature scowl and bunched shoulders. I removed my gloves and wiped my sweaty palms across my jeans. "Rescued again. Thanks."

He grumbled, and his cool eyes assessed me from head to toe. "You don't really seem like the damsel-in-distress type." Unlike most of the men at the ranch, Ray never looked at me in a way that made my skin crawl. Usually he just looked pissed off.

I couldn't help but smile at the way his lips were drawn in a permanent frown. "Not usually, but Montana is proving to be a worthy adversary."

He conceded with a nod. "That she is."

Before he could turn his back to me and brush me off, as he'd done *thousands* of times before, I jumped on the opportunity to talk with him without listening ears nearby.

With his time on the ranch, surely he'd recall a marshal

that could be my father. With enough luck and charm, I could unearth a tidbit of information locked in that thick skull of his. "So, Ray," I started. "You've been here a long time, right?"

He sighed as if talking to me was the last thing on earth he had time for, but he stopped and rested his arms on the handle of the shovel. "Nearly the longest. Who's asking?"

I lifted my palms in innocence. "Just me. I was curious about how all this came to be." I twirled a finger in the air, indicating I meant more than just a cattle ranch.

Ray looked past the field toward the looming mountains in the distance. A storm threatened, with thick, heavy clouds creeping across the sky.

"When I first got here, Laurel Canyon wasn't worth two pennies rubbed together. Downriver from an abandoned button factory, it was two hundred acres of barren fields and broken-down buildings rotting from the inside out." He shrugged. "It was nice."

Ray ignored the soft laugh that pushed through my nose as he continued. His eyes focused on something in the field, and he spat on the dirt. "Dorthea and Robbie took a beat-down old farm and turned this place into thousands of acres of workable land. Provided a place for hard, honest work and refuge. Gave a second chance for people who didn't deserve it. It was Redemption Ranch before anyone thought to name it."

I studied grooves and lines in his face, hardened by age and the sun. Ray was a mystery wrapped up in hackles and mistrust. I couldn't help but fall half in love with him.

His focus turned from the valley beyond the barn to me. "I know who you are."

I raised an eyebrow. "Is that so?" I planted my hands on my hips. "Who am I, then?"

"You're that movie star—Madison someone." His words gave me pause. In nearly two months here, no one had alluded to knowing my real identity. I assumed Gemma and Johnny had been mistaken and no one knew who I was. Apparently, I was wrong on that front. Perhaps everyone in Tipp was just used to keeping their mouths shut.

"That last space one wasn't complete shit."

I stifled a laugh at the near compliment.

"Those other movies where you fall in love with your boss or the one you played the lawyer who ends up stranded in a small town . . . not really my kind of thing."

Humor danced in my eyes. Apparently Ray had watched several movies in my catalog.

"Though I don't know why they had you flouncing around in next to nothing. Anyone knows anything would tell you that dressing like a wannabe showgirl at the Tropicana would never hold up in a space battle."

"Yeah," I admitted. "It was a stretch." I pulled the hair off the nape of my sticky neck to allow the breeze to cool me down. My eyes sliced to him. "I'm surprised you recognized me. So far, I think I have most people fooled."

The old man swiped two fingers in front of his face. "It's the eyes. Hard to forget big eyes like that."

My smile bloomed. "A gift from my mother, though hers are green. But I hope you can keep this a secret between us. Wouldn't want too much attention brought to the ranch."

A sneer marred his weathered face as he examined me. "What's your deal? On the lam? Witness a murder or something? Drugs?"

I smiled. His theories were a lot more interesting than the truth, but in order to continue digging for information, Ma Brown needed to allow me to stay, and time was running out.

"Research for a role." The lie rolled off my tongue with the practiced ease of an Oscar-nominated actress.

His skeptical, piercing eyes moved over me, and goose bumps tightened on my arm. Apparently Ray wasn't as easy to fool as I thought.

"Keep your nose clean, kid." As Ray turned and shuffled away, I continued to organize the tools and wondered who else knew or suspected my identity. I was shocked that a small part of me didn't really care anymore.

I watched the old man shuffle away.

"Is Ray giving you trouble?" Josh walked up behind me, dropping a hand on my shoulder and giving it a gentle squeeze.

I leaned into his touch. "Trouble? That sweetheart?"

"Sweetheart? That's rich. He's the resident asshole. Jaded and downright mean sometimes."

I shrugged as Ray disappeared out the wide front door of the barn. "Seemed nice enough to me."

Josh shook his head in disbelief.

"Hey." I turned to face him and bounced up on my tiptoes. "Can I cut out a few minutes early today? I have some sleuthing to do."

He crinkled his eyes at the edges, as if he was really considering telling me no. "It'll cost you." Josh smiled before planting a kiss on my lips.

"Thanks, boss." The words smashed together as I smiled and kissed him back.

Ray had given me an idea.

16

JOSH

AS SHE HAD DONE for the past few weeks, Effie sat on the couch with her legs crossed, my laptop perched on her thighs and her teeth sunk into her lower lip. She was determined—I'd give her that. Despite Tipp's reputation for its tight-lipped residents and closely guarded secrets, Effie pressed on. I flipped the dish towel over my shoulder and watched her as she studied the notebook in her hand.

For the first time in my life, I was living with a woman. A woman I was sleeping with, no less. It helped that I could be myself around Effie. When I was quiet, too exhausted from a long day in the sun to keep up my cheery facade, she never batted an eyelash. Those nights we sat in companionable silence—at least as quiet as it gets when you were a headcase. I read a book or watched TV while she continued digging into the mysterious past of a father she had never met.

Effie groaned a soft, frustrated sigh. I pushed closed the dishwasher and smiled to myself. "How's it going, Columbo?"

Her annoyed look only widened my grin. "It's not," she pouted.

I walked to the couch and pushed a pile of papers to the side before plopping down next to her. I gestured toward myself. "Hit me with it. Whaddaya got?"

She glanced at her notebook, looking more vulnerable and nervous than I'd seen her. "Okay." She lifted the notebook filled with loopy handwriting haphazardly smattered across the pages. "It's a stretch, but . . ."

When I looked at her patiently, she cleared her throat and sat straighter on the couch. "Ray mentioned an abandoned button factory not too far from here. That made me think about public records. Things that are big news for a small town. Then I remembered some of the marshals lived here. Like your family, right? If they bought a home, there would be public records."

I considered how to be supportive but also realistic. "Tipp is small, but not that small. That's a lot of research. And how would you even know if it's him when you come across the right name?"

She worried her lip. "I know. I need a way to narrow it down." She sighed and rolled her neck. "I know my father was at least partially Greek. My mother said she named me after his grandmother. So I was hoping a super-Greek-sounding last name would be a start." She frowned down at her papers before offering a sad shrug. "Maybe?"

I shifted on the couch, my leg opening a space for her. "Come here."

A pouty Effie scooped up the laptop and loose papers and deposited them on the small table before sitting in the possessive circle of my arms. My hands kneaded the pebbles that knotted in her shoulders. "I know it's hard. The whole foundation of the ranch is secrecy. I think you should talk to Ma."

A low hum vibrated through her as my hands worked to ease the tension in her shoulders. Heavy rain beat against the window. A quick flash and thunderclap made us both jump. Our shared laughter seemed to ease her tension, and my skin got tight. Effie was crawling her way into parts of me I didn't know what to do with yet.

After another crack of thunder, we were plunged into darkness. For a beat, neither of us moved.

"Do you have a flashlight?" Effie whispered.

"Sit tight. I'll check it out." I stood and walked toward the window, and Effie used the dim light from her phone. I peered into blackness. "It's the storm. I can't even make out the lights down at the Johnsons' farm." I turned, Effie's sharp features illuminated in a soft glow. "Nothing to do but wait it out."

My blood ran hot as all the thoughts of what we could do to pass the time raced through my mind.

"It's so quiet," Effie whispered and looked around.

I gathered the emergency candles from a drawer and took the opportunity to adjust my thickening cock, which was pressing uncomfortably against the back of my zipper. I placed the candles around the living room, bathing us in a cozy glow. Giving up on her research, Effie neatly stacked her papers and tucked away my laptop.

I stalked toward her in careful, measured steps, pulled by the invisible tether Effie had managed to lasso around me. My fingers danced across the thin skin on the inside of her upper arm.

"Come here." The roughness of my voice filled the space between us. I dragged my hand lower, capturing her hand in mine and stealing away her phone. I shot her a look and handed it back so she could unlock it.

She bit her lip to suppress a smile as she quickly unlocked it and handed it back without moving her body away from mine. Her sultry, floral scent filled my lungs. I typed quickly, and the opening bars of "Cover Me Up" by Morgan Wallen played from the small speaker.

"Better?" I wrapped Effie in my arms and began to sway to the sensual song I'd heard on the radio, and I immediately thought of her. Together we moved without speaking. I couldn't help but focus on the way her body moved under my hands. I couldn't stop thinking about all the ways my hands had made her moan over the past month. Effie was an ever-evolving mystery, and I'd barely scratched the surface of how I wanted to make her feel.

Pleasured.

Used up.

Seen.

I let the song take us as I hummed along. I eased my hands up her back, and goose bumps broke out on her arms. Something about the way we moved together—whether it was the static in the air from the storm or something more—stacked the tension between us like bricks.

It was only a matter of time before Effie was leaving, and I wouldn't ask her to stay. She had nothing here but a broken-down cowboy who was struggling to hold on to the end of his rope.

"Josh?" Her voice was barely above a whisper.

I smoothed an errant piece of hair away from her face and got lost in her eyes. "Yeah, baby girl?"

"What are we doing?"

I'm falling in love with you.

Unnerved, my words came out throaty and deep. "Just dancing."

I moved my hands to her face and tipped her back before lowering my mouth to hers. Her fingernails scraped against my back as she bunched my shirt. Thick, pulsing heat washed over me at the sting of her nails.

Desire, aggressive and untamed, coursed through me. My hips pressed forward, letting her feel the effect she had on me. Effie practically crawled up me as her arms tightened around my back.

I dropped to my knees. When she looked down on me, her auburn hair tumbled around her face. Her pupils were dilated, her eyes black with lust.

"Take off your shirt."

She efficiently followed my command, and my gaze dropped to her nipples, which poked through the creamy lace of her bra. I pulled her toward me and clamped my mouth down on one tight bud, teasing her through the thin fabric. With the flick of my hand, I released the clasp on her bra. The weight of her tits made my cock pulse as the bra dropped to the floor. Effie's head dropped back as my thumbs stroked.

I moved to the waist of her shorts and let my mouth follow as I dragged them down her thighs. "Turn around."

As she turned, I reached behind me and tore my shirt off my back, discarding it somewhere in the room. Still kneeling, I stroked a hand up her back before bending her in front of me. She braced herself against the arm of the couch.

I wrenched down the zipper of my jeans, pulling my dick from my pants and giving it a good, tight stroke. Eye level with her glistening pussy, I stroked my cock.

"I can't decide if I want to feel you come all over my

face or just bury this cock in you and watch that tight pussy stretch around me."

A shudder racked through her as my free hand moved up the round curve of her ass and squeezed. Her head turned and her gaze locked on my hand, entranced as I stroked my cock.

"You like that?" I flexed my abs for her, and my cock pulsed as she licked her lips.

"Keep going."

At her insistence, I let my hand travel up and down my length. "Spit on it."

The filthy words were out, and my girl didn't even hesitate. Effie turned and used her mouth to soak my cock. I stood, dropping my pants and boxer briefs to the ground.

"On the floor." Lust coursed through me, and I could barely get out more than one or two words without feeling like I was going to ignite.

Desire flushed her pale skin as she lowered herself onto the plush rug, always watching as I stroked my cock in front of her. Her long finger moved up her thigh and disappeared into her pussy. I kneeled over her, pumping away as she fingered herself. Watching me jack off while she played with herself was intense. Erotic.

I needed more of her—all of her.

"Let me taste you."

Her fingers slipped out of her, and she raised them to my mouth. I moaned around her fingers, slipping my tongue between them as her sweet taste fell across it. Seconds away from blowing my load all over her, I reached into the pocket of my jeans and grabbed a condom. Effie leaned back on her elbows and watched as I rolled it down my length.

Effie deserved sensual lovemaking surrounded by flickering candlelight. She deserved a slow hand and delicate touches.

She wasn't going to get it.

Hovering over her, I roughly pushed her knees apart and drove into her, spearing her on my aching cock. Her cry tore through the darkness. She was absolutely owning me with every noise that I thrust from her body.

I smoothed a hand up her torso, then higher until I wrapped my hand around her throat.

"Yes. Yes."

Her heels dug into my ass as I pumped into her. I couldn't get deep enough. Close enough.

"More," I ground out as I thrust. "I need more."

I pulled out as her pussy squeezed around me. Blind lust for that woman filled me. In one move, I peeled off the condom and thrust my bare cock inside her.

Her walls choked my cock in a way I'd never felt before, and I ground my pubic bone against her clit. Effie shot up, wrapping her arms around my neck and moving her hips with mine.

"Oh yes. Fuck you feel good." Her skin had a luminous sheen and she panted against my ear as I drove us both to the edge.

One hand tangled in her hair as the other found her neck, holding her in place. My voice was guttural and raw. "I had to. There's been no one else."

Before my words were out, her pussy clamped down on me, and the hot flood of her orgasm seeped over me. Like the storm outside, her orgasm battered and raged around me.

My teeth ground together when her lips found my ear and her hot breath washed over me. "Do it. Fill me. I want it."

I bucked my hips up, dumping every ounce of myself into her as I came. I had never come so hard in my life. My legs trembled, but Effie kept hers wrapped around me. My rough hand was still wrapped around her slim throat when we both came down from the unexpected high of phenomenal fucking.

We were panting. Shaking.

When my breath steadied, I untangled myself from her. I made quick work of wetting a washcloth with warm water and cleaning up my girl. The playful smile never left her lips, but as her lids grew heavier, I cradled her in my arms.

"You are full of surprises." Her husky laugh had warmth spreading in my chest. I laid her on top of me on the couch, our legs unfurling around each other. For a long while, I listened to her satisfied hums and steady breathing.

When the lamp next to the couch winked on, we didn't bother to move. I traced the curve of her neck with my fingertips, committing every hill and valley to memory. The topography of her body would be memories that haunted me once she returned to her life in LA.

Finally, as the last shred of my heart became hers, Effie's drowsy words broke the silence. "Do you really think my father could have been a marshal?"

"It's possible. From what I remember, it was a small group in the beginning."

I kept an errant thought to myself. The one that had dogged me for weeks now. A seed of an idea that had been planted and was growing wildly despite its unlikelihood.

What if Effie's father wasn't a marshal . . . but a witness?

17

EFFIE

I HAD BEEN ROUGHLY and thoroughly fucked.

Bare.

My stomach whooshed at the memory of Josh tearing off the condom and taking me in a way no other man had. He had *owned* me, and I couldn't seem to get enough, no matter how reckless it was.

When my period came a week later, I tamped down the tiny, unexpected wave of disappointment. It was ridiculous, really. A baby with him would have completely upturned both our lives. Turned my entire existence to ash. I attributed my runaway thoughts on living in the impossible fantasy world where Josh and I could actually end up together.

I looked up from the lunch I'd been picking at in time to see Josh's crooked smile as he sauntered toward me. I looked past him to see the expansive field open up behind him. He was completely in his element on the ranch. I beamed back at him. "Careful. A guy could get used to a pretty girl like you giving him a smile."

I could feel a blush heat my cheeks. It didn't matter how

many magazines I'd covered, Josh's earnest compliments never ceased to send a ripple of giddiness through me. When he finally reached me, he bent down for a familiar kiss. We'd given up trying to hide the fact we were together, and no one on the ranch gave it a second thought.

Josh wrapped an arm around my shoulders and pulled me into his side. "You wanna do something with me tonight?"

I looked up at him. "Of course."

He nodded but then dropped a kiss on the top of my head and walked through the barn doors toward his office.

Later that night, nervous energy sizzled out of him as we sat on the swing on his front porch. His knee bounced, and his thumb drummed a rhythm against it.

"Relax. He's going to have a great time." I ran my fingers through the ends of his hair, amused by the way it was getting longer and flipped out at the ends.

A moment later, a car pulled up, and Malcolm bounded out of the back seat, running full speed at Josh and slamming into him with a hug.

"Whoa! Hey, bud. You remember Effie."

"Of course! Hi, Mad—Effie." Malcolm turned his hug to me and squeezed my legs as I hugged him with one arm and ruffled his hair with my free hand.

"Hey, why don't you go inside and use the bathroom. We're going to head out in a few minutes."

Malcolm raced inside as his foster mom slowly made her way up to the house.

Josh reached out a hand, his charming smile firmly in place. "Ms. Harrison, I'd like you to meet my girlfriend, Effie Pierce."

My eyes sliced to him, but I kept my smile intact.

Girlfriend.

We hadn't talked about a label for whatever this was between us, but the way he said it with such confidence, such possessiveness, did something gooey to my insides.

"Pleasure to meet you, Ms. Pierce. Malcolm spoke very highly of you after the last visit."

Ms. Harrison eyed me carefully, and I turned up the wattage on my smile. "The pleasure is all mine." Her eyes glanced over our shoulders toward the house, and she lowered her voice. "Malcolm is cleared to stay the night with you, and he is very excited. However, there is one issue I would like to address with you."

I looked between Josh and Malcolm's foster mom. "I'll just excuse myself . . ."

Ms. Harrison raised her hand, cutting me off. "I'd actually prefer you to stay, as it has to do with you."

My eyes widened and I looked at Josh, whose face had gone blank.

Ms. Harrison clasped her dark hands in front of her. Her slow sigh was similar to one you'd give a child when your threadbare patience had finally unraveled. "After Malcolm's last visit, he was very excited to tell me all about your new . . . friend." I didn't shrivel back from the slightly raised eyebrow she shot me. "However, when I casually asked about you, he stated that it was a secret."

Oh shit. Josh must have told Malcolm to keep my identity between us.

Josh raked a hand across the back of his neck, and his broad shoulders drooped.

"I'm sure you understand my concern. Our counselors work to ensure that the children are safe. Protected from potential abuse."

"Abuse?" Unintentionally my voice raised several octaves, but Ms. Harrison was unfazed.

"We teach the children that safe adults do not ask children to keep secrets. You can understand how this would be confusing for Malcolm."

"I understand." Josh's voice was harder than I'd ever heard it. Shame washed over me. Josh had asked Malcolm to keep a secret because of *me*. And now he was in hot water with the one person who had a significant impact on Malcolm's care.

Josh's hand raised to the side of his head, where he pressed an index finger into the hinge of his jaw. It was subtle, but I'd seen him do that same odd thing before.

Something was up with him. Stress, most likely. Stress that I had caused.

I took one step forward. "It's my fault. You see . . ."

"It's fine, Effie." Josh redirected his attention to Ms. Harrison. "I'll speak with him about it, and it won't happen again."

Satisfied, Ms. Harrison nodded and turned back toward her car. "Malcolm really is very excited. Enjoy the overnight, and I will be here at ten a.m. to bring him back."

We waved goodbye, but the wind had left my sails. When I turned toward him, all evidence of Josh's upset was erased. He cupped my face, squishing my pouting cheeks together.

"It's fine," he said again. "Let's go have fun."

"I'm ready!" Malcolm bounded down the stairs. Josh scooped him up as he leaped from the bottom stair, and Josh carried his giggling body like a football. He spun as we made our way to his truck, Malcolm's squeals clearing the wildlife within a one-mile radius of the house and helping me forget the worried look that had crossed Josh's features.

The Cedar County Seaside Circus was neither near the sea nor a circus. It was, however, one of the largest carnivals

I had ever seen. The county fairgrounds were packed with carnival rides, food vendors, and tables full of people selling arts and crafts. My favorite was a large platform stage with swags of twinkle lights winking over the wooden dance floor. When a young man walked ahead of us with a very rotund pig on a leash, I burst out laughing.

Josh smiled down at me and flicked a knuckle on the tip of my nose. "Welcome to Montana."

Malcolm could barely contain himself. His dark eyes were wide as he took in the flashing lights. Screams from the rides rolled over us in waves. We went straight to the ticket booth, and Malcolm's jaw hit the floor after Josh purchased him the unlimited-ride bracelet.

"How about you? Up for some fun?" Josh purchased a small handful of additional ride tickets.

"Am I allowed?" Hope danced in my voice.

"Allowed? Of course. We're here to have fun."

Malcolm laced his small hand with Josh's and looked up at me. "Which ride is your favorite, Effie?"

His small, sweet voice tugged at my heart. "Well, actually, this is my first carnival."

Both Josh and Malcolm stopped abruptly.

"What?"

"Seriously?"

Their incredulous voices folded over each other, and I couldn't help but laugh.

I raised my palms. "Sad but true."

Shaking his head, Josh swiveled on his heel and marched back up to the booth. I waited with Malcolm, who only looked at me and lifted his shoulders. Minutes later, Josh came back with two additional unlimited-ride bracelets.

"If we're gonna do it, we're doing it right." He wound

the red paper bracelet around my wrist and gave my forearm a gentle squeeze before releasing me. As his fingertips trailed across the thin skin at my wrist, my breath caught.

"Looks like you're the expert, Malcolm. Where to?"

"Go big or go home?" Malcolm held out his fist to Josh.

Josh tapped his fist on top of Malcolm's, and a devilish grin inched up the corner of his mouth. "Go big or go home."

Malcolm nodded before thrusting a fist in the air. "Gravitron 3000!"

Oh fuck.

~

AFTER TWO HOT DOGS, one funnel cake, a competition between fried Oreos and fried Twinkies, and back-to-back tours of the Tilt-A-Whirl, my stomach pitched and rolled. I pressed a hand to it and willed myself not to throw up in the very suspicious-looking trash can. Desiree would never forgive me if I also contracted the Ebola virus.

"Lookin' a little green around the gills there, Ef!" Gemma's playful voice carried over the crowd as I lifted my head from between my knees. Her hair was piled high in a messy bun that looked effortlessly chic, and a white ribbon wound around it to form an adorable bow in the back.

Despite the warm evening air, Gemma's signature high neckline and long sleeves tugged at my heartstrings. She spoke a few words to the twosome of girls she was with and walked over to wrap me in a hug.

Behind me, Josh called out. "First time."

Gemma held me at arm's length as I swallowed again.

"No shit?" Josh's eyes sliced from Gemma to Malcolm. "Sorry."

Malcolm grinned at her and popped a thumbs-up.

"Yes. It's my first carnival, and I think I overdid it with all the fried foods."

Gemma plucked a fried mushroom from the red-and-white paper basket in Josh's hand. "This is a veggie. Doesn't that count?" She popped it in her mouth.

I'd put on at least five pounds since I'd arrived in Tipp and didn't even want to think about how much shit Sergei was going to give me when I got back. Never mind Desiree or my mother. I'd be getting grief from all sides despite the fact I kind of liked the way my hips filled out my denim jeans lately.

"Josh, can we go on Pharaoh's Fury?" I looked to where he was pointing and saw the Egyptian-style ship swaying back and forth on a pendulum, and my stomach tightened. Josh eyed me over, hesitant to answer Malcolm.

I waved him off. "You two go. I'll be fine to sit this one out."

Gemma jumped in. "Effie can hang with us for a while. We're going to walk and listen to the band."

Josh positioned his body into my space and lowered his voice to me. The rough texture of it flowed over me, soothing my quivering belly. "You sure?"

Relief flooded over me. *Thank god I don't have to go on another spinning ride.* I nodded once. "Definitely. He's having a blast, and I don't want to ruin it for either of you."

Josh dropped a kiss on the top of my head before looking at Gemma. "Take care of my girl."

I rolled my eyes, but Gemma stood straight and gave him a jaunty salute. "Yes, boss."

Malcolm grabbed Josh by the hand, and I watched them

walk together toward the ride. A balloon in my chest expanded, making it harder to breathe.

Gemma's friends walked up to join us, and we all watched Josh walk away. "He is *so* cute with him."

"Adorable." The short redhead with a riot of curls pressed her freckled hand to her chest and sighed.

"I think my ovaries just exploded." The leggy brunette fanned herself with a spare napkin.

We all laughed, and Gemma made quick introductions with her two friends, Kate and Sophie. Kate stared for a beat too long, and I wondered if there was a hint of recognition there. She let it go without questioning, and I followed the group as they wound through the crowd toward the stage.

I glanced back only once to see Josh looking over his shoulder at me, Malcolm's hand in his, grinning.

Fuck me. I am in deep shit.

18

EFFIE

THE CEDAR COUNTY SEASIDE CIRCUS knew how to throw a party. Music thumped through the speakers as the crowd's collective boots stomped to the beat. Whoops and hollers rose for songs about country living, lost love, and something about women finding tractors sexy—which, three months ago, I would have completely scoffed at, but after seeing Josh dismount a tractor at the ranch, and the way he looked with the big machinery beneath him . . . I get it.

"This band is so good. Who is it?" I sipped the beer Kate had handed me.

"Colin McCoy and the Dirty Pidge Boys. Locals from a few towns over. Good, right?" Sophie had to lean in and yell to be heard over the crowd's excitement.

I nodded. They were excellent and mixed country classics with songs I'd never heard before. The singer's voice was rich and deep and *very* sexy.

I glanced at Gemma, who was mouthing the words and tapping her foot. I'd heard her sing once before and knew she was talented. The look of longing that crossed her features told me there was definitely more to that story.

"If you look there," Kate added, pointing to a gorgeous blonde in the corner of the stage. The woman was staring at the lead singer with lust in her eyes, a little kid wearing noise-canceling headphones propped on her hip. "That's his wife. They're obsessed with each other, and it's so swoony."

The singer looked directly at his wife, singing each song for her. A pang crept into my chest cavity. *What must that be like? To live a life where your significant other is so devoted to you that everyone else just falls away.*

Josh's face, with his signature smirk and the way his eyes crinkled at the edges, popped into my mind. There was potential there. Had I been born into a different life—as a different person entirely—I could see building a life with him so easily. But what kind of life would that be? I had no discernible skills outside of my acting and using my looks to make money. My value had been tied to the facade since I was a child, my mother having shoved me into every beauty pageant she could find.

If I abandoned that life, what would I have left?

"Hey, since this one stole our Josh off the market"—Kate slung a thumb over her shoulder at me—"let's go shake that ridiculously sculpted ass of yours!" With a hard smack to Gemma's backside, Kate was pulling her toward the dance floor. I glanced down at said ass and noted I somehow missed how fit Gemma was. I smoothed my hands down my hips and reminded myself that things like fried carnival food and beer were not *Sergei approved*.

Sophie slugged the last of her plastic cup of beer and tossed it into the nearby trash can. "All right. You too. Let's go."

Before I could protest, she was pushing me from behind toward a crowd in the middle of the dance floor. The music had shifted to an upbeat song I could more or less sway to.

The crowd was happy, but I also found them overwhelming. My head scanned the crowd, snagging on a handful of faces who'd paused their conversations to gawk. I wasn't the best dancer, but I was not so bad it would warrant the looks and whispers being sent my way.

No. That's recognition on their faces.

Sure enough, the points started. Like a wave, more and more people began centering their attention to me, and the little semicircle of clueless, dancing women.

I swallowed past the sandpaper that coated my throat. I leaned toward Gemma, squeezing her upper arm. "I'm gonna sit this one out."

Before she could answer, I let the curtain of my hair fall over my face, and I pushed toward the outskirts of the dance floor. Before I made it to the edge, a large frame blocked my path.

"Holy shit. You're Madison Colt."

I lifted my chin. My heart ricocheted around my chest, but I managed a cool smile. "Ha! Flattering, but no. I get that all the time."

I attempted to sidestep the man, but he mirrored my movements, blocking me from leaving. "Bullshit. I can't believe it's you!" He barked over his shoulder. "Dude! It's the fucking hot chick from *Stardust Guardians*!"

More heads turned my way as the murmurs turned into a full-blown swell of conversation. I looked around, hoping for any way out of this situation, and my eyes caught Gemma's. Her lips tightened, and she started moving her way through the crowd.

"Sorry to disappoint," I said to the man. "I'm not her."

As I went to move again, the asshole stepped forward and into my space. Panic skittered over me when Al, the skinny, tattooed bartender from The Rasa, stepped in front of me. In shock, I stared at the long white braid that hung down his back. A hand wrapped around my elbow, and as I flinched, Gemma moved into my side. Together with Kate and Sophie, we stared at the scene unfolding in front of us.

Al stood, chest puffed out, as a small crowd of onlookers gathered, some pulling up their phones and pointing them in my direction. In front of my eyes, the slightly annoying, aging man transformed into a frightening motherfucker.

"There a problem?" Al's voice was cold and hard as, one by one, Tipp residents stacked behind him. I scanned their familiar faces and wished I'd done a better job at remembering their actual names.

Kate leaned down to whisper to me. "Al used to be in a motorcycle gang. Before giving up that life and settling in Tipp."

I could see it so clearly. The scars across his knobby knuckles, the way he twitched and flexed his hand—ready for the fight. I didn't recognize half the faces who stood behind him in solidarity, but they stood at my defense. Protecting me from the accusations the man had thrown in my face. From the truth.

He threw a hand in my direction. "It's Madison Colt!"

Al glanced over his shoulder to look me up and down before tossing me a wink. When he looked back at the man, he shook his head. "Not even close, man. That's our Effie, and she ain't no movie star. Go on and leave 'er alone."

He looked over Al's shoulder at me, unconvinced.

When Al's back went rigid, intensity rolling off him in waves, the guy finally relented. "What the fuck ever, man. I don't want any trouble."

He turned and disappeared into the crowd, his group of friends pausing to get one last look at me.

Only once the crowd had dissipated could I let the

breath of relief I'd been holding whoosh out of me. Al started to walk away, seemingly unaffected by what he'd done for me. I walked up to him, shoulders straight and fire in my eyes. His widened fractionally as I placed my hands at the sides of his face and plated a smacking kiss right on the lips. The crowd behind him hooted and hollered. It lasted only a fraction of a second, but a blush bloomed across his ruddy face, and he pulled me into a hug.

"Go on," he demanded.

I smiled up at him and turned to find Gemma and her friends laughing as they pulled me into their circle.

"Jesus, that was a close one." Gemma was laughing. "Let's go find your man, superstar."

~

I CHOSE NOT to mention the almost incident on the dance floor to Josh. Knowing him, he'd want to find the faceless man and beat the shit out of him—or feel indebted to Al on my behalf or something equally chivalrous.

The carnival wasn't about me, and I didn't want the tiny blip to ruin his outing with Malcolm. The spike in adrenaline had me wide awake as we drove our way back to Josh's house. Malcolm was a chatterbox as he replayed each ride he and Josh bested. His excitement was infectious, and the little giggles that erupted from him pulled at my heart.

As the lights of the carnival faded and the darkness of the winding country roads enveloped the car, his eyelids sagged, and his voice got quieter. In the front seat, Josh's hand found mine and squeezed.

Once back home, the three of us settled on a movie—not one of mine, thank god. Josh said he needed a minute and would happily make us popcorn as we got set up for the movie. I glanced back at him to see his arms braced on the counter, his head hung low. The urge to go to him, comfort him, and ask what was wrong was overwhelming. He shook his head, and I whipped my focus back to Malcolm.

After the incident on the dance floor, the need to apologize to Malcolm—and Josh—for thinking they had to keep my identity a secret was unbearable.

"Hey, kiddo." His deep-brown eyes met mine. "I owe you an apology."

His little eyebrow tipped down.

"You don't have to keep my identity a secret. If someone finds out, I'll just deal with it."

He lifted his shoulders. "Josh said when it's someone else's secret, we shouldn't tell."

I thought for a moment. As much as I wanted to press Malcolm and fish around for more about what was bothering Josh, I couldn't do it. Only the lowest scum of the earth would use a kid against another person, and no matter how many times I may have bent and manipulated my morals in LA, I couldn't do it.

"That's true. A part of trusting someone is knowing they always have your best interests at heart. But it was wrong of us to ask you to keep my secret. I'm sorry for that."

He paused his flipping through channels to look at me again. "A sign of a good person is someone who can apologize." Warmth filled my body. I bumped Malcolm's shoulder with my own.

"That sounds like some good advice."

"Josh told me that."

My smile broke free as I took in Malcolm's sweet face. "He's kind of great, right?"

"I think I love him more than my own family." The sadness and wisdom infused in his little voice hollowed me out. What comfort could I provide? I'd never met my father, and my own mother used me to feel an ounce of fame she'd never reached. The woman would sell her soul if it meant she was the one who had made it big. I gave him the only real truth I had come to know.

"Family are the people who love you. Sometimes that's not always the people you're born to." He leaned his head on my shoulder, his tight black curls tickling my cheek as I leaned against him.

"Room for one more?" Josh entered the living room with a bowl overflowing with buttery popcorn. Malcolm inched toward the center, allowing Josh a seat on the end. We snuggled in together as Malcolm pressed play for the movie.

Josh and I made bets on how long Malcolm would last. Turned out, he won at exactly fourteen minutes. He and I continued to watch the movie with Malcolm tucked into Josh's side. Josh kept his arm slung over the back of the couch toward me. His thumb drew lazy circles at the base of my neck, sending warm tingles down my back.

A while later, Josh's breaths deepened to a slow, lazy rhythm.

This is what it could be like.

Unexpected tears sprung at the corners of my eyes. For the first time in my life, I hated the choices that brought me here. The fame. The money. The need to hide out while gossip blew over. Even the drive to find my father.

This pretend life I was living was a cruel glimpse of the kind of happiness I could never keep.

I thought back to a movie I'd once made early in my career, *Fractured Time*. In it I played a woman who traveled back in time to save her son's life but inadvertently made everything in the future worse. I considered what an alternate timeline would be like. One where I had come to Tipp and found my father. Maybe my mother and I would have stayed. Josh and I could have had our childhood friendship develop into something more over time. Everything would be different.

My eyes dropped to Malcolm. He wouldn't have been a part of that timeline, and my chest ached even thinking about it. He was special. He and Josh deserved each other.

I may not have had the ability to go back and change my timeline, but I also knew Josh and Malcolm were exactly where they needed to be—cuddled together on the couch after a night of too many carnival rides and too much sugar.

Knowing it would be most appropriate for Malcolm to wake up and not find me in Josh's bed, I covered them with a soft blanket, walked to my room, and wept.

19

JOSH

I DON'T THINK Effie or Malcolm realized I had heard their entire conversation when I'd excused myself to the kitchen to make popcorn. Effie's words about family being the people who loved you flayed me open. I knew right then and there I was in love with her.

Malcolm was a great kid—the best. He deserved more than unreliable adults and random visits with me at home and at the ranch.

Shit needed to change. The kind of shit that added permanence to his life.

Would Effie be a part of that?

I knew the answer was a resounding *no*, but I didn't stop myself from letting the image of us raising Malcolm together wash over me.

I might not be able to give him a mother and a complete family unit, but I could give him a home. One that was permanent and full of structure and love, one where he never had to question the intentions of the adults in his life.

Setting the wheels in motion, I hung up the phone and leaned back in my office chair. A satisfied glow washed over me. I couldn't wait to see the look on Malcolm's face when I told him.

I just hope he wants me back.

The familiar panic of self-doubt slipped through before I could squash it down. I definitely would need to have a serious conversation with him soon. Make sure he wanted me as much as I wanted him, and that together we could make a go of it. There were a shit ton of hoops to jump through before it became a reality, but if he was game, I was *all in.*

Effie's smile flashed in my mind, and I rubbed the raw spot in the center of my chest. If only it were that simple with her. Anxiety crept up my neck, and the familiar buzz between my ears grew to a roar. I needed to get out of the stifling four walls of my office. I needed air.

I walked through the large barn out into the open expanse of the Montana valley. I ignored the fact that the July summer heat was peaking, and soon the first signs of fall would start creeping in.

Time was almost up.

"You got a problem."

The familiar sound of Ray's scratchy voice broke me from my darkening thoughts. "Afternoon, Ray. What's up?"

His weather-worn face grew more weary every year, but his crystal-blue eyes were still sharp. He was a grumpy asshole, but he worked hard and cared about the ranch and its animals as much as I did. So when he saw an issue, I tended to listen.

"Coupla stragglers in the south field. They didn't wanna come up. Lethargic."

I pressed my lips into a thin line. Ray also had a keen eye for the animals. *This is not good.*

The buzzing between my ears roared louder. I did not

need the additional heap of stress that sick animals would pile on.

I steadied my breath.

Nicest guy in the room.

"I'm on it. I appreciate your attention to detail."

Ray rolled his eyes and muttered something akin to *ass kiss* as he turned from me. I grinned at his back. It must be hard work to be that disgruntled—almost as hard to consistently make the right choices.

After making the rounds and getting my eyes on the cattle myself, I discovered Ray was right. Something was definitely wrong with those cows, which meant quarantining the entirety of that particular herd.

Ma was not going to be happy with the delay—and cost—that would cause.

Scrubbing my hand over my face, I made my way to her office. Her door was open, and she was behind her computer screen, glasses perched on her nose.

After I knocked, her eyes met mine, and she gestured for me to enter, then lifted her eyebrow, waiting for me to speak.

"Just giving you an update. We've got a herd out. A couple of sick ones. The vet'll be in to check them out."

"A whole herd?"

I leaned on the arm of a chair across from her desk. "More than a few looked weak. Slow. The best bet is to separate the whole herd to contain whatever it is."

She pressed her thumbs into her eye sockets and sighed. "I do not need this shit today."

I stood to my full height. "You and me both."

My gruff tone tore Ma's attention from the computer screen.

I was always good at reading people—a skill passed

down by my US marshal father, I suppose. Ma Brown's cheek twitched. She did not need or want me voicing my opinion on the matter. No, she wanted the Josh Laredo everyone knew and loved. Agreeable. Kindhearted. Selfless.

Just say, "Yes, ma'am."

"Do you trust me?" I asked her.

She considered a moment before leaning back into her desk chair. "You've been here almost as long as the rest of us. In my line of work, I trust very few people."

Effie's confidence and bravery to step out of her old life and explore her past lit a fire in me. I looked down at Ma. "I've earned it."

"You have."

In two words, my bunched shoulders relaxed.

"As head stockman, I won't be running this type of thing by you anymore. You've got more on your plate than necessary, and I am more than capable of managing the animals and my workers without you." My bold statement earned me another raised eyebrow, but Ma Brown stayed silent. "If there's something that would affect production or is a matter of federal protection, I'll let you know."

My heart hammered as I waited for her response.

"Dismissed."

Ma's attention went back to her computer as I exited her office in two strides and strode down the hallway.

Nice-guy Josh was gone. There were things in my life I wanted—responsibilities. Respect. People.

I was taking them.

~

THE BRAKES on my old truck squealed as I parked it beside a tree. It was hidden enough that you couldn't see it from the road. A short hike along the mountain and the familiar clearing came into view.

Effie clutched my hand as we wound around the rocky path and toward my favorite spot.

Our spot.

I stopped to admire the steam that rose from the pools of hot springs and sucked the misty forest air into my nose and held it in my chest. Effie squeezed my hand as I exhaled.

Walking closer to the pool, she turned to face me. "How has no one found this before?"

I set down the cooler of food we'd packed and leaned against the rock face. I lifted a shoulder. "I'm sure someone somewhere has. I've never run into them though. I like to think it's mine. Shrouded in mystery."

She grinned and stepped into my space. Her crystal-blue eyes sparkled up at me as her head leaned back to meet my gaze. Her body pressed against mine, and nothing had felt so right. I ran a hand down her spine, then traced a knuckle down her impossibly straight nose.

"Wanna jump in, or should I feed you first?"

Effie leaned into my touch, and a warm hum vibrated through her slim throat. "Mmm. Hot spring first."

I dropped the pack that had our towels and took one last loop around the perimeter to ensure we were, in fact, alone. Effie's long fingers slipped open the buttons of her dress as she shot me a hot look from across the steaming spring.

The feral beast inside of me perked to life, and a low grumble rumbled in my chest. One look at that woman made me lose my damn mind. I made quick work of pulling my shirt off my back and dropping my jeans, never taking my eyes off Effie as she piled her fiery hair into a high bun.

In the steam, she was ethereal. A siren calling me to the depths of her waters. In slow, measured steps, Effie lowered herself into the pool. I followed her, entranced by the dips and curves of her neck and shoulders.

"Coming in, cowboy?"

I moved toward the hot spring, her thick voice making my heart pump faster. The warm water lapped at my legs as I lowered myself next to her. A deep, heavy sigh moaned out of me, and I gave in to the heat.

Effie rubbed the water up her arms. "I swear, this water just does something miraculous to my skin. It feels so soft."

My palm found her shoulder and stroked down her arm. "It's the minerals in the water. Millions of years of moving through rock and sand."

"Johnny needs to bottle this up and sell it at The Rebellious Rose. He'd be put on the map for finding the actual Fountain of Youth."

I smiled and kneaded the muscles that bunched at her shoulders. "He's a good guy. I'm glad you're making friends here."

My hands smoothed over the toned muscles of her back, and I willed myself to not press her against the rocks and explore every inch of her.

No. Today was something else entirely. The air between us was different. *Charged.*

I turned Effie's shoulders so her back rested against the rock face. Lowering my body, I ran my hands down her torso and hips. Farther still until I felt the tender skin of her thighs. Effie quirked an eyebrow, and I shot her a cocky smirk.

Lower and lower my hands moved until I lifted her foot to my chest and ran a thumb into her arch.

"Oh fuck." Her head lolled back as she enjoyed my touch. I kneaded and rubbed, her toes poking up out of the water, and I lowered my mouth to kiss the tops.

"You're too good to me."

I shook my head once. "You deserve so much more. Turn around and let me get your back." Effie obliged and propped her arms on the ledge of the spring, her cheek resting on top of her hands. Once she was pliant and finally relaxed, I took the space next to her, mirroring her pose.

Effie's eyes were closed as the hot water lapped over her shoulder. "We're friends, right?"

Her eyes stayed closed, but I couldn't take mine off her. "I think so."

"Who's your best friend?" Before I could answer, she continued, "The last best friend I can remember is Rita Alsip in the sixth grade. It was right before we moved from Vegas to California. In LA, I was too busy with pageants, modeling, and acting classes to make many friends. I remember Rita loved drawing and crafting, and we had these little matching friendship bracelets made out of that embroidery floss."

"Cute." I gulped past the thickness in my throat. I thought hard about her question. "Haven't had one in a long time either, I guess." If I said *Ray*, that would be depressing as fuck. Her eyes fluttered open, the steam curling between us. "But everyone loves you."

I wanted to agree. But I couldn't lie—not to her. "Everyone loves parts of me."

A small, sad laugh escaped her nose. "The parts you let them see."

My lips pressed together. The woman had burrowed under my skin, and there wasn't a damn thing I could do about it.

"What parts do I get to see?" Her long lashes were darkened by the moisture in the air. A soft smile played at her lips as I inched closer.

"Effie Pierce." I wound my arm around her, pulling her into me. My mouth hovered over hers as my heart slammed against my ribs. "You"—I rubbed my thumb across her cheekbone as she toyed with her lip—"are my best friend."

My wet lips pressed into hers, and she mewled, arching into me. My breath caught. Blood surged to my cock. Effie's nails raked down my shoulder blades, stinging as they dug into the flesh. Her leg hitched up to my hip, and I grabbed the back of her knee. Heat rose around us as I licked and sucked at the tender skin of her neck.

"More," she panted. "I need more."

I reached down to palm her breast, capturing the diamond tip between two fingers. I pinched and rolled as her moan was swallowed by my kisses.

"Get up here." I wound her legs around my torso and moved up the ledge and out of the hot spring. I lowered us to the towels in the soft grass. Effie propped herself on her elbows. Lust filled her eyes. I knelt between her knees, drinking in the sight of her glorious, naked body.

She sucked in her lower lip as I ran my hands down her inner thighs, kneading her muscles. "I've never wanted anyone as much as I want you. So I'm going to tell you exactly how this is going to go." Breaths sawed in and out of her, lifting her full round tits. "First, I'm going to tease you and taste you. You'll be as close to the edge as you can get before I warm you up with my fingers. You'll be aching for more." Her knees dropped open, and her breathing got heavier at my words. "You'll be hot and wet and begging for me to fill that greedy little cunt."

Effie dropped from her elbows as I lowered my head. After pushing her knees apart, I lowered my mouth to the thin skin at the top of her thighs. I licked and nibbled, letting my hot breath wash over her pussy. Seeing her glisten as I worshipped her made my cock pulse. Unable to resist, I slicked my tongue over her opening. Her sweet flavor washed over my tongue, and I moaned into her, pushing into her opening. I flattened my tongue and ran up her split to her clit. I flicked pressure over the nub, loving how vocal and responsive she was.

My cock begged to slam into her. Take her. I fisted myself and squeezed once, reveling in the mounting pressure between my legs. My balls ached for release, but I wasn't nearly done with Effie.

I kissed and licked and sucked until her tiny inner muscles were pulsing around my tongue. Only then I dragged two fingers around her clit, adding a gentle squeezing pressure.

"Josh. I'm close." Her breathless pants only fueled my efforts. A few more pulses and I'd have had her tumbling over the edge, but not yet.

Not yet.

I released the pressure from her clit and dragged two fingers down to find her opening. "You want to be full, baby girl? Should I warm you up for this cock?"

"Yes. Please, yes."

I pushed two fingers into her, and her groan echoed through the forest canopy. Soft light filtered through the trees, illuminating her body in the dusky light as I sucked her clit and added a third finger. Stroking and moving, I found her G-spot, that fleshy interior nub, and moved over it. Wetness seeped out of her around my fingers, and I hummed in approval.

"Good girl. So fucking wet for me." I bent down to taste her, pulling her even closer to the edge. "I've been thinking all day about that tight pussy squeezing me—milking this cock."

"Oh my god. Oh fuck."

"I want it too. I want all of you." I slipped my fingers from her and lined my throbbing cock against her core. I ran a teasing line up her slit with the head of my cock. I paused to reach my jeans and pull out a condom.

"No. Bare. I want you bare."

A guttural groan moved through me as the head of my cock slipped inside her tight body.

"I can feel every inch of you."

I slipped in deeper, stretching her open. "Not yet you don't." Inch by torturous inch, I filled her. Her pussy clamped down around me and gripped. I started pumping out a rhythm, surging in and dragging back out.

"Baby." I stared at her, waiting for Effie's lust-clouded eyes to meet mine. "Are we making love or are we fucking? Because I'm about to lose my damn mind." I pumped harder into her and held as my cock went as deeply as it could go.

"Both." Effie reached to grab my ass, holding me inside her, and squeezed. "It's both."

I grabbed her wrists and pinned them above her. Slamming my hips against her, I fucked her. Hard. Pouring every ounce of love I had for her into each thrust. Filling her with the same incomprehensible, scary-as-fuck love that had wound its way into my very soul.

No one but her understood how rough, hard sex could also be making love. A show of how deeply my body ached for hers.

No one but her.

Pressing her—spearing her—into the hard ground, I lowered my mouth to her nipple. Teasing and biting and sucking as her clit ground against the base of my cock. Her hips bucked beneath me.

"There. There. Oh fuck." Effie's orgasm tore through

her as I moved my hips, teasing her clit until my own release was right behind hers. Her wetness mixed with mine and flowed over my cock as I filled her.

I collapsed around her, sucking in desperate breaths as thoughts slammed through my mind like a Ping-Pong ball.

I love you.

I need you.

The words clogged in my throat. Finally I managed to gain control over my voice. "It's never been like this for me."

Effie's smooth leg stroked along the back of mine as she let out a satisfied hum. Her arms hung heavily at her sides, and I scrambled to compose myself. Effie didn't say *me too* or *I know how you feel*. Instead, she breathed deeply, and I fought the tiny voice of insecurity that taunted, *You're nothing special to her.*

I rolled off her, taking her with me and tucking her into my side. The soft grass tickled my back.

"I can't feel my toes." Her deep, throaty moan shot tingles through my chest. Her fingers traced the lines of my chest and abs as I stared at the light filtering through the trees above us.

After a few quiet moments, Effie spoke. "Tell me about your family."

I considered. "My mom and siblings live closer to Bozeman. Less rural. More to do."

"You have a brother, right? The construction guy who helped you build the house?"

"Brian. And Mandy is my sister. She teaches fifth grade. Married and has two kids."

"Your mom never remarried?"

My palm stroked her smooth skin. "Dad's been gone a long time, but he was larger than life. His presence is still very much *there*, you know?"

She nodded, but I wondered if her thoughts had turned to her own father and her quest to find out more about him. My dad was the cornerstone of our entire family—he shaped each of us in his own way, and I couldn't imagine growing up without his guidance. It seemed everything in my life would have been different.

"Hey." I nudged her gently until her eyes met mine. "Come with me to meet them."

20

EFFIE

THE WIDE-OPEN TERRAIN of Montana's valley slowly morphed into rows of carbon copy houses and perfectly rectangular city blocks. The mountains still loomed in the distance, but even the air was different. Suburban. Pine Valley was stuck somewhere between the Old West and a modern-day city.

I could see why Josh preferred the wild, untamed country of Tipp.

The familiar city sounds flowed over me. The whoosh of car tires. A honking horn. The shrill cry of an ambulance in the distance. In many ways, it was much like LA.

I watched the houses—a mixture of ranch-style homes and more modern colonial styles—flash past me. "Did you live here too?"

"Mom moved here after Dad died. I stayed a month before calling Ma Brown and begging for a job." Josh kept his eyes trained on the road ahead of us as he battled intermittent bouts of traffic. He radiated barely stifled nervous energy. Whether it was the traffic or the fact I would be meeting his whole family for dinner, I wasn't sure.

Whatever it was, it made him quieter on the ninety-minute trek to Pine Valley. We listened to music, and I enjoyed the late summer sunshine as it danced across the mountains.

Josh pulled his truck into a flower-lined driveway and parked. He didn't make an effort to leave the cab of the truck, so I stayed still. My curious eyes searched his face.

"I won't tell them." *We can keep your secret.* The words remained unspoken, but I understood his meaning. He lifted my hand and smoothed a kiss over my knuckles. His eyes searched mine, and emotion bloomed in my chest.

I seriously don't want this getting out.

Nothing good could come from a leak to the tabloids about my whereabouts. "I don't want to lie to your family." My lips pressed together in a small smile. "Really. It's okay."

Relief washed over him. Josh was a good person. One who didn't deserve the secrets and lies that were a part of the deal when you attached yourself to a celebrity. He exited the cab of the truck, but before he could round the hood, the front door opened. A woman—his mother, I presumed—stood smiling, while two young boys pushed past her and ran toward us.

"Uncle Josh!" The younger boy squealed and launched himself into Josh's arms. His deep, warm laughter pinched my heart as Josh swung the boy onto his hip, flipping him upside down and shaking him.

"Who is this?" Josh asked as the boy laughed in delight. "Who is this strange creature?"

"Uncle Josh, it's me! Kayden!" Giggles erupted from him, and Josh continued to shake.

"What? No way. You're, like, seven feet tall already!" Josh righted Kayden and set the little boy on the ground. He turned toward the older one. "Caleb." They shared an intricate handshake of snaps and fist bumps and slaps. "My man."

Both boys talked over each other as Josh's mother stood in the doorway, smiling at the scene. Josh tipped his head toward me, gesturing to *come on* as he walked toward the front door.

"Hey, Mom." He lowered a kiss to her cheek, and she patted his chest.

"Hi, honey. How was the trip?"

He herded Kayden and his brother inside as I walked up behind him. "You know. Slow. Mom, there's someone I'd like you to meet." He stepped back, opening his frame to me, and I moved closer. "This is Effie Pierce. Effie, my mom, Patricia Laredo."

I smiled and held out my hand. "Mrs. Laredo, it's a pleasure to meet you."

Tears welled in her eyes as she swatted the air between us. "Oh, hush. Call me Patty. And come here." She moved forward, enveloping me in a tight hug. She was about my size, and her arms wound around my shoulders. At first I froze, unsure what to do. But then something shifted and clicked inside me. Warmth spread in my chest. Her gentle embrace held me in place, and I wrapped my arms around her back. With a quick squeeze, she released me.

A man who I assumed was his brother, Brian, walked up behind Patty. He was taller than Josh—thicker in the chest and stomach but still fit. His hair was darker and shorter. While he was handsome, he was somehow more reserved—holding back that overt goodness that radiated out of Josh and made everyone instantly comfortable.

"Come on, Mom. Don't scare off the first girl Joshie's ever brought home."

I turned and raised an eyebrow to Josh. *Joshie?*

He pinned me with a subtle glare. *Don't even.*

I stifled a laugh and smiled at Brian and offered my hand. "Effie."

"Brian. The older, handsomer brother, but you can see that for yourself." His long arms stretched wide as if it were benevolent for him to let me gaze upon his glory.

Josh sucker punched him in the gut. "Dick!" Brian clutched his stomach, and Patty smacked him in the back of the head, making Josh laugh.

"Mouth."

"Sorry, Mom."

Patty turned to me. "I'm sorry for these two. They were raised by wolves. Come in. Come in. Mandy's just inside helping with dinner."

We all gathered in the kitchen, and it was a flurry of introductions to Mandy; her husband, Tom, who was entranced by a baseball game on TV; and her two boys. Patty and Mandy seemed to have a routine around prepping dinner, so I focused on the two rowdy boys in the living room while Josh and his brother traded brotherly insults.

Being around Josh all this time, I was surprised to find Brian was the more gregarious brother. Tom's eyes never left the television. Mandy was quiet, and Josh landed somewhere in the middle. Every now and again I'd catch Mandy eyeballing me over the kitchen island. She'd look away before her curious eyes would slice back to me. I caught the same look from her mother when they traded whispers over the salad.

I couldn't decipher if they recognized my face or if I really was the first girl Josh had ever introduced to his family, as Brian had teased. As a family, they were loud— talking over each other and having half conversations before the topic veered in a different direction. No one seemed to notice, but before long, my head was spinning.

The backyard to Patty's house was small, but when Tom complained to Mandy that he couldn't hear the game over his rambunctious boys, all but Tom moved outside.

Brian stood at the patio door. "Beer?"

Josh raised his hand and looked at me. I lifted my shoulder and smiled. *Sure.* I could suffer through one shitty beer in the name of going with the flow.

Patty jumped up from the brown patio chair she had occupied. "We've got wine or . . . maybe we could make a cosmopolitan or something."

"Mom . . . ," Josh started.

I laughed lightly. "A beer is fine, but thank you."

Patty looked relieved and sat back into the plush patio furniture.

Brian had returned with the cold beers, and as I took my first, tentative sip, Mandy asked, "So when's the next movie out?"

I sputtered and nearly choked on the Coors Light just as Josh pinned her with a glare. "Dude."

Mandy's eyes looked innocent as she shrugged. "What? You are Madison Colt, right?"

"Oh shit! I knew she looked familiar." Brian's forearm pushed into his little brother. "Hell yeah, Joshie!"

Josh thumped a hand on my back as he glared at his brother and I coughed, trying not to choke. *I should have taken her up on that hard liquor.*

Regaining use of my voice I settled my patient, practiced smile into place. "I go by that stage name, yes. But you can call me Effie. I guess my new hair wasn't much of a disguise." I touched a hand to my natural auburn locks.

"What brings you to Montana, dear?" Patty was still a

little shell-shocked, but she was trying her best to salvage the situation and maintain her composure. Mandy lifted an eyebrow. She knew the tabloid stories—I was sure of it.

"I'm looking for my father." I took a tentative sip from the bottle and was relieved when it went down my tightening throat. "I believe he may have been a US marshal. Much like your late husband."

A somber silence fell over the group.

Fuck.

I looked to Josh for help, but his eyes were downcast, just like the rest of them.

Double fuck.

"Mom! Mom! Mom! Can we walk to the pond?"

Mandy looked to Patty for an answer. "Dinner still has a bit to go," Patty told her.

"Fine. Get your shoes on." Mandy stood.

"Can Uncle Josh take us? Please?" little Kayden begged.

Brian opened his arms and looked offended. "What am I? Chopped liver?" The boys giggled in response.

"The men can take the boys. We can finish here." Patty raised her finger. "But be back in thirty."

After a peal of laughter and a kiss on the head from Josh, they were gone, and I was left to the Laredo women.

"You know they're going to come back filthy. All four of 'em." Patty watched as the foursome disappeared around a corner.

"Yep." Mandy nodded.

I followed the women into the kitchen. "It smells delicious. Is there anything I can help with?"

Dear god, please say no.

"I think we're all good here. I hope lasagna is okay. I didn't think to ask Josh about a special diet. You're not *vegan*, are you?" She whispered the word *vegan* as if she was horrified, but she left out the *not that there's anything wrong with that* her question implied.

I couldn't help but laugh. "Lasagna sounds amazing, thanks."

"Another beer?" Mandy asked.

I shook my head, and we settled into the chairs around the small kitchen island.

"Effie, we are thrilled to meet you. Josh surprised us with the news he was dating." Her warm, motherly smile had my insides tumbling.

"He likes to keep to himself and play cowboy up at that ranch." Mandy's tone was teasing, but I didn't miss the judgment laced in her words.

My hackles started to rise, and I smoothed a hand over my thigh. "Josh is amazing at his job. He's respected by the men and women who work for him."

"Yeah—criminals and idiots."

"Mandy." Patty chided her daughter.

"His knowledge of animal care is second to none." I jumped to his defense. "He seems to really enjoy the work he does."

"I guess," Mandy conceded. "All I know is I couldn't work there. Too many ghosts."

Patty sighed as if she knew exactly what Mandy meant. She turned her attention to me. "So tell us, What is Hollywood like?"

I considered her question a moment. Not *How did you meet my son?* or *How long have you been together?* but about the glitz and glamour of Hollywood.

I wasn't surprised, just disappointed. I provided the safe, surface answers I'd been trained to use and tried to steer the conversation to safer ground.

"Your boys are so cute, Mandy. Have they met Malcolm yet?"

Her eyes narrowed. "Malcolm?"

Fuuuuuuck.

I cleared my throat as my brain scrambled. I was saved by Kayden and Caleb throwing open the door. It banged against the wall, and I jumped from my seat, excusing myself to the bathroom.

I was coming back when Patty's soothing, motherly voice stopped me in the hallway. "Are you sure you're okay, honey?" I peeked around the corner to see her hand patting the center of Josh's back.

"I'm fine, Mom." Josh kept his voice hushed, but I could pick out the annoyance in his tone.

"Have you followed up with Dr. Bennington? He really thinks—"

"I said I'm fine."

Doctor?

"Okay. Okay. I'm a mother. It's my job to worry about my babies. You seemed a little off is all." She changed the subject, and I silently cursed her for it. "Effie is delightful."

"She's a good time."

My heart jumped in my throat. *A good time.* We'd never promised each other more than that, but my stomach soured at how cavalier he made our relationship sound.

"I'm just hoping one day I'll get some more grandbabies. Ones that look like you, maybe. Lord knows Brian is in no hurry to settle down."

"I don't need a wife to have a family." His tone was clipped, almost bitter, in a way I'd not heard from him before.

Patty laughed, a soft rolling sound that carried with it

the *oh you silly thing* tone only a mother could perfect. "You know how babies are made, right?"

My thoughts immediately went to Malcolm and how much Josh loved him. Patty didn't know. And clearly, Josh didn't see me fitting into that equation anywhere.

My stomach plummeted to my feet.

I had heard enough.

Making my entrance a bit louder than necessary, I plastered on a perfect veneer to survive dinner while my heart actively cracked in two. I acted the shit out of that family dinner—laughing at Brian's slightly off-color jokes, complimenting Patty on her cooking, praising Mandy for her boys' good manners.

I never wavered, even when Josh would slide me a glance or gently squeeze my knee under the table.

It was the performance of my lifetime.

Inside, I was a mess.

Josh was more relaxed than I'd seen him. Not once did he have to take a steadying breath or pause before answering someone's question. Here, in his mother's home, he was *himself*. It was a strange and beautiful thing to witness. All I could think was how exhausting it must be for him to always be so perfect at the ranch. To do what was expected without a fucking break.

Because by the time I'd made it through dessert, I was a caged animal—crawling the walls and desperate for escape. I couldn't keep up the act.

I clearly wasn't built for family. They were messy and in your business and full of secrets and old truths. Even Josh admitted to his mother that he didn't see me fitting into a family unit.

"You okay?" The quiet ride home was my opportunity

to stuff every last feeling into a box and let them rot in the corners of my mind.

"Of course." I smiled at him, my weariness rapidly overtaking me like a wilting flower. "Just tired."

Josh raked a hand through his hair. "Sometimes they're a lot to handle."

I shook my head. "Your family is great." I swallowed past the growing lump clogging my throat. "Really great."

21

JOSH

"SHE WOULDN'T GIVE YOU *ANYTHING*?" Gemma crossed her arms over her chest and pouted as she sank back against the couch.

I walked into the house to find Effie, Gemma, and Kate sitting on the floor of my living room, blankets and pillows creating a cozy workspace as they sifted through papers scattered in front of them. They were focused on the newspaper articles Effie had printed from the library and the pages of notes she'd scribbled down as she searched for any information she could find regarding her father.

I made my entrance as quietly as possible, noting they were getting low on snacks and drinks. I toed off my work boots before heading to the kitchen.

"Nothing." Effie sighed and rolled her neck. "That woman is a steel trap."

Gemma nodded in assent. "Ma is hard to crack. I just can't believe she wouldn't give you anything at all to go on. She usually has a softer side than that."

"Well, she clearly doesn't have a soft spot for me."

Annoyance twisted Effie's face, and my chest tightened for her.

"Let's regroup," Kate suggested. "What do we know?"

Effie gathered some of the notes she'd written and took a deep breath. "I think my mother met my father in Vegas. She was a struggling performer—a showgirl at the Tropicana. She may have known him before, but I was born in Nevada. From the little she's told me, they had a volatile relationship, and it didn't last very long. My whole life we moved around a lot until we finally settled in California."

"I'm putting these in chronological order." Gemma started arranging the articles on the table. "How did you end up in Tipp?"

I pulled out a wooden tray and started arranging fruit, crackers, and some cured meats Effie had picked up. It was a sad little charcuterie board, but those women were determined, and if they were going to make any headway, they needed some sustenance. I also pulled the bottle of chardonnay from the fridge and walked toward them.

"Hi!" Effie brightened as if she was just noticing me. I was relieved at her knee jerk reaction to my presence. After our visit with my family, something had shifted. Effie was quieter on the car ride home, but she wouldn't admit to anything bothering her. In the time since, I would catch her lost in thought, but she never let me in. Seeing her relaxed and surrounded by her friends made me smile.

Effie looked around at the scattered papers around the group. "We're just, um . . ."

I smoothed her hair with my hand and kissed the top of her head. "All good. I brought you some snacks and a refill on the wine."

"Swoon." Kate held her hand over her heart and looked at me while Gemma bumped her shoulder.

I set the board down beside them. "I can give you girls some space."

"Stay?" Effie asked. "For a minute, if you can. Maybe you can help."

I curled myself behind her, sucking in a lungful of her floral shampoo and then kissing her shoulder. "Okay. What do you got?"

"I was just going through the timeline." I nodded for her to continue. "When I was twelve, my mom got it in her head that she was finally going to find my father. It led her here. I was so excited to meet him. Things with my mom were always . . . hard. I craved any connection with my father. But she wouldn't let me meet him. We got into a huge fight in the car, and I took off."

That was when Effie had run into the woods and found the hot springs. It was where we had shared our first kiss and I'd fallen head over heels for a girl I'd never met. I gently squeezed her hip, letting the knowledge of our meeting go unspoken—a secret just for us.

"Did your mom talk with your dad? You know for sure he was there?" Gemma's brow was furrowed.

"I do. She tracked me down, shoved me into the car, and left Montana. I cried so long and so hard as we drove away."

Kate rested a hand on Effie's knee. "I'm sorry."

Effie only nodded. She was good at keeping her emotions at bay, but I didn't miss the tightness in her voice. She was barely holding it together.

"She got tired of my anger and tears, and she said, 'The man I married doesn't exist.' Before that, I didn't know they'd ever been married. My mom dug into her purse and tossed me a little pebble and told me he'd asked her to give it to me. I think she only gave it to me to shut me up, because she had no intention of giving it to me before that."

"Jesus. That's rough." Gemma shook her head.

An idea snagged in my brain. "Hey, if they were married, would there be a marriage certificate? Something like that is public record. At least you'd get his name."

"Hey, that's a start!" Kate prompted.

Effie turned her head to smile at me. It was full and bright and hopeful. My stomach twisted. I knew I'd do anything to keep that look on her face.

"It's something." Effie reached for a new piece of paper and scrawled the words *Marriage record* in hurried handwriting. She underlined it twice.

"Once I have his name, I can ask around town too." The determined furrow was back in Effie's brow.

Gemma considered a moment. "The town is pretty protective over the people who live here. I just don't know if they'd give up much information."

Kate chimed in. "I'm not even *from* here and have learned it takes a long time to earn trust. Half the time Al still acts like he doesn't recognize my face when I'm trying to get a drink at The Rasa."

"If you had his name, a little more information, maybe Ma Brown would be more open to talking with you about it."

"True." Effie thought about it for a moment. "If I have his name and can prove that I'm his daughter, surely she'd at least confirm he was a federal marshal and worked here."

"You're sure he worked at the ranch?" Gemma prodded.

I stiffened, knowing Gemma must be thinking the same thing I was.

"I mean, why else would he be here?" Effie laughed as if any other option was absurd, but Gemma and Kate shared a silent look.

"What?" Effie demanded.

"Just looking at all possible options," Gemma finally said before shooting me a look. The pit in my stomach hollowed out. Gemma and the girls had the same troubling thought I had. The more information we got, the more likely it was that Effie was going to be unhappy with the truth about her father.

∽

A BUZZY KIND of energy tingled down my arm and into my fingers as I hung up the phone. My tongue felt thick. I was really doing it. I whooshed out a breath and slid my clammy hands down the thighs of my jeans.

A social worker had walked me through the lengthy and laborious process of adopting Malcolm. When I spoke with his foster mom, she remained conservative but supportive. Without hesitation, she had agreed that Malcolm would be overjoyed and that she saw the love and connection between us.

Ms. Harrison had also warned me that it would be a difficult process. She gave me the contacts I would need and offered to write a letter of referral to help my case. There would be paperwork, a home study. From there on out, I was determined to make sure everything was perfect. Nothing would stand in my way from giving Malcolm the life I knew he deserved.

I couldn't wait to talk to him about it.

"There you are!" Effie's singsong voice filled the office. Bit by bit she was taking up all the empty corners in my heart, which raced just thinking about her. "Tonight's a Malcolm night, right?"

I shoved down the warning bell that the more I shared

her with Malcolm, the harder it was going to be on him when she left. "It is."

She wound her arms around my neck, and I got lost in the warmth of her embrace. The smell of Montana mountain sunshine on her skin. "Is it a boys' day or can I tag along?"

"We'd love to have you." *Forever*. I smiled at her, letting her happiness replace the growing unease in my gut.

By the time Malcolm arrived, my truck was loaded down with fishing gear, a picnic basket, and Effie's gigantic bag. No fucking clue what she packed, but it weighed more than Malcolm himself.

We turned into Redemption Ranch, and I followed the winding dirt roads past each building and through the vast property. The truck bumped along the road as Malcolm told Effie an animated story. She laughed at his jokes, and I flexed my hand to keep from reaching for her every ten seconds.

The stream that fed into the larger river cut through the property and had several deep spots that were prime fishing. I parked the truck at an angle near a copse of trees. We took our time setting out a large blanket, weighted down with the cooler and Effie's bag. Out of it she pulled a giant hat and plopped it on her head. The wide brim shadowed her face and shoulders.

She looked up at me. "I know. It's very *extra*, but I need some reprieve from the sun."

I lifted my shoulder. "I thought you looked cute."

Her smile bloomed, and I bit back a grin.

"Hey, Mal," she called. "Come over here." I watched as Effie pulled a bottle from her bag and slathered him with sunscreen. He wiggled and helped to smear the cream around his skin.

Shit. I hadn't thought of that.

I chided myself for forgetting something as simple as sunscreen and added it to the mental list titled *Dad Shit* I'd been keeping in the back of my mind.

"Josh, can I get in? Please?" He was already taking off his shoes and socks before I answered.

"You'll scare all the fish away."

"Just a toe? One toe?" he pleaded.

Effie stifled a laugh and looked at me with wide eyes. "It's just *one* toe." Effie's graceful limbs unfolded as she rose. "I'll go with him."

"Whose side are you on?" I grumbled. Unable to say no to either of them, I nodded. He grabbed Effie's hand, and they raced to the shallow bank of the stream.

I joined them with a set of fishing poles and some bait. As I approached, I noticed that Effie had ditched her sundress and was splashing in the knee-deep water with Malcolm. Her hat did its job of keeping her face protected from the sun, but I could still make out the fresh freckles that dotted the tops of her shoulders.

I stood back and watched as they splashed each other and giggled. Every bit of love inside me was captured in that moment. I wanted to freeze time and remember everything perfectly—his playful giggle, how his dark skin was a beautiful contrast to her pale shoulders, the way she held his hand and twirled in the water. I reached into my back pocket and pulled out my phone. I snapped a picture of Effie crouched down to inspect a rock he'd lifted from the water. It was the moment everything felt complete, yet so utterly lacking.

Malcolm deserved permanence. A father and a mother who would love him and be there for him like mine had done. I needed to convince everyone that I was the type of man who could do that for him.

Effie was leaving in a matter of weeks. We hadn't talked about it, but I knew she'd be due to return to her life for the premiere and press tour.

I shoved down the anger and annoyance at how unfair it all seemed. Effie was the one person who made me feel at ease, free to actually be myself, who quieted the incessant, restless buzz in my head, and she was someone I couldn't manage to hold on to.

"You just gonna stare all day, or are you coming in?" Effie's wide smile pulled me from my own head.

"I thought you said just a toe?" I crossed my arms and feigned annoyance.

Effie shot Malcolm a playful look and lifted her shoulders. In one swoop, she bent down and pushed a wave of water toward me. Malcolm rushed in my direction, laughing maniacally. I scooped him up and tickled his ribs before he could splash me again.

"Traitors!" I bellowed.

We laughed and splashed, and I did my best to retaliate, but with two against one, my clothes ended up soaked through. Malcolm's attention was drawn back to the rocks and shells that poked our feet. His hands dug through the water, pulling up stones smoothed by the watershed and time.

"Whoa! Jackpot!" Malcolm's grin split his face as he held up his treasure.

"What is that?" Effie moved closer to inspect. "Josh, have you ever seen anything like this?"

I moved toward the duo. In Malcolm's cradled hands was a large mussel half shell. It was perfectly intact save for nine perfectly round holes.

"Oh yeah," I said, turning it over and inspecting the shell. "Great find. It's from the old button factory." I pointed upriver. Malcolm and Effie looked at me, so I continued. "They'd use the mussels from the river to stamp out buttons. The leftovers were tossed back into the river. They wash up every once in a while, but usually they're broken up a bit."

"That is so cool!" Malcolm ran his fingers over the iridescent inside of the shell. He poked a pinky through one of the holes. Effie continued to stare down at it, a soft line forming between her eyebrows.

"They don't make them anymore?" Malcolm asked, handing it over to me.

I shook my head. "Nah. I think plastic buttons became popular. Cheaper to make." I tossed the shell back to him. "You should keep it."

He beamed up at me and sloshed through the water to set his treasure on the shore. Effie tracked his movements, and by the time he was back, the intense furrow was gone.

We played in the water until Malcolm grew bored and decided on a picnic lunch. After we ate, I led them down a winding path that hugged the water, and Effie perched on a shaded rock while I showed Malcolm the basics of fishing. It was a deep hole that I knew had small fish for him to catch. We got lucky and they were biting.

By the time the sun sagged in the afternoon sky, my phone was full of pictures from the day—Effie looking like a goddess, Malcolm holding up the small bluegill fish, a selfie of the three of us making silly faces into the camera.

This is the best day of my life.

I was greedy. I wanted a million just like it.

That night, after filling Effie with slow, gentle strokes, I lay awake, staring at the ceiling as my fingertips drew lazy circles on Effie's back.

"Have you ever thought about having kids?" I asked into the darkness.

She was so quiet. Her body rose up and lowered in a steady rhythm. I almost assumed she was sleeping when her tiny, sad voice broke into the darkness. "I'm not sure I'd be very good at it."

I swallowed past the gravel in my throat. *I think you'd be amazing. We'd be lucky to keep you.*

The words clogged in my throat. Effie's life was halfway across the country—waiting for her to return to her life in LA. It was unfair of me to even consider asking—begging—her to give that up and live a simple life in a town no one's ever heard of.

I was a coward, and I let her disappointment hang in the air.

22

EFFIE

I STARED down at Desiree's name on my phone. She'd called three times in the last week, and I'd ignored every one. Since the day with Josh and Malcolm, I'd been a mess. Playing and swimming in the stream and watching Josh teach him how to fish was one of the most relaxing days I could remember.

Those two adored each other, and Josh wasn't the only one I was falling in love with. Malcolm, with his sweet laugh and gentle spirit, had stolen a chunk of my heart too. When my phone buzzed again, I knew Des wasn't going to let me get away with ignoring yet another one of her calls.

"Hi, Desiree."

"About damn time." She was pissed. "I know you think you're hot shit, but don't forget I'm the one working my ass off here to make sure your career doesn't go completely off the rails. Unbelievable!" She started muttering to herself as I tried to placate her.

"I'm sorry, Des. The service here is spotty, at best."

"Well, playtime is over. I need you back in LA."

My mouth went dry. I sputtered and tried to find the words.

No. No. It's too soon.

"I'm not due for the press junket for another three weeks." I calmed my voice and did my best to sound assertive.

"And I need to prep you. A lot has been happening here while you've been playing cowgirl in some Podunk, backwoods town."

I resented her patronizing tone. She didn't know anything about the people or the lifestyle in Tipp. My spine stiffened. "No. I'll be back in LA after the first week in August, as we agreed. Don't forget this whole scheme was your idea."

Before she could argue, I disconnected the call. A hot coal formed in the pit of my stomach. Acid burned up my throat. I was used to people handling me and managing my career. I trusted them to make the majority of the decisions, but I couldn't fathom leaving Tipp just yet. I was so close to getting more information about my father, and I wasn't ready to give up my time with Josh.

My heart thudded. How was I ever going to say goodbye to him?

My palms were sweaty. My mind was racing. I needed fresh air.

Threading my hands through my hair, I lifted it off my hot scalp. I was up against a wall. Time was not my friend. If I knew Des, I'd just royally pissed her off, and it was only a matter of time until she got her way. I had no way of knowing exactly what she would come up with, but she was ruthless. If she wanted me in LA earlier than we'd agreed upon, she'd stop at nothing to make it happen.

I needed to see Josh, but he was running an errand in town.

A spark of an idea hit me, and I dashed to the bedroom. I snapped a racy picture of the lace top of my panties, the swell of my ass just barely visible in the shot, and sent it to him.

Josh: *I'm coming home.*

Excitement danced under my skin. I dashed into the bathroom and refreshed my makeup. My hair was a little flat from the humid air, but after bending over and tossing my fingers through it, it was passable as casual bedhead.

Ten minutes later, Josh pushed through the bedroom door. His feet were bare, and his fists were clenched at his side. The tight shirt stretched across his chest and clung to his body. My eyes moved down to his tapered waist, and my breath hitched when I saw the top button of his jeans already undone.

I stood in the doorway to the bathroom, leaning against the doorframe. When I bit my lip, Josh needed no further urging. The air shifted, and cocky, lighthearted Josh was gone. In his place was a man looking at me with such intensity, such tenderness, that a swell in my chest squeezed so tight I felt it might burst—splitting me open and spilling every secret I never dared to share, even with myself.

He moved toward me in two strides and grabbed my ass, lifting me off the ground so I could wind my legs around him. He pushed me against the wall as his hips pressed against me, and he sucked hot kisses up my neck and over my ear.

My skin was hot and a ball of need bloomed low in my stomach.

Josh shifted his weight and moved toward the bed. When he set me down, Josh reached behind his neck and pulled his shirt over his head before returning his attention to me. He ran his hands over my body as though he needed access to more of me.

All of me.

I groaned and shivered against his rough palms. When his hand stopped above my breast, my heart hammered against his touch.

"I feel this."

Tears burned at the back of my eyes. I placed my hand over his heart. "I feel this," I repeated.

"Effie."

One word. My name—my real name spoken with such reverence—and I was done for. My body knew what my heart had already decided. There was no walking away from this man.

I loved him.

I loved him and, incredibly, he loved *me*, and no one was going to keep that love from me.

Josh sank his fingertips into the skin of my thighs and gritted his teeth. "Everything about you is perfect." He inched his nose down my sensitive skin, lower and lower, stopping at the edge of my panties. His breath fanned over my heated skin.

I pulled him up toward me. I needed him to see what I couldn't bring myself to say out loud. I had never been good at revealing my true self. People wanted the refined *Madison Colt* version so much more than the chaotic unsure *Effie* parts of me.

Everyone but him.

As our limbs tangled, messy kisses gave way to fumbling hands as we stripped each other bare. He finally positioned himself at my entrance. Looking into my eyes, he sank deeply, filling me as I wrapped myself in him.

We moved together, slow and sensual. Connected in a way that was familiar but altogether new. I cried out his name, and he held me closer, rocked by his own orgasm.

Overcome by emotion, fresh tears slipped past my lashes.

As our heart rates leveled, he swiped the tear away with his thumb. A deep line creased between his eyebrows.

"Did I hurt you?" His worried eyes scanned me.

I shook my head. "No. I'm good." I offered him a watery smile. "I'm really, really good."

He breathed a sigh of relief as he braced his weight above me. "Me too, baby girl. When I'm with you, I'm good."

I whispered the only words racing through my mind. "I don't want to leave."

His cocksure smile bloomed across his face before he kissed me firmly. "Then don't."

∽

"THIS IS NOT what I expected when you invited me to girls' night." Sophie entered the house and looked around the kitchen to see papers and notes scattered across Josh's kitchen island.

"We've got wine." Gemma lifted the bottle and gently shook it in her direction.

"I was just finishing up before you got here." I started scooping the papers and arranging them in a haphazard pile.

Sophie approached, rolled her eyes, and grabbed one of the sheets of paper with my notes scribbled across it. "Well, what is it?"

"Effie is trying to find her dad." Kate's eyes gleamed as

she leaned across the marble. It had been a week since I had let Gemma and Kate in on my secret research. It was only fair that Sophie knew too.

"Oh shit. Really?" Sophie looked harder at the notes.

"I know he was here in Tipp at one point. Never met him." I shrugged. More and more it was feeling like I was chasing a ghost. Every new lead was a dead end. Every question I asked was met with either information that didn't help me or silent indifference.

Determination set Sophie's lips in a hard line. "What do we know?"

My chest bloomed with an uncomfortable feeling. *Had I ever had girlfriends? Ones who didn't want something from me other than friendship?*

Gemma squeezed my hand, and I looked up to meet her eyes. She knew what it was like to be here—new and out of place. She had found her way and made a home here with a job and friends and *happiness*.

Could I do the same?

I cleared my throat and shuffled through the papers, unsure of where to start. "I know a few things."

"We have his name," Kate cut in. "High-er-ray-me . . . something?" she said, attempting to sound it out.

"Hieramias Adamos," I corrected. Kate blushed and I shrugged. "I googled how to pronounce it."

"Effie is Greek, right?" Gemma asked.

I nodded. "Euphemia."

"So that's definitely him," Kate concluded.

"Unless my mother secretly married some other Greek guy." It was entirely possible. My mother was a mystery wrapped up in a tacky veneer.

"You'd think that name would ring some bells." Kate

chewed her lip as she looked over another piece of paper. "What else do you have?"

"Besides an unreliable timeline?" I reached into my pocket and pulled out the small circle. After the day with Malcolm and Josh, I realized I hadn't needed to carry my worry stone with me in weeks. When I pulled it out of the drawer I'd tucked it into, the familiar whoosh of comfort settled in my bones. It also confirmed my suspicions. The circle was a perfect match for the shell Malcolm had found in the water. It *had* come from the river. There was no way that was a coincidence.

"I also have this." I pulled my hand from my pocket and opened it to reveal the small circle. My thumb pressed into the delicate divot. "My mother told me that he asked her to give it to me. It's really all I have. But the other day, Malcolm found a shell with holes in it that matched this."

"The old button factory," Sophie confirmed.

I nodded. "So I know at least that was the truth. I *know* he was here." I stared down at the small circle in my hand. Gemma stepped beside me.

"Hey, I've seen this before." The way her voice dipped sent a cascade of shivers up my back. "The wine has to wait, ladies. We're leaving."

Minutes later we were piled into Gemma's truck, barreling down a country road and holding on for our lives. Gemma's reckless driving was a perfect match for how my insides were tumbling and reeling. Kate and Sophie squealed with excitement as we pulled under the large wooden sign that read Laurel Canyon Ranch.

Gemma leaned out her open window to smile at the guard who patrolled the entrance. He smiled back and moved aside to let her pass. Instead of parking near the main lodge, as I'd expected, Gemma turned the truck up the dirt path toward the row of cabins by the large barn.

"Where are we going?" Kate whispered. As darkness settled around us, our collective excitement waned, and eeriness seeped its way into the truck.

"Okay, this is bugging the shit out of me." Gemma parked the truck outside of the main barn and turned in her seat to face me. "I've seen it before."

"The stone?" I asked.

"It's not a stone. It's a shell, like you said. And even around here, they're pretty rare. We'll find the occasional blank—like Malcolm did, but it's *really* rare to find the actual buttons."

"How do you know all this?" I asked.

"Scotty, right?" Kate offered. Gemma whipped her head in Kate's direction, her blonde hair flying across her shoulders. "Sorry." Kate raised her hands. "The asshole," she corrected.

I pinched my brows in question.

Gemma sighed. "When I first got here, I was hurt and scared. I *hated* being here. He was a marshal, but he became more like a lifeline. We were friends. He was kind to me—"

"And super fucking hot," Sophie added.

I quirked an eyebrow but let Gemma continue. She glared at Sophie, who only smiled. "He left. *But*," she emphasized, "before he left, he showed me something."

Gemma exited the truck and we all followed. Darkness was descending on the ranch, and only a dim light illuminated the outside of the barn door. Gemma pushed open the heavy door and slipped inside. Kate, Sophie, and I exchanged wary glances before following.

The rich, heady smells of animals and dirt greeted us. Under the blanket of night, the barn I'd spent weeks working in was transformed. Long shadows slanted across the floor, creating black pools and menacing shapes.

On the outside, I smoothed my face into calm indifference, but inside my nerves were rattling like rusty chains. Kate gripped my hand as her eyes widened in the darkness.

"Gem . . . ," Sophie whispered. "This is really fucking creepy."

"Hang tight. There's a light." Seconds later a dim light flicked on, blinking to life.

"How did light make it *more* creepy?" Kate sank closer to me.

My eyes cut to Josh's office across the barn. While it wasn't locked, it *definitely* felt like we shouldn't be creeping around the barn at night.

"Here." A door groaned open as Gemma stepped aside. The four of us huddled at the entrance, peering into the dim storage closet that stretched back. Along the right side, three shelves ran the length of the space. A chainsaw, some hand tools, and boxes of nails were neatly organized. On the left, shovels, brooms, and other gardening equipment were leaned against the wall. On the far end was a small desk and chair.

"Come on," Gemma urged. Our feet remained planted, but Gemma gently rolled her eyes and urged us forward. We inched behind her. A hard *BANG* cracked through the darkness, and we all screamed, clutching onto one another. After we whipped around us to see a broom had smacked the cement floor, we dissolved into a fit of relieved laughter.

"Holy shit. I think I peed my pants." Sophie was wiping away tears.

I pressed a hand into my hammering heart.

"Look," Gemma urged.

We approached the small desk. Above it was a little

shelf, and on the shelf were a few broken pieces of shells—button blanks—like Malcolm had found. Beside it: three circular buttons, exactly like the one tucked in my pocket.

My eyes went wide as I pulled mine from my jeans and held it in my palm next to the others.

"They're exactly the same." Kate's voice dipped low as she squeezed my shoulder.

"I knew I'd seen them before." Pride filled Gemma's voice.

"This is unbelievable. Where did these come from?" I asked.

Gemma stepped aside to point to the weathered brass nameplate resting on the desk.

My stomach pitched and rolled. My heart plummeted.

Ray.

23

JOSH

YOU'RE NEVER GOING *to have it all.*

You'll have to choose.

I closed my eyes and pinched the bridge of my nose. My elbows dug into the wood of my desk, and I focused on the sharp pain. A buzzing crept up my neck and settled between my ears. I tried my usual techniques—deep breathing, music, focusing on *anything* else but my constant companion revved to life.

Ever since Effie's girls' night a week ago, she'd been different. On the surface, everything seemed normal, but she was preoccupied and a little distant.

Probably planning her exit strategy.

I buried myself in work. Ms. Harrison had spent hours on the phone mentoring me, answering my questions. I pored over research online in any spare moments of my day. I did everything I could to learn about the process and anticipate any roadblocks.

The Army had instilled the need for order and rules. Checklists were my companion. I was determined to be the kind of man any social worker would be thrilled to endorse. Gold stars.

My gut soured when I let the truth seep in. I wasn't the man I'd spent most of my adult life projecting.

Easygoing.

Normal.

Honest.

Fuck.

I still hadn't told Effie my intentions to foster and eventually adopt Malcolm. A thousand times I'd tried to mention it—feel her out and see if there was a way to get her to see how perfectly she could fit into our lives.

Would she run?

Nausea roiled in my gut as the buzzing turned to a high-pitched ring. I slammed my fist into the desk and roared, "FUCK!"

The container of pens rattled under the jolt. I steadied my breath.

Get. Your shit. Together.

"Everything okay in here?" Effie's hand curled around the frame of the door as she popped her head into my home office.

I swallowed hard. "Yeah. Sorry. Just a . . . I don't know."

Her eyes softened. "Hey . . ." Her gentle voice soothed as she entered the space and walked behind me. Her hands found my bunched shoulders, and she kneaded the tension that resided there.

My head slumped forward. "I'm sorry I've been busy, but I've been meaning to talk to you."

Effie's hand worked on the knots across my back. I craved her touch. "Same," she said. "There's so much I need to tell you."

I swiveled my chair. Effie stood above me, her hands

resting on my shoulders. Hope and affection swirled in her eyes.

You're it for me.

Defeated, I leaned forward and rested my forehead on her stomach. Her hands pushed into my hair, raking her nails across my scalp.

"You first," she urged.

I gathered my strength to bare it all to her. The delicate touch of her hands on my scalp infused me with courage to finally tell her the truth.

All of it.

"I'm not well," I admitted, unable to look her in the eyes. Not yet.

Her hands stilled in my hair. She used her control over my head and neck to tilt my head back and force me to look at her. "You're sick?"

The worry and panic was evident on her face. "No." *It's so much worse than that.* "I'm not ill, physically. Just here." I tapped my forehead like Malcolm had once done—back when he told me I should have told Effie the truth about my condition. The kid was always smarter than me, that was for damn sure.

"I don't understand."

I stared down at her feet. She made no effort to pull away from me, so I forged on. "When I was in the Army, I worked with heavy artillery. It left me ... damaged."

"What do you mean?"

"Not physically, really. Tinnitus—a buzzing, sometimes a ringing."

A heavy sigh released from Effie's lungs. "Oh," she breathed.

She didn't understand. She thought it was no big deal. That I was normal. I pressed on. "It's always there. A constant, incessant monkey on my back. Stress and anxiety make it worse, but even when I feel okay . . . I don't."

A thumb smoothed over my cheekbone. "Have you talked to someone? A doctor or specialist?"

I nodded. "There's nothing they can do. It's incurable."

"That can't be true." Effie shook her head.

"It is." My voice was harder than I'd intended, so I took a breath. "I can use a white noise machine. One doctor suggested a hearing aid to help." I shook my head. "Nothing works."

"That's okay. It's okay."

"It's not. There's more. I—" I swallowed hard. I had planned to tell Effie about Malcolm when the timing was perfect. I could pitch to her the life I was building, one that included both Malcolm *and* her, and it would be so perfect and complete that she couldn't refuse.

That was all crumbling at my feet.

Her expectant eyes had the truth tumbling out of me. I was bruised and raw, and the hope that shone in her eyes was poking at the tender parts of my heart.

"I want Malcolm. Forever." The truth spoken out loud was a balm to my aching chest. "I want to be his dad."

Effie ran a hand over my temple. "Oh, honey. I know. Everyone knows. Anyone who looks at you two can tell you were always meant to be his dad."

I fought back the burn of tears and pressed my tongue to the roof of my mouth to hold my shit together. I grunted to clear my throat. "It's not that simple. There's a lot of fucking hoops to jump through, and even then I might not be cut out to do it. That's why I've been wrapped up in this." I gestured toward the desk with my computer and papers. "I need to make sure it's perfect. That *I* am perfect."

Silence stretched between us. "That's why you do it.

You're always putting on a show. You project happiness, even when it's not always the truth, so no one knows what's going on inside of you."

Effie pressed her hand into my chest, and emotions welled inside me like a tidal wave threatening to crash over us both. She got it. She got *me*. I couldn't speak. I couldn't *breathe*.

I stood to my full height, pulling Effie into me.

Her arms wrapped under mine, pulling me closer. Tears thickened her voice. "You are not broken, Joshua Laredo."

"I don't know how I'm going to keep you both," I whispered into her hair. She gripped me tighter but didn't speak. I wanted her to tell me she'd stay. To declare that she was choosing me over LA. Over the life she'd admitted no longer sparked joy.

My thoughts returned to Malcolm. He was getting attached to Effie nearly as much as I was. It wouldn't just be me who suffered when she finally left us.

When the aching silence became unbearable, I cleared the emotion from my throat again and whispered, "What did you want to tell me?"

She hesitated until her voice went soft. "I think Ray is my father."

24

EFFIE

"THIS IS QUITE POSSIBLY the worst idea I've ever had." I stared at Josh through the mirrors as I smoothed my hands over the full white skirt of my dress.

He walked up behind me, placing his hands on my shoulders, and kissed my neck. "Relax. You look great."

I stared at my reflection.

Half criminal. Half self-centered wannabe socialite. Total disaster.

My stomach pitched and rolled as I looked for anything out of place in my appearance. The all-white lace dress hugged my torso and then flared slightly around my hips. The high neckline kept it demure, yet chic, and once I saw it had pockets, I was sold. As always, Johnny came through and was able to find the perfect combination of cute, comfy, and stylish.

Lately I kept my clothing simple with jeans and T-shirts. The structured lines and tight fit of my previous clothing no longer felt as comfortable as they once had. I still loved to dress up, and date nights were no exception; however, something about today felt bigger.

Important.

I smoothed a hand down the front of the modest dress as it mocked me from the mirror.

Who are you anymore?

"It's just a barbecue." Josh finished the last few buttons on his shirt and rolled his sleeves, showing off one of my favorite parts of him.

After racking my brain for how to approach Ray, I suggested hosting a barbecue in the backyard. Being surrounded by people was well within my comfort zone, but the prospect of seeing Ray again and *knowing* there was a good chance he was the father I had never known had me reeling. Josh didn't say anything when I'd decided to stay home for a few days to plan the party. Mostly I was avoiding any accidental run-ins with Ray on the ranch.

Much to my dismay, I wasn't able to secure any decent party rentals that were local or available with less than a week's notice. Instead, I scoured the local stores for plain-white paper products. I dug through Josh's cabinets and decided that mismatched jars would be adequate for floral centerpieces. He didn't need to know about the jelly I scooped into the trash because the jar was perfect.

The menu was simple but perfectly complementary. When Josh planted a large bag of red Solo cups on the table, I gritted my teeth to keep my eye from twitching.

I kept myself busy and greeted everyone with a practiced smile, and after the fourth person brought food that went completely against the overall palate of the menu I'd created, all my plans went out the window.

Individual caprese skewers alongside pretzels and beer cheese dip. Classy.

"You're doing that weird eye-twitch thing." Josh

gestured toward his face, a smirk playing at the corners of his mouth.

I looked past him to be sure no one could hear me and gestured toward the table of mismatched potluck food. Josh grabbed a pretzel and swiped it through the beer cheese dip.

"So good."

I rolled my eyes at him and repressed a smile while I rearranged the dishes for the tenth time.

"People are here to enjoy themselves. No one cares that the beer cheese dip doesn't go with the grape-jelly meatballs."

I eyeballed the Crock-Pot and scowled at it.

"Hey," he said, placing his hands on my shoulders and softly kneading the bunched muscles. "People are here to spend time with their friends. Relax and maybe you can have a good time too."

"Is he here yet?"

Josh shook his head. "He doesn't always show up to these kinds of things. I hounded him about it all week, but there's no telling with him."

I swallowed and nodded. The doorbell rang, and I plastered another cool smile on my face before moving past Josh.

Before long, the backyard was full of small groups of people chatting, red Solo cups in hand, or playing one of the yard games Josh had set out. Low music played out of the backyard speakers, and everyone seemed relaxed.

Happy.

Everyone except Ray, who looked like he'd been dragged here and it was the last place on earth he wanted to be. I hadn't seen him arrive, and my heart rate spiked when I noticed him. Sitting at a small table with another older ranch hand, Ray peered into the crowd. I took the opportunity to look over his weathered face. His lips tipped down in a scowl. Years of work outside had deepened the lines around his eyes and mouth. His hands were dark and leathery.

I'd hoped for something, *anything*. A spark of recognition or something in my DNA that recognized that man as my father, but I felt . . . nothing. When his companion got up to refill his drink, I heaved a deep breath.

Now or never.

Rounding my shoulders back and down, I took a steadying breath, smiled widely, and marched over to Ray in quick strides.

"This seat taken?" My hand touched the back of the chair next to him.

His blue eyes—*Had I ever noticed they had the same gold flecks as mine?*—shifted to me. He only tipped his chin, and I quickly sat beside him.

"Thanks for coming," I started.

Ray's shoulders bounced in a silent chuckle. "Didn't feel like I had much of a choice. Josh rode my ass all week about coming out."

My smile pinched, and I rubbed my finger across the small, circular shell in the pocket of my dress. I gently cleared my throat. "You've mentioned you have been in Tipp a long time. But where did you grow up?"

His eyes sliced to me, and a tingle of nerves had goose bumps sprouting on my forearms. "Who's asking?"

I kept my friendliest smile secured. "Just making polite conversation, Ray."

He harrumphed but stayed silent. "Grew up in Natchitoches, Louisiana. From all over, really."

"I moved around a lot too." I smoothed my sweating

palms over the skirt of my dress. "How did you end up in this remote corner of the world?"

"Bad choices."

Stunned by his gruff, yet honest, answer, I paused. Then I slipped my hand into my pocket, clutching the small shell in my hand. "But you've been here a long time, right?"

"'Bout eighteen years, I suppose." His cool blue eyes shifted around the guests at the party, but his voice remained aloof. Uninterested.

I pulled the shell from my pocket and opened my palm. His eyes immediately landed on the button blank. "I was hoping you could tell me a little more about this."

Ray's voice was quiet, but hard. "Where did you get that?"

"It was a gift. My mother says it was a gift from my—" The words snagged in my throat as emotion welled inside me. "My father."

His gaze flew from my hand to my face and back down again. Recognition flickered over his aging features before anger rose, a visible tide washing over him. "You steal that off my desk, girl?"

"I was twelve when my mother, Terese Pierce, gave it to me. She said it was a gift from my father." I repeated the phrase I had practiced in front of the mirror all morning.

Ray pushed to his feet, slow and aching.

"Please." I raised my hand. "I just want to talk."

"I got nothing to say to you."

I stood, staring at his back as his labored steps opened a chasm between us. My eyes burned as the party continued around me. I looked about, and no one seemed to notice my facade was crumbling at my feet. After my eyes met Josh's, he pushed past the small group he'd been talking to. His feet ate up the distance between us, and he pulled me into his arms.

"Hey." His voice was balm on my tender insides. "What happened?"

I gathered my resolve as people's attention slowly moved to us. I blinked away the tears and buried the raging emotions. "Nothing. I'm fine."

"Eff—"

My eyes flew to his. "I said I'm fine."

He took one step back. "Okay. I'll just go get you some water."

Thankful to be alone to gather myself, I took a breath.

You can do this. It's a performance. Get through it.

My smile was perfect by the time he returned with a cup of water, and I walked to a small group of people gathered by the dessert table. Josh followed my lead and let our conversation drop, but I could feel his concerned eyes on me. I slipped away and headed toward a small circle of women I didn't recognize, save for Gemma.

"Hi, ladies. Having a good time?" I asked.

"Hey, Effie." Gemma smiled. "These are a few girls that I go to class with." We made introductions, and they continued with their conversation without me.

Finally, one turned to me. "So what's it like living with the most eligible bachelor in Tipp?" She lifted and lowered her eyebrows suggestively.

I blinked once and shot her a demure smile. "Josh is very accommodating. He gave me a place to stay while I'm here."

The blonde bumped shoulders with her friend. "Train him right so he'll be ready for market once you leave." She gestured toward Josh and the small group of guys he was laughing with. "God, living with a woman like you definitely upped his husband-material status."

"Like he needed much help," her friend quipped.

"Come on." Gemma clipped the conversation short, noting my uncomfortable silence and the death stares I was shooting into the sides of their faces. "He's a nice guy, not a piece of ass. Effie isn't going anywhere." Gemma mouthed, *Sorry,* over their heads.

I didn't miss the appreciative way they looked over Josh. A surge of protectiveness rolled through me. They didn't have a fucking clue what the real man was like. Sure, they saw the kind, funny, accommodating man who filled out a pair of Wranglers like nobody's business, but they had no clue that beneath the surface was a wolf clawing his way out.

Gemma shifted their conversation to an upcoming course they were all taking, and I sat back, only half listening. I quietly assessed the group but kept my smile in place. There was no doubt they would yelp at the sting of his hand across their petite asses and be horrified. No one seemed to understand that Josh was layered and complicated and more than just a handsome smile and a helping hand.

The blonde was short and cute in a *farmer's daughter* kind of way. Her button nose and natural, loose waves oozed girl-next-door sex appeal. Something I'm sure the men in town fell over themselves for. She looked . . . safe. Like the last thing she'd ever do was leave the quiet mountain town. She was bred to bake pies and have babies and live a quiet existence with the lucky man who came home to her every night.

She was nothing like me. *Josh* was nothing like me. I lived in a town that functioned on appearances and social climbing. Josh and I had created our own little bubble, but in reality, he would have a very hard time fitting into my existing lifestyle. He would be charming, sure, but he wouldn't stand for the backstabbing and gossip culture of Los Angeles—the way I had to mold myself to meet expectations.

He deserved a woman who would bake and have a garden in the backyard and have his ridiculously handsome babies. My hurt from Ray's reaction piled on top of the realization that Josh and I were just so *different*.

"There you are." Josh's soothing voice pulled me from my darkening thoughts. The girls ate him up with their eyes, and I moved closer to him.

"Yeah. All good," I lied. His arm lay across my shoulders and pulled me into him. I sagged into his warmth. I wanted to wrap him around me like a blanket. To be buried and wake up in the morning with only his scent and his touch to keep me company. I wanted to forget about Ray's harsh dismissal and perfect girls next door and leaving Tipp to return to a town who'd likely already forgotten about me.

After the doorbell rang, Josh and I exchanged curious looks. So far everyone had either done a one-knock and entered or walked around to the backyard and joined the barbecue that way. He didn't leave my side as we walked through his house.

My heart plummeted when Josh pulled open the front door. Standing at even height with Josh, his perfect smile gleaming in the afternoon sun, was Benjamin Cross.

"Madison!" He moved forward and pulled me into an awkward embrace. "How's my girl?"

25

JOSH

IF I CLENCHED my jaw any tighter, my molars would have turned to dust. After that asshole pulled Effie from under my arm and smashed his body against hers, he had the balls to reach out his hand.

"Hi there, handsome. Benjamin Cross."

I glared at him and his perfectly straight nose. I wanted to ram my fist into it. *I know who the fuck you are.* Despite the barely contained rage coursing through me, I shook it. Of course. "Josh."

He turned his attention back to Effie, moving her shoulders so he could look her over. "Look at you! Des is gonna flip when she sees how soft Montana's made you. Fuck, it's good to see you."

I took a half step at his dig, but when Effie wound her arm around his torso and squeezed him back, I paused. The wave of buzzing filled my head, like locusts descending and devouring everything in their path.

I didn't think I was the jealous type, but the oily coating roiling around my stomach said something else.

Effie turned her head to look at me, that douche's arms still around her. "This is such a surprise." She nodded, keeping my gaze, and spoke slowly as he kissed the air on either side of her head. "I had no idea, Benjamin. Really."

"Just because you gave up on social media doesn't mean it gave up on you. There were pictures all over IG of you dancing at some county fair. Desiree finally gave in and sent me the address. But really? Cowboy boots?"

Effie rolled her eyes and I'd had enough. I hooked a thumb over my shoulder. "I'm going back to our guests."

"Right, I'm sorry." Effie offered me a small smile. "I'll be right there."

Dismissed and more than a little annoyed, I walked through the house and into the backyard.

"All good, man?" Evan Walker stepped beside me and handed me a beer. About my height, Evan folded his heavily tattooed arms across his chest. A witness who'd come to the ranch and started a new life. I didn't know much about his past, and I didn't ask—as was the way at Redemption—but he was a solid friend. He had proved to be a good man. His wife, Val, was also a cop who'd become a marshal.

A criminal and US marshal. Surely if they could figure out how to make it work, Effie and I could stand a chance.

"Fine," I gritted through my teeth. What was supposed to be a good time with music, beanbag toss, and a few beers had dissolved into something else entirely.

Evan eyed me suspiciously. "If you say so. I don't think I've ever seen you so worked up before, man."

The ringing blared in my ears, and I tried to push it away with a swig of my beer. "Just a weird day." I forced a smile, and when the game in front of us ended, I tipped my chin. "We've got winner."

The beanbag toss had been a welcomed distraction. Evan wasn't very good, and I enjoyed giving him shit about the one thing it seemed he wasn't great at. He scowled and tried to muscle his way through. Thankfully, I'd grown up with backyard barbecue games and carried us to a win.

My eyes clung to the door, waiting for Effie to come back outside. Wondering what the *fuck* they were doing in there. After she walked out onto the patio—alone—I exhaled in relief.

Evan chuckled and shook his head. His voice was low, but I caught it anyway when he said, "Shit. You've got it bad, man."

"You have no idea." I left him to intercept Effie as she busied herself with clearing cups and rearranging bottles of water on the drink station she'd set up outside.

"Everything go okay in there?" I asked, trying to sound casual and not completely unhinged.

"Benjamin and I are going to dinner tomorrow."

I tempered my simmering jealousy. "I see."

She turned to face me, her eyes wide. "You're coming with."

~

I STILL COULDN'T BELIEVE I'd agreed to be a third wheel on a date with my woman and her ex-boyfriend. But it was better than the alternative—her on a date with him *alone*. Fuck that.

Effie had explained that Benjamin insisted they have dinner in order to talk about the upcoming press junket. I was content ignoring the looming deadline and continuing to live in the fantasy world where Effie was in Tipp forever.

I'd suggested The Rasa, eagerly looking forward to Al's

special brand of customer service, but Effie stated that Benjamin wanted something more *intimate*.

Prick.

I reluctantly agreed and suggested Ruthie's, a restaurant at the edge of town. It was mostly for those passing through or date nights, but the food was decent and the beer was cold. Effie looked stunning in an off-the-shoulder top. It gave perfect access to the thin line of skin where her fiery auburn hair stopped and the swoop of the shirt began. I trailed my fingertips across that strip of skin, and she leaned into me.

"Thanks for this." She smiled but it was forced. It seemed she wasn't looking forward to this dinner any more than I was.

We'd beaten Benjamin to the restaurant and gotten a table, but when he finally did show up—twenty minutes late—the conversation died. Clinks of silverware and hushed voices followed him, and he made his way toward our table. Benjamin glanced around the restaurant with a grimace, almost like he was afraid to touch something—or worse, that something might reach out and touch him.

He was clearly out of place. He'd had the decency to wear a jacket, though Ruthie's wasn't nearly fancy enough. His shirt was unbuttoned two buttons too many, and his gold necklace flickered in the candlelight. His slacks were pressed and stopped above his ankles, his bare feet slipped into loafers. I took stock of my own button-down shirt and slacks. My entire outfit probably cost less than his belt, but the appreciative way Effie's eyes roamed over my forearms and chest was enough.

When he finally made it to the table, we stood, and Benjamin kissed the air at the sides of her face again. "Darling."

I stifled an eye roll. Benjamin looked at me, and I didn't bother to offer my hand but only nodded to acknowledge his existence.

Ignoring me completely, Benjamin stood next to his chair. When it dawned on him that no one would be pulling it out for him, he used two fingers to drag the heavy wood chair against the floor. We glanced at the menu, and when Tenisha came to get our order, he closed the plastic menu and pushed it away from him.

"Do you have any vegan options?"

Tenisha looked at me in shock, and I just raised my eyebrows, amused.

"Um . . . I think we have a vegetable soup?"

Effie cut in. "That's fine. I'll have the southwest salad with grilled chicken. Dressing on the side, please."

I frowned. Effie never ordered a salad. She had been more of a strip-steak-and-veggies kind of girl. I don't know why that annoyed me as much as it did. I ordered the loaded baked potato and steamed vegetables with a steak, rare, just to watch Benjamin pale and stifle a gag.

Effie carried the conversation, making small talk and asking surface-level questions about what she had been missing in LA. From what it sounded like, not much, but she was enthralled by his recounting of the drama surrounding Hollywood's elite.

"Madison. Maddy." Benjamin reached across the table to grab her hand, and I stiffened. She slipped her hand away gently, and I relaxed a little in my seat. I sure as hell didn't appreciate the way he talked to her like I was fucking invisible. "We both know you're better than this town."

He looked around with disdain, and I was seconds away from hauling him over the table and beating the shit out of him. Effie's eyes sliced to me, and she rested one hand under the table on my thigh, holding me in place.

"People haven't forgotten about us, love," Benjamin continued. "You can't buy publicity like that. If we show up at the press junket, together, people will lose their minds."

He stood to his full height and adjusted his sports coat before rounding the table and standing at her side. In one swift move, he dipped his hand into his pocket and dropped to his knee.

"Madison Colt, will you marry me?"

"Oh, fuck no—" I stood, scraping my chair against the wood floor as Effie gasped.

"Benjamin, this is—" She was cut off by the murmurs of the other patrons. A few people even had their phones out, and I assumed they were recording or snapping pictures.

"This is ridiculous. Get up." The color in Effie's cheeks rose and my heart ticked faster.

"Don't make a scene, darling," he gritted through his perfect smile.

"*I'll* make a scene," I cut in. "She said no." Technically, she hadn't, but when Effie didn't correct me, I let my clenched fist relax.

Resigned, Benjamin rose to his feet and turned on his heels, but not before sending me a scathing look. I hardened my stare and didn't move until he was out the door. When I turned to Effie, she was wide-eyed, but her plastic smile remained intact.

"Well." Effie huffed out a breath and slapped her napkin across the plate. "That was *not* how I expected my marriage proposal to go."

No shit. Watching another man get on his knee for her wasn't what I had envisioned either.

She looked up at me and her smile shifted. Her real smile crinkled the corners of her eyes.

I wound my arms around her, and she scrunched her nose at me. "How does LA sound?"

26

EFFIE

I'M sure to Josh LA sounded like a goddamned nightmare, but somehow he still managed to put me at ease. Benjamin's ridiculous display at Ruthie's had undoubtedly made the news. Grainy photos of him on one knee, me looking horrified, and Josh looking like he was about to murder Benjamin were too tempting for the tabloids to resist. Someone leaked the photos, and "Are They a Throuple?" and "The Cowboy and the Cassanova: Who Will She Choose?" headlines started popping up online.

I had to deal with this swiftly, before the location was leaked and Ma Brown came for my ass. My insides were still tender and bruised from the swift rejection of Ray, but I couldn't deal with that yet. Right now I needed to get the media under control, salvage my career, and figure out what the hell was next for me and where Josh fit into it all.

Joshua Laredo had his charm dialed up to eleven when, a few days later, we made the trek from Tipp, Montana, to sunny LA. We had plans to stay downtown for a few days. I didn't want the paparazzi to get wind of my return, and they had already been camped out in front of my house since the pictures of Benjamin proposing surfaced.

From the flight attendants, to the driver, to the hotel staff, he was attentive and engaging and *genuine*. People were drawn to his slow, subtle twang and good manners. When an older woman bumped into us in the hotel lobby and he dipped his chin and drawled *ma'am*, I swooned right alongside her.

I caught the not-so-subtle glances from every woman eighteen to eighty-two as we walked through the hotel. Dreamy sighs and heart eyes were exploding around their heads. If I thought the female attention was bad at The Rasa, it didn't hold a candle to the effect Josh had on women in LA. As soon as he started speaking, the women—and a few men—fell all over themselves to accommodate him.

Some women may have felt jealousy for all the attention their man was receiving, but not me. I loved it. Josh was completely clueless to what was unfolding around him, and his genuine, kind nature was amplified in a town where everyone was always looking out for themselves. When I made a comment about it, he only shrugged and said he thought he was just being polite.

I grinned, knowing he was mine. Who could blame them? He was delicious, and only I had the pleasure of knowing the dominant, demanding lover beneath the modest cowboy exterior.

"Well, shit." Josh dropped our bags just inside the hotel room and looked around. His hands bracketed his hips as he surveyed the room. It was a luxurious suite with French doors that tucked away the fluffy king-size bed.

"Nice, right?" I slipped out of my heels, cursing how uncomfortable they seemed now that I wasn't so used to wearing them. I walked to hang my garment bag on a hook and noticed the chilled bottle of champagne waiting for us.

Being in LA left an odd twist in my gut that I couldn't shake. The air wasn't as clean as I remembered. The sun not as shiny. I had been hiding from the real world, living a completely different life while I was in Tipp. I hadn't been *Madison Colt* in months, and Effie Pierce was someone I was just starting to get to know.

Famous and beloved in LA was something my mother and I had always worked for, but Tipp was a reality I never knew could exist. It reminded me of the little girl I was before talent agents and directors and my mother molded me into the woman I needed to be in order to be successful. The hopeful little girl who always wondered whether there was just a little something *more* had been buried for so long.

My head swam with confusion. I couldn't just walk away from the life I'd built here, but being back in Los Angeles made me realize it wasn't quite as shiny and perfect as I'd made it out to be. Where would I go? Live in Tipp with no job? Live in the same town as a man who may or may not be my father but refuses to even have a conversation about it? I had plenty of money but not enough to retire at thirty. It would run out eventually if I didn't have another option. I also knew enough about myself and that I would need *something*. I would never be happy being a kept woman with no purpose, and I certainly wasn't interested in shoveling cow shit for the rest of my life.

Time moved slowly in Tipp. I could breathe. Back in LA, it felt like my choices were catching up with me, and sooner, not later, I was going to face some difficult decisions. I glanced at Josh, who'd toed off his boots and sprawled sideways across the bed. His denim jeans were slung low on his hips, and with his arms stretched behind his head, his T-shirt rode up and teased me with the scrap of skin stretched over the muscles that created a perfect V.

I smiled. We would meet with Desiree and sort out this whole mess before preparing for the press junket. It meant so much that Josh was by my side. I felt braver and more self-assured. I tucked myself into the crook of his arm, and he shifted to pull me closer. He was dozing, but not quite asleep, and I breathed him in. His stubble was rough against my cheek, and he smelled so damn good.

I pressed a kiss to his throat, and the vibration of his low groan sent little sparks radiating down my spine. His muscles bunched and he pulled me closer. I swung a leg over his hip and shifted, pressing myself against his side. When I shifted again, my body responded to his arms around me, and Josh pulled me on top of him.

His eyes opened, devouring me with one heated look. I loved how he saw me—craved me. Despite the long day of traveling, my body awakened. I braced his hips between my thighs and inched up against his growing erection. His hand slid across my cheek and into my hair, gripping the back of my neck and pulling me down for a hot kiss. His tongue moved over mine, sensual and deep. We moved together, grinding and touching and moaning.

I broke the kiss and inched down his body, shooting him a wicked smile. When my fingers tickled the skin above his waistband, his abs twitched and heat spread throughout my body. I pushed his shirt up to get a better view, and when he flexed his abs for me, I swallowed a groan. I palmed the hard ridge of his cock and pressed my tongue on the vein that started just on the inside of his hip and disappeared. Josh sucked a breath between his teeth.

I smiled up at him, loving how my touch could make him fall apart. His belt buckle clinked as I unfastened it. I unbuttoned his jeans and slowly inched the zipper down. His cock was thick and hard. I ran my tongue over my lip as I slipped his underwear down.

I wanted my mouth on him. To feel him fill me in every way. Pressure built between my legs, warm and insistent. I teased the head of his cock, swirling my tongue and paying special attention to the sensitive underside. His throaty groan spurred me to duck my head, taking him as deeply as I could. His hips shifted, pushing deeper as I gripped the base with my hand, and a groan broke free from his throat.

He easily overpowered me, shifting his hips and flipping me to my back. Sprawled across the bed, I watched as he dropped his pants and underwear and pulled his shirt from his back before crawling over me.

"Your mouth is fucking magic, but I want to drag this out."

My core tightened at his promise, and I shifted my knees to accommodate his body. Fully clothed, Josh's unashamed nakedness was erotic. He ran his hands down my breasts to my knee. Moving my skirt up as he stroked higher, I arched into his touch. Every nerve ending was on fire, and my eyes ate up every inch of chiseled muscle. He kissed me deeply, his tongue stroking mine as his fingers teased the seam of my underwear. I tried to scissor my legs, but his hips prevented me from the pressure I needed. His soft touches on the thin skin of my inner thigh made me shiver and moan.

His palms covered my knees as he pressed them apart, stretching and baring me. "This pussy is mine."

Without hesitation, he pushed his fingers deep inside me. I hissed a breath and arched against his hand. He pumped into me as he leaned forward and sucked on my bottom lip, his teeth biting down.

"Josh. Yes. You feel so good."

He leaned his head so his lips brushed my ear. "I'm going to wreck you."

At his filthy promise, butterflies erupted in my belly. His rough hands flipped my skirt and yanked my panties down. He sat back on his heels, his cock jutting up between his muscular thighs as he looked down on me. "You're so fucking perfect."

Josh brushed his fingertips delicately over my pussy, the feather-light touch teasing me. "Who owns this pussy?"

My voice was strained and breathless. "You. You do."

A cocky smile pulled at his lips before he leaned his head down and spit directly on my aching pussy. A dirty little thrill raced through me.

"You're fucking right I do," he growled before running his tongue up my slit.

My hands drove into his hair as he devoured me. I gripped his hair and bucked my hips. His moans encouraged me to move against his face. Swirling and teasing his tongue, he moved from deep inside me to my clit. Sparks ignited under my skin as I pulsed around him. Tension rose from my toes all the way up my spine and out the top of my head.

He worked me over and over until I thought I was going to dissolve. He slid two fingers inside me and I cried out and arched against him. One hand shot up, his fingers spread as he pinned me in place on the mattress. I writhed beneath him.

"You'll want for *nothing* when you're with me."

Warm, hot pressure against my clit stacked and built until I was tumbling over the edge of ecstasy. Wave after wave rolled through me as my pussy throbbed around his tongue and fingers. Josh growled into me, and I let the orgasm drown me.

I lay panting and soaked on the bed as he peppered slow, wet kisses between my legs and the inside of my thighs. When the fog cleared, the deep, aching need to be completely consumed by him was overwhelming. I looped my arms under his and pulled him up and on top of me. Spreading my legs wider to accommodate him, my hand gripped his cock and guided him to my entrance.

"I'm not through with you yet, cowboy." My voice was heavy with lust and anticipation.

Josh slid his hips forward, and my pussy sucked him in deep. I stretched around him to accommodate how thick he was.

"How do you feel, baby girl?" he asked as he slowly pumped in and out of me.

"Full." I wound my arms around his back, pulling him closer to me. Our hearts beat wildly. My nipples pinched, and I cursed the fabric between us. As he looked down at me, the air in the room shifted. Gone was the possessive, frantic wolf who was desperate for me, and in its place was a different kind of desperation. The kind that destroys your heart because you're so desperate for more that the mere thought of losing it sends you reeling. The intensity in his stare had pressure building in my chest and between my legs.

One hand moved over my frantic heartbeat. "I asked, How do you feel?" he repeated.

My hand moved to trace his eyebrow and feel the rough stubble on his face. "I feel seen," I admitted quietly. Slow, languid thrusts allowed me to feel every inch of him as he slowly moved inside me.

"I see you." His eyes never left mine, his hand still

planted over my heart. "I see you and I love you."

I arched my back to take him deeper. He slowly pumped in and out. Even at a languid pace, he unleashed on me. He was primal and raw and intense. On a cry, I pulled him closer, and tension bunched the muscles in his back. I wrapped my legs around his hips to pull him farther inside me as he emptied himself with steady pulses. I held his body to mine as his orgasm overtook him, and I let my mind forget everything—the demands of my agent, leaving for the press junket, the uncertainty of what comes next. With Josh it all melted away. His pants slowed. He raised his head to look at me.

I moved the strands of hair that tumbled over one eye.

This man is incredible and he loves me. A bubble of laughter tickled my belly. It was absolutely absurd.

Confusion and intensity flashed across his face. "Why is that funny?"

My grin widened. "Because I love you too, and it's absolutely unbelievable." I let a small laugh roll out of me. Josh huffed a relieved breath and bundled me closer, his light laugh mingling with my hair and the bedsheets.

When he shifted, he took me with him so he was sitting back on his heels and I was held in his arms. "You almost gave me a heart attack."

I let a satisfied moan roll through me as he ran his hands down my back. We sat, tangled in each other, the outside world shuttered away. I soaked him in. All of him—from the tender strokes of his fingertips to his filthy mouth to the warm corners of his golden soul.

It was only the shrill ring of my phone that tore us from each other. Desiree's name flashed on the screen, and I groaned and braced myself to morph back into Madison Colt and face the press with Benjamin Cross.

27

JOSH

I WOULD NEVER UNDERSTAND Los Angeles. Parts of it were pretty, sure, but it was loud and fast and everyone was on top of one another. I could see the appeal of sunny skies and palm trees swaying, but it was nothing compared to staring off a butte into the vast Montana wilderness. You could stare into the forest or across the plains and have an existential crisis while knowing very few had stood in that exact spot. Like you were *lucky* to have seen it at all. LA made you feel like it would swallow you up and spit you out without a second thought. Like you were just the next one among the long line of poor, lonely souls.

LA even made Effie different, and for that I hated the city. She constantly checked her phone and email, waiting to hear from her agent about what to do next. I couldn't even flick through the television without seeing the pictures of Benjamin down on his knee or old clips of them holding hands and smiling at each other. Photos of her dancing at the carnival had surfaced too. I was sure Ma Brown was in full-on damage-control mode as everyone prepared for Tipp, Montana, to be leaked to the press.

"I have to meet with Des this morning." Effie had been getting ready in the bathroom for over an hour before she walked out. Her hair was straightened, and she had on a full face of makeup with dark eyeliner and bright-red lipstick. She looked gorgeous, just . . . not like my Effie.

"I can find something to do." I uncrossed my legs and stood to wrap her in a hug. "You take care of what you need to. I'll be here."

Her face transformed, and beneath the makeup, I could see my girl. "Come with me?"

My heart skipped a little at her wanting to keep me at her side. "Course. You ready?"

When we left the cocoon of the hotel room, the air shifted. Effie kept her head down and face hidden. She left a respectable distance between us, and when I reached for her hand, she shifted casually to adjust her sleeve. It didn't go without notice.

We took a private elevator to the parking garage, and a driver met us with an SUV with blacked-out windows. He barely spoke save for when I offered my hand and a thank-you. When we arrived at DS Talent, our entrance was just as discreetly swift as our exit from the Hotel Bel-Air had been.

Nervous energy radiated off Effie, but she kept it stuffed down. Her index finger drummed on the outside of her thigh as we waited. The lobby was huge, an all-white open space with a wall of windows showcasing the city. Effie was recognized immediately as we entered.

"Ms. Colt," the receptionist greeted her and swiftly picked up the desk phone.

A large, curving staircase climbed three floors, all of which opened to the waiting area below. In the lobby, couches and chairs were arranged in sections with comfortable seating. Offices with glass walls and matching white-and-wood furniture dotted each floor as I looked up and around. Large portraits lined a long hallway, and I saw Effie's—no, Madison Colt's—smile shining back at me. I bumped her shoulder and discreetly pointed at it while giving her a small smile. She rolled her eyes, and I got the real Effie smile in return. My chest pinched.

My girl is still in there.

Loud clacking heels announced someone's arrival. "Ms. Spice is ready to see you. She apologizes for any wait."

Effie released a soft breath and hooked her arm in mine. "Let's get this over with."

I followed quietly by her side as we walked down the portrait-lined hallway toward the expansive office at the back of the space. When I passed Benjamin Cross's portrait, in which he gave the camera an intense, smoldering stare, I flexed my fist to keep from driving it through his stupid fucking face.

Desiree's office was just as opulent and tidy as the rest of the agency. Her obvious distaste of my presence didn't faze me as Effie charged in.

"I cannot believe you told Benjamin where I was."

Desiree rolled her eyes. "First of all, when pictures surfaced of you dancing at some hillbilly hoedown, I squashed the story. Denied it was you and buried it. So you're welcome."

Desiree's intensity had Effie wilting a bit in her presence. Effie released a measured breath and folded her hands in front of her. "Thank you for that. Now what do we need to do to clean up this mess?"

"Mess?" Desiree looked positively giddy. "This is something we can work with. People are now questioning your breakup with Benjamin, but you're no longer the villain."

Her dark glare pinned me in place. "But this"—her hands gestured between us—"is a problem." Her eyes flicked to me. "No offense."

I just shook my head and stood in relaxed attention. She may be intense, but the Army had made me immune to someone barking orders in your face and cutting you down.

"Benjamin proposing was a brilliant move. It creates drama. Interest. Now everyone in America is wondering, *Who will she choose?* or *Will they fight for her?* and *Who is this mystery man?* It's perfect."

"I'm with Josh. Not Benjamin. There is no choice to be made." Effie gripped my hand and I squeezed back.

"I don't give a shit," Desiree shot back. "It's not about the truth. It's about perception." The woman rounded her desk to pick up her phone. "You have a very important press junket and premiere coming up. You need to be seen. Here in LA I have a lunch scheduled, and there's a party tonight. You'll make an appearance."

"I won't deny my relationship with Josh."

"No one is asking you to stop . . ." She paused and barely stifled a sneer. "Whatever this is. I don't give a shit what you do in your private life. All I'm saying is that you need to leave a little to the imagination. Let the 'will they, won't they' mystery hang for a little while. Hold his hand but don't openly kiss. Touch his arm but pull away."

Effie opened her mouth to speak, but only a small squeak came out before she slammed her lips together. "And if I say no?"

Desiree's dark eyes moved over her, and my back stiffened. The air in the office cooled by several degrees. She ignored Effie's question completely as she assessed Effie again. "I'm also booking an appointment with Sergei."

Effie swiveled on her heels, fuming, and I moved toward the door with her, holding it open so we could leave that hellhole.

"And you."

I turned, and Desiree pointed directly at me. Not since Mrs. Anderson's third-grade class had I felt more discomfort and nerves from a single look.

"Don't fuck this up for her."

~

THE REST of the afternoon I kept my mouth fucking shut. I knew that Effie was stressed out, and I didn't want to add to that. She asked if I wanted to go shopping before her lunch, and I declined. I could meander through the city alone while she played her part and shopped for a new outfit for the party appearance Desiree had arranged. I wanted to support her, but I also wasn't interested in being part of some fucked-up, imaginary love triangle.

Effie was mine, but Madison Colt was not. A heavy rock sat in the pit of my stomach.

When she returned from shopping, she had enough bags to stock The Rebellious Rose. Not only had she gotten clothes for herself, but she had picked up a pair of slacks and a button-down shirt for me. It was fancier than anything I owned, but the fit was great, and it brought a smile to her face.

We were ready to navigate the shark-infested waters of an LA party in order to be "seen." It was a far cry from anything I'd experienced before, but I knew my role, and I was willing to do what it took to show Effie I was in her corner.

She looked stunning. She'd picked up a short black dress that shimmered when she moved, and her heels made her almost as tall as me. Her auburn hair was piled high on her head, with small pieces escaping around her face. The access to her long, slender neck begged for my mouth to drag across her delicate skin. I wanted to worship every inch of her.

I ran my hand down my chest. She'd told me a hundred times how good I looked and that if we weren't careful, I'd be the one getting all the attention.

Jesus fuck, I hope not.

We arrived at the secluded entrance of a venue, and a young woman greeted us. She was so tall and so thin I was afraid she might blow over. The poor girl looked like she needed a snack. "Everything is set. They are aware of your arrival, and a select few photographers have been granted access. They agreed to be very discreet. Just go in and have fun." The woman turned to me and frowned. "Hmm. We thought you might dress in your own clothes. Lean into the country charm a bit." She waved a hand. "It's fine. This can work."

Effie only nodded.

"Benjamin Cross will also arrive. He attended with a small group, and one model will be paying him special attention. Tasteful." She winked at us. "Let's keep everyone guessing."

The absurdity and complexity was mind numbing.

It was like a chess game when you'd only ever learned checkers.

As the woman moved away, Effie leaned into me. "I'm

sorry for all this. Let's just get through it. If it gets really bad, I'll feign food poisoning or something."

A small chuckle escaped me. I reached for her hand and pulled her knuckles to my lips.

Before she could speak again, Effie was ushered toward the side entrance of the building. Like a broken-down stray dog, I followed.

28

JOSH

"IF YOU COULD JUST TURN to the left. Gorgeous." Effie lifted her chin and followed the reporter's directions as he snapped photo after photo of her. Her perfect smile never wavered. My back was tense, and I shoved my hands in my pockets to keep from fidgeting.

"Now you." One photographer snapped his fingers at me, and I ground my molars together. "Lean in and whisper something in her ear."

I looked at her in question. She stepped closer and dipped her chin in a slight nod.

I leaned into her, brushing my lips against the shell of her ear. "That man's soul must be blacker than the inside of a cow."

Effie pulled back, and the corners of her lips twitched as she struggled to contain the bubble of laughter rising in her throat. She let loose, her gorgeous smile cutting through the fake one before she slapped a hand over her mouth to hide it. I pulled her into me and squeezed. Her closeness reassured me that no matter what happened tonight, my Effie was still in there.

We made our way slowly down the long hallway. I assumed it was meant to look natural, like we were arriving at the event, but Effie was instructed to stop. Pose. Smile. Laugh.

It's all bullshit.

"Madison, have you spoken with Benjamin Cross since his proposal?"

The reporter next to the photographer was furiously scribbling down notes as Effie spoke through her smile. "Benjamin and I have spoken. His proposal was a surprise, but we're working things out."

The fuck?

We moved on, creeping our way toward the back of the building as Effie posed and vaguely answered any questions the reporters slung at her.

"Are you ready to stake your claim and let Benjamin know Madison is yours now?" the reporter asked, turning his steely gaze on me.

I opened my mouth to set him straight, but Effie jumped in. "We've known each other since we were children."

Before I could say my piece and let him know that Effie was more than capable of dealing with Benjamin, but that if it came down to this, hell yeah, I'd put him in his place, we were moving.

My back ached from stiffness. The hallway was endless as she posed with me—without me. Laughing. Smiling. Answering questions with the same half truths and vague responses. Her voice was foreign and lacked the warmth and genuine joy I'd come to love.

I kept my mouth shut, offering only the occasional nod to the reporter or photographer. I was a pawn, and I hated it. When my eyes sliced to hers and she threw me a wink, my shoulders relaxed.

"He's here." The photographer whipped his camera toward the end of the hallway, acknowledging the arrival of Benjamin Cross.

The reporter nodded at Effie, and the pair moved back down the hall, leaving us in a moment of peace. I took a deep breath.

"You were great." Her hands smoothed over my shirt, and she picked invisible lint from my shoulder. I concentrated on her face, my eyes searching to find the smattering of freckles that were hidden under the layers of her makeup. "The worst is over. Now we can just enjoy ourselves inside for a minute and head back."

In the back room, dozens of people were in the throes of a party. I recognized a few faces—socialites and celebrities from the covers of magazines and movies. The lights were too low, and the music was too loud. Back by the bar, high-top tables were set with fancy linens and flickering candles. Groups of people stood together, and the dance floor in front of a DJ was already full.

I needed a drink. I had leaned in to talk to her when someone pulled her into a conversation. No one acknowledged my existence, let alone tried to engage me in conversation. I adjusted my shirt sleeves and cleared my throat. Effie was greeted as Madison, and I was disgusted by how fake and insincere everyone seemed. I knew Effie's stage name was something she always went by, but it still grated on me.

We worked our way around the room, me as the puppy in her wake. Despite how she shifted in her impossibly high heels, her smile never wavered. A photographer in the crowd caught my eye.

Son of a bitch, they're still lurking around. When she attempted to include me in a conversation and smiled tightly, tipping her head in the photographer's direction, I realized exactly what she needed from me.

The nicest guy in the room.

It was what everyone always expected of me, and she was no different. So I turned my charm up to eleven. I pushed down my judgment and disgust at how plastic everyone seemed. I could be just as fake as the rest of them.

Once I shifted from sulking shadow to the Joshua Laredo everyone loved, Effie visibly relaxed. Her smile started to reach her eyes, and I knew I'd made the right choice for her. I shook hands and let my accent thicken, just a bit. My manners on full display, I morphed into the man she needed me to be, despite how unsettled I felt.

Confident I was nailing my performance for her, I whispered in her ear. "Back in a second."

Effie lifted an eyebrow, and I shot her a wink and a smile, hoping the cameras caught it. As I walked toward the back bar, my eyes flickered over the exit, and I wondered if she would even notice if I just up and left. I'd been introduced to dozens of people, most of whose names I'd already forgotten.

My eyes found Effie again, and I noted someone had refilled her drink for her. I leaned on the bar, ordered a whiskey ditch—then had to explain it was a whiskey and water while the female bartender smiled and looked me over. I knew that look. She appreciated what she saw, but my mind was focused on the stunning redhead making her way across the room.

"You're about as good of an actor as the rest of them." I shifted toward the voice to find Effie's manager, Desiree, holding a highball glass of brown liquid. She raised it in salute, and I clinked mine against hers.

Her natural coiled hair curled dramatically around her

large eyes. She looked more like a movie star than a talent agent. Her dark eyes assessed me, and I met her stare.

"If you ever want a career here, I can make that happen for you. With your body and that face combined with this whole rugged cowboy thing you've got going on? Give me six months."

My eyes shifted around the room. Not a single thing could entice me to want this life, save for my girl. "I'm good, thanks."

"You are good. I'll give you that. I saw that performance you gave. Nearly charmed Anna Holliday out of her Spanx, that much is true."

We both looked at the famous actress I'd spoken with earlier. She was leggy and waif thin and just as fake as the rest of them. My eyes found Effie again. She was in a small group, and I saw Benjamin walk up and join them.

My back clenched, and my fist curled around the sweating glass in my hand. Out of the corner of my eye, I saw Desiree's smile widen. Apparently my inner turmoil made for delightful gossip. They were standing close, talking with the group, and then she smiled *Effie's smile* for him, and I nearly shattered the glass in my hand.

"The plot thickens . . ." Desiree's voice was deep and quiet. Her hand rested on my forearm as I drilled a hole in the back of Benjamin's head and plotted how I could bury his body on the back forty acres of the ranch.

Desiree sighed beside me. "Unfortunately for me, you seem like a good man, so here's a tip. Run as far from LA as you can."

She sauntered away, so I picked up my whiskey and moved in Effie's direction. She was still with the same small group, Benjamin glued to her side as I approached. He leaned in, placing a hand at her lower back, and I leveled him with a hard stare. A wave of possessiveness burned up my throat.

Benjamin didn't acknowledge me in any way, but he withdrew from the group and cast his attention on a woman one table over.

"Well that's a look I didn't know I was into." Effie smiled at me, but it was thin and practiced.

What the hell are these feelings?

It was exhaustion and anger and disgust. Confusion, maybe, too. I had never asked Effie about her relationship with Benjamin, and I didn't follow Hollywood gossip close enough to really know.

Clearly, he'd thought their relationship was serious enough to warrant a marriage proposal. The only time we'd talked about it, Effie had brushed it off and said that it was unexpected and rash. I'd been operating under the assumption Benjamin was a total dumbass, but the way this entire party seemed like a setup for rumors of a reconciliation made my gut turn.

Would she go back to him once she went home to LA?

I'd fallen for her, hard, and I was willing to put in the work, but we hadn't gotten to the point where we talked about how to navigate her life in LA and mine in Montana. The prospect of a long-distance relationship made me sick, but life without her felt damn near impossible.

Effie had never said she was staying in Montana. After things with Ray blew up, I had known it was a tender subject and that it hurt her to discuss it. Then Benjamin, with his ankle pants and loafers with no socks, showed up and created chaos.

As the conversation circled around me, my thoughts filtered back to Malcolm. I was making good progress on the paperwork that would allow me to foster and adopt him. It was a mountain of paperwork and a thousand hoops to jump through just to prove I loved the kid enough and that he was best with me.

Would this fuck it up for us?

The laughter around us was shrill and fake. I was deeply uncomfortable with the thought of Malcolm coming anywhere near these people. It was shockingly clear I didn't know as much about Effie and this very large part of her life, and I hated that. Hated myself for not acknowledging who she was before she blew into our lives. Effie was an award-winning actress. She was poised and engaging and, at least on the surface, seemed at ease with everyone at the party. On the ranch she laughed and worked hard, got dirty, and charmed everyone she met. It made me wonder which version was the real Effie Pierce.

Malcolm deserved better than the man I was being. He deserved a father who had a strong moral compass. A man who could be kind and accommodating without sacrificing his honor in the process. My palms started to sweat, and it felt twenty degrees hotter. The buzz in my ears grew to a roar, and my head pounded. The air was stifling.

This isn't me.

"Are you almost ready?" Even to my own ears, my voice was raw and hurried.

Effie blinked at me, and her smile never faltered. "A few more minutes if that's okay."

"I'll meet you at the hotel." Before she could argue, I placed a kiss on the slope of her shoulder and stormed away. If she said anything in response, it was drowned out by the high-pitch ring that followed me everywhere.

I was a coward, but I couldn't stand to be there for a single second longer.

29

EFFIE

HE LEFT ME. He *actually* left me standing at the party, staring at his broad shoulders as he stalked through the crowd and out the side door. The crowd parted, mouths agape as he barreled through them, radiating fury.

"That was perfect!" Desiree hissed into my ear, and she looped her arm in mine. "The photographer got some amazing shots."

My head whipped in her direction. "Did you do this?"

A pleased smile played on her lips as anger rose like a tidal wave in my chest. My cheeks burned, and I calmed my breath before I spoke. "Where did he go?"

She lifted a slim shoulder. "Don't worry about it. The driver will get you home. Let's have a drink."

"Fuck the drinks." I kept my voice under the thump of the music, but my glass snapped against the table as I set it down. "I'm leaving. Get me a ride. *Now*."

By the time Desiree arranged for a driver to discreetly get me back to the hotel, the wind had left my sails. I recalled how Josh had been so obviously out of place and uncomfortable, yet he had managed to rally and turn it around. Everyone loved him. He was engaging and endearing and perfect. Both the men and women were eating out of his gorgeous, charming hands.

When he left to get a drink and Benjamin slid in next to me, my skin had felt slick and oily. He stood too close, whispered too softly. I was aware the cameras were capturing our every move, so I'd opted to appear aloof. I didn't need any more attention on this *nonrelationship* than necessary. I only wanted to ride it out until the tabloids sank their teeth into the next front-page gossip.

However, the way Josh had glared at Benjamin told me he didn't understand the subtext or what I was going for. He wasn't used to attending an event with a specific agenda.

His soul is too good for that.

When I made it back to the hotel, it was dark. Josh was curled up in the king-size bed with his back to me. I was as quiet as I could manage as I showered and scrubbed as much evidence of Madison Colt off my face as I could. I slipped into the bed and curled myself around him. His skin was hot, and his muscles rippled under my fingertips, but he didn't stir.

I sighed and noted his rhythmic breathing. I could have woken him to hash out whatever weirdness was blooming between us, but the truth was, my mind was swirling. Madison Colt and Effie Pierce crashed together, and those two lives were so completely opposite that I was left feeling exhausted and out of my element. I wasn't sure what to do about all of it.

∼

THE NEXT MORNING, things went from bad to worse. The images from the party had already hit the press, and everyone was talking about us. Again. The mystery of who Madison Colt was sleeping with was public fodder, and my phone pinged with calls and text messages from so-called friends I hadn't heard from in months.

Josh awoke in a better mood, but he was still distant. I knew he was itching to get back to his life in Montana. He ordered room service for breakfast, and we ignored the discomfort rapidly filling the hotel room. The unanswered questions between us weighed on me. I needed to find a way to reconcile my life before Montana and the unexpected joy I had found there.

When Desiree called for the third time in an hour, I excused myself to the hotel balcony.

"Answer my calls the first time I ring you." Her tone was clipped and angry.

I rolled my eyes at the urgency in her voice and took a measured breath before lacing my voice with kind patience. "What is it, Des?"

Thankfully, she softened. "I'm updating your schedule. We are right on track. I let Trish know her vacation is over. Your assistant will be ready for instructions by tonight. You've got nails at two p.m. I also booked you a spray-tan appointment—hopefully we can cover those sun spots—at four. Social media is showing they actually like the red hair you've got going on. I fed the story that it's a whole Rita Hayworth or Christina Hendricks vibe, so that's a relief because your colorist is in Beijing."

"Wait a minute. Hold up. What are you talking about?"

She let out an exasperated breath. "We are striking while the iron is hot. Everyone's talking about your little love triangle. The studio is adding an additional week to the press junket!"

My stomach dropped, and my breakfast threatened to

come back up. I swallowed the bile that rose in my throat. My mind was scrambled eggs. "I can't do that. I won't do that. There are some things in Montana I need."

"It's in your contract, sweetheart. Don't go diva on me now. This is happening. Unless you want to get blacklisted by the most influential studio in Hollywood, you'll fall in line. We'll have your shit shipped back to you if you need it that badly."

I was numb as Desiree bulldozed over my feelings and continued with an endless list of appointments to make me presentable. Interviews, photo shoots, podcasts, and conference calls. It had been over a year since I'd had to prepare for the whirlwind of a big premiere, and the thought of it alone was daunting.

I wasn't ready.

Desiree Spice didn't give a single fuck. And she had a point—refusal meant dousing my career in gasoline and lighting a match. I'd filmed a scene just like that once, and while in the film it looked badass, in real life, there were significant consequences.

I fought back tears as she hung up without even saying goodbye.

The balcony door opened, and Josh stood in the frame with only a towel wrapped around his hips. My eyes followed a droplet of water as it trailed down the planes of his stomach. He raked a hand through his damp hair.

"Almost ready? We need to leave in an hour if we're going to catch our flight."

My face was hot. My stomach pitched and rolled as I struggled to find the right words. I looked down at the black screen of my phone.

"What is it?"

"I just got off the phone with Desiree. The studio is

moving up the timeline for the press junket. It was a business decision to capitalize on the tabloid attention."

"Move it up? How soon?" His voice was calm, but I could see the muscle in his jaw flex and release.

I couldn't look him in the eye. "Immediately. Today."

"I see."

I sighed. "I'm trying to see what I can do. Maybe we can extend the flights and have a few more days so I can figure it out."

"I don't have a few more days. I have Malcolm tomorrow."

My heart sank. As much as I wanted Josh by my side as I was thrown to the sharks, I knew how important his time with Malcolm was.

"Right," I said. "But maybe just this once, you can move the date or—"

"No."

I blinked at him, trying to process the gruff tone in his voice.

"No." He took a breath. "Look, this wasn't how I was planning to tell you, but I've officially moved forward with the paperwork to foster Malcolm. To eventually adopt him."

My heart stuttered. "Josh, that—that's so great." Overwhelmed with emotion and love for them both, I was stunned silent.

Josh plastered on a small smile, and my stomach tightened.

Did he see me fitting into that plan somewhere?

My mind raced. I was split between my contract as Madison Colt and the scary, unknown prospect of a life as Effie Pierce. I wanted to cry and throw up, all at the same time.

"I understand if you have to stay. That's your choice,

but I'm getting on that plane and going home." His thinly veiled restraint was palpable. Was it anger? Disappointment? I couldn't read past the nice-guy routine he was dishing out.

I took a deep breath and smiled through the riot of emotions welling in my chest. "I know you're upset but—"

"I'm not upset." He snapped back and turned into the room.

I took a breath. I didn't want to get into a fight when he was leaving, and I had a day full of obligations I didn't even want to be a part of followed by weeks of smiling for cameras and answering questions for the upcoming premiere.

Frustration burned through me. "Don't walk away. Talk to me."

By the time I reached him, he had pulled on a pair of pants and was shoving his clothes into his suitcase. "Talk about what? How I have to go back to my life and you're staying in a town with your ex? That you're pretending to be in some fucked-up love triangle with the two of us?"

My eyes widened in shock. His words slapped across my face. "What?"

"How many times have you denied—*publicly*—a relationship with Benjamin? Have you told anyone that we're together?"

"You know the truth." My face was hot. Anger bubbled beneath the surface but also mingled with shame. He wasn't wrong, and my walls went up to protect myself from that truth.

"Do I?" Clearly angry now, his facade had dropped, and he was ready to hash this out in the middle of a hotel room at eight in the morning. His arms spread between us. "Tell it to me, then."

"I love you. We're together."

"And is that something you're proud of? That you can scream from a mountaintop and not hide from a single soul?"

I paused.

He huffed a humorless laugh. "That's what I thought."

After pulling on a shirt, he zipped the suitcase and dropped it on the floor.

"It's not that easy. There's a contract, and I have obligations and—"

"Fuck your contract! Jesus." He dragged both hands through his hair and tugged at the ends. "This is your *life* we're talking about, not pretending to be Madison Colt."

"Madison Colt is my life!" My anger bubbled over. "I didn't ask for any of this."

"And I did?" Josh stepped forward, and his frustration rolled over me. My nipples hardened beneath my shirt. Damn it, he was hot when he was angry. "Let me get through the next few weeks. Once the premiere is over, we can go from there."

"The next few weeks of you pretending to be someone else's woman. Are you going to deny it when they start printing more rumors of you sucking his dick or spreading your legs for him?"

Every filthy, angry word that flew out of his mouth caused a tug low in my belly. We were one wrong move away from a rough, angry fuck, and he knew it too. I inched forward, my chest brushing against his crossed arms. The air between us smoldered. My body wavered closer to his.

"It's my job to act. This bullshit story was brewing before we even met. Am I supposed to answer for every relationship I had before we met?"

His lip twitched, and I half expected him to shout that,

yes, my past mattered to him—that ever since we shared an innocent kiss when I was twelve, I was his.

My eyes flared. *Don't you fucking dare.*

Even though the thought of Josh being so possessive only fueled the simmering heat between us. He stopped himself before saying anything more.

He dropped his arms and sighed. "I can't compete with this. I can't and I won't."

His words drained all the fight out of me. I was tired and angry and more than a little hurt. What the hell was I doing? I *wanted* to fight with him. For him to pick me and fight for my attention. It was fucked-up. I wanted the passion between us to ignite and let us tumble into bed and fuck the frustration right out of the both of us. It would be too easy to use sex as a way to placate and pretend we were okay.

We are so fucking far from okay.

Josh had a life. A steady job. A little boy who was counting on him. Those weren't things a man like Joshua Laredo would ever walk away from.

He deserved so much more than a woman who didn't even know who she was half the time. Whose life was built on pretending to be someone—anyone—else but herself.

My eyes dropped to the floor, but his hand cupped my cheek, and I looked up.

Don't cry. Don't cry. Don't cry.

"I understand. Fulfill your contract. Smile and let them see all the parts of you that make you special."

He sighed and looked at me like a stranger, and my heart cracked open wider. I didn't deserve a man with such a good heart, let alone one as selfless as Josh.

I was so lost.

I leaned into his hand but knew I couldn't speak without completely losing it and sobbing all over him.

"You're going to be great. At the end of this, everyone's going to love Madison Colt."

Then he kissed the top of my head and walked out the door.

30

JOSH

I STOOD outside the hotel door and listened for Effie's sobs. I was ready to turn around. Pound on the door and gather her in my arms and promise to get her through whatever mess was waiting for her.

I was met with only silence.

I set my jaw and flew home alone. I had a ranch full of animals to take care of and a mountain of paperwork in order to ensure Malcolm was settled.

The entire flight I replayed the morning on an endless loop. Over and over I dissected every look. Every touch. For a minute, I thought we might throw ourselves at each other and fuck into oblivion—the tension was so thick. But the moment I'd thrown her relationship with Benjamin in her face, it was game over.

Everyone's going to love Madison Colt.

I was a prick for using her stage name. I'd done it on purpose and was an asshole for it. Trouble was, I was already in love with Effie Pierce, and it didn't seem like those two parts of her could peacefully coexist.

Los Angeles had opened my eyes to the realities of

being a Hollywood superstar. Her life wasn't her own, and as cutthroat as movies made it seem, reality was ten times worse. I was too stubborn to hear her voice and beg for her forgiveness, so I opted to text her once I'd made it home.

Coward.

∼

THREE WEEKS HAD GONE BY, and the strain between Effie and I hadn't eased. She was busy with the press tour, barely having time for a quick text or a stilted phone call. I'd heard her voice only four times in nearly twenty-one days.

I was sick. Distracted. Fucking miserable without her.

My head ached, and I couldn't rein in the buzzing and clicking of my tinnitus. It was as relentless as my self-loathing at the moment. I spent the rest of the day scrubbing the house clean and making sure it was as presentable as possible.

Malcolm's visit was coming on the heels of an appointment with his social worker, and I wanted to be sure everything was perfect. I was relieved when the social worker didn't stay but rather presented me with her business card and the promise that we'd have an informal meeting before the official home study.

Malcolm loped out of the car, his grin wide as he fist-bumped me before beelining it straight into the house. I patted his back as he went by and watched as the social worker drove away down the long driveway.

I found Malcolm at the back of the house, popping his head out of the back door and into the yard. "She's still not back?"

I schooled my face. "Effie has some things in LA she's taking care of. Work stuff."

His face fell. "She didn't say goodbye."

I tried to sound comforting. Hopeful. "It's just temporary. The movie premieres soon, so there are a lot of interviews and meetings. It's taking a little longer than she'd hoped."

"Okay." He lifted his shoulder. "You coming?" Malcolm ran outside to play. Just like that, he'd accepted my word with blind trust. My heart squeezed tighter.

Is it the truth? Is she coming back, or did I just lie to his face?

We played in the backwoods for a while, and I tried to not let stress and worry gnaw at me. By lunchtime, we were sitting on the back steps of the deck, finishing up our ham-and-cheese sandwiches.

My denim-clad legs stretched in front of me. Malcolm had waded down by the creek, looking for crayfish, so we'd both ditched our shoes and rolled up our pant legs in search of some.

Without luck, we headed toward the house and refueled for whatever the afternoon would bring us.

I thought about Effie often. I hated not knowing what she was up to and hated her not being with us even more.

"I lied for you." Malcolm's voice was small, but my back straightened at his words.

"You lied? About what?" Nerves had my blood pressure thumping.

"The social worker asked me if you ever get angry or frustrated or annoyed."

"Hmm." I considered my words carefully. "You had to lie about that?"

Malcolm toyed with a blade of grass. I waited for his

answer as endless possibilities tumbled through my mind. "You hide it." His eyes cast down to the dirt. "But they don't like that."

Fuck.

"I see. What did you say?"

"I told them that it's not always, but sometimes you get frustrated—but that's okay."

Malcolm covered for me. He knew I often pretended to be someone else to placate people, and he saw right through me.

How did I think that was a good idea?

I cleared my throat and rubbed the back of my neck to ease some of the tension that settled there. "You're right. I haven't done a great job at showing you how I deal with my emotions like a grown-up, but you don't have to lie for me. Promise me you'll only tell them the truth from now on?"

He only shook his little head, and I pulled him in for a hug.

"I'll fight for you." *Like you didn't fight for Effie.* I stuffed the guilt down. "No matter what. But let's make a deal. No more lies, okay?"

"No lies." We shook on it and looked out into the yard. "She's not coming back, is she?"

Sadness bloomed between us as I was caught off guard. "I don't know, pal. I kind of made her mad."

"What happened?"

I considered how to explain this to him. Baring my soul and the complexities of a relationship like ours to an eight-year-old was out of my depth. "Her life is really different there. She's super famous. People write things about her that aren't always true. I got mad about it, and we got into a fight."

"That's scary." Of course he thought an argument between adults was terrifying.

"It wasn't that bad. I didn't have the right words and raised my voice. We love each other, but it happens sometimes. It doesn't have to be scary, even though I feel like shit."

His head whipped to me at the curse.

"Sorry," I mumbled.

"It's okay. You *look* like shit."

I couldn't help but laugh and pull him into another hug. "Thanks. And watch your mouth."

~

AFTER MALCOLM LEFT for the day, I settled into the couch with a glass of whiskey. Each goodbye with him got harder and harder. I'd tried calling Effie, but it went straight to voice mail. My conversation with Malcolm had shifted my perspective in a big way, and I needed to talk with her. To apologize for being an asshole and hope she hadn't already given up on me. If anyone was worth baring my soul to, it was Effie and Malcolm.

I was so used to stifling my feelings and presenting only the polished parts of myself that I had no idea what to do in the face of Effie seeing the parts of me I tried to keep hidden. She'd seen more of me than anyone before. She had said she wanted to figure things out, and I didn't give us that chance. Managing her life in LA and mine in Montana would be messy and complicated and hard, but I knew she was worth it.

I'd hurt her when I threw her past in her face. She'd had an entire existence before coming to Montana, and we'd never talked about it. It was easier to ignore who she was in order to live in the safety and seclusion of Tipp—where she was Effie, looking for her dad and a place to work, and I was the man falling all over himself to keep up.

The real world was a lot more work.

As I sipped my whiskey, I let the slow, warm burn spread through my chest. Across from me on the mantel, Effie had framed the picture I snapped of her and Malcolm at the river. Malcolm was so proud to show her a rock he'd found in the river, and she had smiled at him in a way that sucked the air out of my lungs. In the sunlight, her hair looked like fire whipping in the wind. She radiated happiness.

I picked up my phone and did a quick search for *Madison Colt*. The press junket for *Terminal Justice* was in full swing, and snippets of the interviews were popping up online. She was poised and confident and gorgeous, but her smile didn't reach her eyes. I hated not knowing if she was tired or frustrated or overworked. I watched each clip a dozen times and loved the fact that each time Benjamin Cross made a quip or remark about their "friendship," she inched away or pressed her lips into a terse smile. I could read her now and could see, plain as day, that there wasn't any attraction or longing coming from her.

I knew what I needed to do.

It was going to take a few days, a little convincing, and a whole lot of fucking luck, but I had to do it.

Inspired, I rushed to the kitchen and tore a piece of paper off the notepad. I could head to the ranch to take care of business, then drop a line to Malcolm on the way out of town. He would see what a man was willing to do for the woman he loved. In my blocky handwriting, I wrote him a one sentence.

I'm going to get our girl.

31

EFFIE

IT WAS hours before the sun would rise, but my phone was already blowing up with calls and texts. The premiere of *Terminal Justice* was today, and once I acknowledged the messages, the day wouldn't end until I collapsed on the bed, wrung out.

It didn't matter. I hadn't slept a full night in over three weeks and was running on caffeine and sheer stubbornness. While we hadn't actually broken up, Josh and I didn't talk about his abrupt exit after our trip to LA either. Despite only an hour time difference, we struggled to both be available to have more than a few minutes over the phone. Even those calls were strange and stilted.

Everything felt . . . off.

Every night, though, without fail, Josh would text me seven words that were a balm to my bruised and aching heart.

I see you and I love you.

Every night, except for last night. I flipped through the texts to make sure I hadn't missed it, but it wasn't there.

Dread pooled in my stomach. Something wasn't right. Josh had probably realized I was too much work.

My phone rang—notification from the outside gate. I checked the camera and allowed the black town car to enter. Moments later, a swift knock at my door had me dragging my aching body upright in my bed. I'd busted my ass at my agent's insistence to lose the several extra pounds I'd gained over the summer. My body ached down to my bones from the sessions at the gym. A personal chef and tight schedule ensured I was fueled, barely, with only the cleanest, healthiest meals. My stomach rioted against its emptiness.

I pressed my hand to it and groaned into the pillow. I'd strangle someone for a basket of fries from The Rasa and whatever magical seasoning dust they put on them.

The knock came again, more insistent this time, and I peeled my eyelids open. As I padded across the plush carpeting of my bedroom and down the stairs, I readied myself to endure the whirlwind of a Hollywood red carpet premiere. *Madison Colt* would be dialed up to eleven, and she was expected to shine.

Not bothering to change out of my pajamas or put on a bra, I opened the front door to find the driver waiting stoically at the entrance.

"Miss Colt." He flashed his identification. "Ken Williams. I'll be your driver to the hotel, miss."

"Come on in." I turned my back on him and yawned, not bothering to close the door, and I assumed he followed.

Ken, dressed in a classic white shirt, black slacks, and black tie, stood at attention just inside the door in my foyer. He was older, with his salt-and-pepper hair buzzed close to the scalp. He had weathered lines on his face, which reminded me of Ray, and my chest pinched.

Though Ken looked about ten shades kinder than Ray's signature scowl.

I meandered up the stairs to my bedroom. Last night I had packed a small bag of toiletries, but anything else I needed would be provided at the hotel where I would be getting ready.

Hair.

Makeup.

Social media updates.

Premiere-dress final fitting.

After-party-dress final fitting.

More updates.

Jewelry.

Shoes.

Shapewear.

I was exhausted just thinking about it.

It was almost guaranteed I'd be photographed by the paparazzi arriving at the hotel in my baggy T-shirt and sweatpants without makeup. Desiree would be appropriately horrified, but I didn't give a fuck.

The speculation regarding my relationships with Benjamin and Josh was still tabloid fodder—fueled primarily by my agent and the studio themselves. Keeping us in the spotlight drew only more attention to *Terminal Justice*.

How was this ever a life I wanted?

More and more I succumbed to restless, intrusive thoughts about the choices I'd made that had brought me to LA. It felt like a hard truth that while my mother shoved me into the spotlight as a young girl, I wasn't young anymore. I was *choosing* this life for myself. Being Madison Colt entailed thousands of tiny decisions I made every single day. In many ways, it was easier being her than being myself.

Madison was alluring and mysterious. Capable and in control. Wanted. If no one knew Effie Pierce, then I could insulate her from their criticisms and judgments. But after spending so much time in Montana, I found LA lacked the allure it once had. Being a different person wasn't as easy once someone claimed to love the real version of yourself.

I see you and I love you.

"It's about that time, miss." The driver urged me to stay on schedule, and I nodded.

The ride from my home to the swanky hotel downtown was quiet. I hadn't bothered to close the partition between Ken and me. Truth was, it was nice to share the silence with someone.

I sighed heavily and watched the palm trees speed past.

"Big day, miss."

I looked up to see Ken's eyes flick to me in the rearview mirror.

"Long day," I corrected. When he fell quiet again, I felt like a jerk. He was just trying to be friendly, but in Los Angeles, it seemed everyone was out to use you for something. I was sad, really. I couldn't even trust a driver.

I thought for a moment. "Ken, have you lived in LA long?"

"About twenty years, miss. My daughter wanted a shot at an acting career, so my wife and I moved from Arizona."

"Is she still acting?" I wondered if I'd met her.

"No, ma'am." He paused before continuing. "Turned out it wasn't in the cards for her."

"It's a tough town, that's for sure."

"She had a few minor roles, and we were very proud. Every casting director had notes about her weight or hair or nose or height. Allison is stubborn. She wasn't about to bend because someone told her to."

I stared out the window. *Smart girl.*

"But she's learning real estate and is much happier. My wife and I liked the weather and change in scenery, so we stayed to be close to her."

"She's lucky to have such supportive parents." She probably had no idea how lucky.

"Thank you, miss. I'm sure your parents will be watching with pride in their eyes tonight."

I swallowed thickly. My mother would be watching comfortably from home with friends—no doubt thrilled with the uptick of media attention and how she could brag to her friends about it for months. And my father—

I pressed a hand to my chest. I knew it was Ray. It *had* to be. I had so many questions.

Ken pulled into the private entrance to the parking garage and shifted to park. When he didn't move to open his door, I looked up. He had shifted in his seat to face me through the opened partition in the town car.

"Can I ask something of you, miss?"

I pressed my lips together in a tight smile, ready to sign whatever thing he'd inevitably ask me to sign.

Ken cleared his throat and his eyes found mine. "When you're out there tonight, think of the girls, like my Ally. The ones who tried to stand in your shoes."

My jaw popped open, but before I could squawk out an answer, Ken was out of the car and opening my door. Back straight, shoulders set.

"Finally!" Desiree pushed through the doors and halted. "What the hell are you wearing?"

I looked down at my sloppy shirt and pants. "Clothes."

A quick flare of her nostrils gave her temper away, but she was already furiously tapping out a message on her phone. She turned to Ken and snapped her fingers. "You." I flinched at her rude disregard for the kind driver. "You need to drive around the block, then pull up at the front entrance. The paparazzi will likely think someone special is in the car, and we can get this hot mess upstairs." She waved a dismissive hand at all of me.

Before I could thank Ken for driving me and for our conversation, he was in the car and driving away. I stood, arms crossed, and waited for Desiree to finish putting out whatever new fire had flared.

When her attention finally returned to me, she placed a hand on her hip. "You know, I really thought this country-bumpkin routine was going to be a phase." Her eyes rolled to the concrete ceiling of the parking garage. "Sending you to that godforsaken town has got to be the worst decision of my life."

And the best decision of mine.

"Let's go." She snapped at me, and I sucked in a breath to keep from flipping her off. "Everyone is waiting for Madison Colt."

32

EFFIE

THERE WAS ALWAYS A MOMENT, right before I stepped one foot out of a limousine onto the red carpet, that I paused. That I wanted to run. It didn't matter if it was my first time or twentieth, the feeling never went away. This premiere was everything that I had worked for, and the unsettling feeling still crawled its way up my back.

Desiree and I had parted ways at the hotel, thank god, and I had a seven-minute car ride in peace. I'd been hopeful Ken would be my driver, but he'd been replaced with someone else who looked about as friendly as a snake.

I kept the partition up.

As always, I took a deep, steadying breath, plastered on my elusive smile, and allowed myself to be assisted out of the limo. Immediately I was surrounded by handlers and assistants. One woman in a black shirt and slacks held a sign that read, *Madison Colt: Female Lead*. She would walk in front of me, alerting the camera crews and reporters of my name and role.

My eyes scanned the crowd, but I knew I wouldn't see any of the familiar faces I'd grown to love over the past three months. Josh had called to wish me luck, but between the fittings and stylists, our conversation was very public, so I kept it brief.

I would have loved nothing more than to have him walking beside me tonight. He would have been completely miserable, no doubt, but he also would have worn a tuxedo and held my hand.

I had refused the studio's idea that Benjamin and I arrive together. I had put my foot down, and they'd conceded and opted to play up the *Strong, Independent Woman* angle. All I knew was I needed to think long and hard about my life once my contract for *Terminal Justice* was up.

Reporters and fans shouted my name as I stepped from the limo and hit my first mark in front of the backdrop. My handler adjusted my dress—another flex of my independence. Everyone scrambled after I refused to bleach my hair back to platinum, and fans seemed to like it. According to my stylist, Tomàs, the natural auburn of my hair was *an absolute disaster* combined with the punchy, bold orange of the original Dior dress we'd selected months ago. In less than a week, we had been forced to select an entirely new look.

My dress was simple yet elegant. The long sleeves contrasted with the deep center V. Floor length, the emerald green dress pooled at my feet yet had a high cut up to my hip. It hugged my body and showed off the last of the curves that hadn't been whittled away by Sergei and starvation.

It was the perfect representation of how I was feeling. Simple and comfortable, like Effie. Yet elegant and show-stopping, like Madison. Somehow this dress embodied both sides of my personality perfectly.

I smiled. Posed. Waved to no one in particular. Laughed at nothing. All for various photo opportunities.

Moving down the endless length of the ruby carpet, I landed my second mark. Posed and smiled and waited to be ushered through the flashing bulbs and incessant shouts in my direction.

I scanned the sea of faces and paused. My practiced smile never wavered, but my heart stopped in my chest.

Standing in the crowd behind the barrier, nudging his way closer, he was there.

Ray.

An assistant moved closer, cupping my elbow and whispering in my ear. "Move forward."

My feet were rooted. I couldn't stop staring at the old man's weathered, craggy face. My mind went blank.

"Ms. Colt." The woman's voice grew impatient. "Please. Move forward to your next mark."

Ray lifted a hand. I swallowed. "Stop." I pulled my elbow from her grip. "That man." I pointed right at Ray, and he stood taller. "He's with me. Bring him here. Please."

The assistant's eyes flicked between Ray and me. I placated her with a tight smile. "Thank you."

She moved toward the barricade as a murmur rolled through the crowd. With help, she moved the metal barricade, and Ray stepped through. My hand flew to my pounding heart.

He was in a tuxedo.

I pressed my tongue to the roof of my mouth to maintain my composure. Tears flooded behind my eyes, and I blinked them away. Ray took a tentative, shaky step in my direction. His steps were stiff and slow. Cameras took their lenses off me and focused on the old man as he made his way across the carpet in my direction.

Finally, Ray stopped to stand in front of me. He tugged at the collar of his tux and looked so deeply annoyed that a barking laugh rose up from my chest.

Reporters started shouting over each other. "Who is this?"

"Madison, is he a fan?"

"How do you know the man?"

Ray turned back toward the pulsing crowd. "Fuck off. I'm her dad."

Emotions crashed over me. I pressed a finger to the inside corner of my eye to keep my tears from spilling and ruining my makeup. "Hi, Ray."

His crystal-blue eyes shone back at me. "Effie." He smiled and tried to stand a bit straighter. "Got something I been meaning to talk to you about."

I laughed again. I couldn't believe it. My head and heart crashed together in a confusing mix of questions and emotions. "Yeah. I guess so." My hand dipped into the pocket I'd requested be sewn into the dress, and I held the button in the palm of my hand. Ray looked down and smiled.

I looked around at the curious faces and endless row of paparazzi and gestured toward them. "I kinda have a thing though . . ."

Ray offered his elbow, and I wound my arm with his. "It would be an honor."

∽

"I STILL CAN'T BELIEVE you're in California." I shook my head, Ray sitting across from me in the low lighting of my kitchen.

"Well, believe it. Suffered through a miserable plane ride just to be here."

I laughed and bit into a slice of pizza, stifling a low moan as my stomach grumbled.

Holy shit, carbs are life.

I wiped the corner of my mouth. "I appreciate it. I do. I'm just in shock, I think. How did this even happen?"

Ray shot me his signature scowl, and the air between us grew silent. "I didn't mean to hurt you when you asked about the button at the party. It caught me off guard."

"I'm sorry I sprung that on you." I studied his face, still searching for any sense of recognition or confirmation that he was, in fact, my biological father.

Ray's weathered hand trembled as he wiped it with a paper towel. "Made bad choices my whole life. That was no exception."

I waited, needing more. Anything.

"I knew Terese for a long time. We had good times and bad times. Our relationship was volatile. Hell, those *were* the good times."

"When did you meet?"

He shook his head. "I came from Natchitoches. Met your mother for the first time in New Orleans when she was bartending, I think. But I was involved with organized crime. We were expanding, so I went where the money was. New Orleans, Las Vegas, New York."

All places my mother and I had lived.

"You had a relationship with her all that time?"

My head swirled with new information. My mother had maintained a secret relationship with him for far longer than I'd realized.

He nodded. "Yep. We would hook up for a while. Even got

married once in Vegas after I won at the craps table. It only lasted a few weeks. Neither of us was the marrying type. Things would be good until they weren't. We'd implode and move on."

Blood drained from my face as realization dawned on me. "We moved all those places because she was following you? You were there the whole time?"

He shook his head. "Hard to say. Seems Terese would show up a few months later in whatever city we'd gone to." His sad eyes met mine.

"I was born in Nevada, but we moved around a lot. Mom would say it was because she was tired of the heat or wanted to live by a beach or whatever. I'm assuming it was to meet up with you." I pulled my hands through my hair and exhaled. "I just can't believe she kept up the lie this whole time."

"I swear to you, Effie, I had no idea about you until I was in Montana. In a moment of weakness, I told her where I was. Part of me knew it was the end, and I wanted to say goodbye. She showed up here, and things went south between us. I never saw your mother again after that."

My mother had been moving us around the country my whole life to follow Ray. My father, whom she had kept a secret until I was twelve years old, had lived in the same cities my entire life.

How could she be so evil and selfish?

Anger rose inside me at the decisions the adults in my life had made. I clenched my jaw at the injustice of it all.

"She went to Montana and finally told you about me, but did she keep me from you?"

Ray's rounded shoulders slumped further. "I didn't claim you."

A heavy weight pressed into my chest at the truth of his

words, and the back of my eyelids burned. Even when my mother had told him about me, he didn't want me.

"I see." I schooled my voice to be calm, but it still trembled.

Ray's crooked fingers reached out, and he placed his hand over mine. "It was the greatest mistake of my life."

My eyes flew to him. Tenderness was not something Ray was known for—far from it—but anguish was all over his face.

"I'm a fool. I didn't want to believe her. Truth is, I wanted a clean break. A fresh start. Hieramias Adamos needed to die. Deserved to die, really. I took the shortened name Ray, a new last name, and never looked back."

"You gave up everything"—*including me*—"for Redemption Ranch." His honesty, his truth, was tearing me apart.

"Dorthea and Robbie took a chance on me when I became a rat."

"A rat? A federal witness, you mean."

"Rolled over to testify against my friends to save my own ass. They woulda done it to me if they had the chance."

A long stretch of silence hung between us. For years, *years*, my father had lived in the same city, and my mother had kept it from me. Only when she realized he was leaving her behind for good did she tell him about me, and *still* he was just out of my reach. A tear broke free and I swiped it away.

"Now I ain't telling you this because you're crying and I want you to feel better. But I thought about you every day. I wondered if you favored your mother. If you looked like my sister. You do, by the way." He flipped a hand in my direction. "That hair and those eyes."

Ray shook his head. "Shoulda seen it the minute you stepped on the ranch."

I pressed my hands to my cheeks and let out a breath. "This is so wild. I can't believe it." My finger traced over the small shell button on the counter between us.

"Before she stormed out, I stopped her, asked her to give you the shell from me. I had no idea if she'd thrown it in the dirt or gave it to you."

I smiled. The shell button was the one thing that confirmed I was his child. "She did. I don't think she wanted to, but I was so hurt and angry at her that she relented. I'm not sure why, but I've always kept it with me."

His story, our story, was a lot to take in—my mother selfishly keeping us apart, his criminal past, witness protection . . .

Blood drained from my face and pooled in my gut. "Ray." I touched his weathered arm and was relieved when he didn't pull away from my touch. "The cameras. Aren't you afraid? That someone will recognize you? Coming here was dangerous."

Ray dismissed my concern with a shake of his head. "Honey, the people who were looking for me are dead or too old to do anything about it. I testified and moved on a long time ago. I figure I don't have many more years left on this earth. I told the truth when I said I thought about you every day. Buncha times I almost started looking. Then figured, 'poor girl doesn't need a criminal looking for her.' Then Josh showed up and changed my mind."

"Josh." My heart twisted. We were so off course I wasn't sure how we were going to figure things out.

"That boy came stomping around. Tore me a new asshole."

I laughed at the picture Ray created. "Josh did?"

"I was shocked too. I watched that boy grow up in the shadow of his father. Good man, but serious. Tough. Timothy Laredo was a hard-ass marshal. Never gave an inch of room, and I'd guess he was the same at home. When Josh was real little he'd be on the ranch and pitch a fit. Man, could that boy holler. His father wouldn't have it. Barking orders and getting him in line. I think Josh learned pretty quick that it was safer to not let those big emotions get the best of him. Probably why he took to the Army the way he did."

I tried to picture confident, agreeable Josh as a bratty kid and could only laugh.

"Well, that man came fighting for you. I saw the same fire in him that he'd snuffed out a long time ago. He stomping and pacing and yelling that I was throwing away the best thing in my life without even giving it a chance. Not sure he was talking about me or himself though."

I looked at him and he raised an eyebrow.

"That boy is a fool for you," Ray continued. "I told him he should come here himself. Get all dressed up for you, but he insisted that it would mean more for me to show up. So here I am."

I grabbed Ray's hand and squeezed. I smiled through the blurry tears and poked beneath my ribs. "Here you are."

33

JOSH

SENDING Ray to California had been a mistake.

It was the only explanation I could come up with for why I hadn't heard from Effie since the premiere two days ago. I scoured the internet like a stalker in order to get a glimpse of Effie. She was stunning. Heartbreakingly so. Even the dolled-up version of her twisted my heart. I'd do damn near anything to see her again, but I thought sending Ray instead of myself was the right call. What she needed rather than what I so desperately wanted.

My soul ached for her, and I couldn't find a way to keep her. I couldn't ask her to leave her life in LA behind.

I wouldn't.

Hunched over my forgotten coffee, I exhaled. I willed the ringing in my ears to quiet, but, of course, it didn't. The weight of uncertainty was gnawing at me. When there was a knock at the door, my jaw clenched. I was at the end of my rope.

What now?

I pulled open the door and stared. The air was pulled from my lungs, and I couldn't move.

Effie.

My Effie.

"Hi." She beamed at me, her hair in a loose braid and her jean shorts just the right amount too short. "I'm moving out."

I blinked. Excitement at seeing her and dread at the understanding of her words swirled in my gut. "What?"

Her smile widened. "Can I come in?" She pushed past me and into the house before I could answer. She turned, bouncing on her heels, and spread her palms wide. "I'm moving out," she repeated.

"Okay." I drew out the word, not understanding how she could be so happy while she ripped my heart to shreds.

"Here's the thing." She stepped forward and placed a hand on my cheek. "God, you're cute when you're confused."

She looped her arms around my neck and let her fingertips play with the ends of my hair. "I'm moving out because if we're going to get Malcolm, I think his transition will be better if it's just the two of you for a while. I've been doing a *lot* of research, and stability is important for children in transition. I want everything in place for your home study, and I won't let some social worker with old-fashioned ideals let the fact that we are unmarried and living together stand in our way. I've already worked it out with Ma. I can have one of the cottages on the ranch. It's perfect."

My grin spread, slow and wide, as I realized what she was saying. "So you're moving out."

A giggle erupted from her chest. "I am."

I stepped forward, scooping her into my arms. "That's good. That's really, really good." I let my mouth drop to hers, and in one kiss, my world tilted on its axis.

She's finally home.

Her soft little moans as I ran my hands up her back drove me wild. I wanted to consume her in the front entryway, but a level head pulled me back.

Her eyes shone back at me as I looked down into her blue eyes. Her sweet smile. "I still can't believe you're here."

Mischief flashed in her eyes. "I take it you didn't see the last leg of the press junket."

I wrinkled my brows. I hadn't seen it. I had realized watching every snippet on YouTube was only making my uncertainty and heartache worse, so I'd forced myself to stop.

Effie sank back down to her normal height as her smile, *her real smile*, widened and cracked my chest open. She leaned back against the entryway table, her fingers drumming at her sides. "I was getting a lot of questions about what's next for me. My next role and what happens after *Terminal Justice*."

My heart squeezed.

"When Alicia Winters from *The Morning View* asked that same question for the billionth time, I knew. I'd known my answer all along, but there I was, on syndicated television, telling her that *Terminal Justice* was my last movie for a while. I am planning to settle into early retirement. I would consider only very select jobs and *only* if they fit within my family's schedule."

She'd done it. Announcing her retirement was the Hollywood equivalent of flipping a table and walking the fuck out.

My woman, the rebel.

Pride and love for her swelled, filling my chest. "What about your contracts? Whatever you had lined up after this?"

"My contract with the studio is fulfilled. I have a few

modeling gigs that don't take too much of my time, and once those are done . . ." Effie shrugged. "We'll just see. If Demi Moore can live her best life in Idaho, so can I. Though I think Montana suits me just fine."

In two strides, I was towering over her. "It suits you."

Effie's hands slid up my chest. "That is, if you and Malcolm will still have me. I need you to know that I am so sorry for what happened in LA. I shouldn't have ever gone along with Des's plan. You deserved so much more than that."

"I know. I'm sorry I wasn't ready to see that part of your life."

"My old life. A chapter I was glad to experience, but I'm ready to start a new one. A less chaotic, more *Effie* one. The *best* one."

My nose gently rubbed against hers. "I'm ready for a new chapter too. No more stuffing down hard feelings or pretending to be agreeable when I'm not. I'm just gonna work on being me for a while."

She pressed a hand over my heart. "I see you and I love you."

I kissed her lips to keep the sting behind my eyes at bay.

FAMILY DINNER WAS a big to-do for Ma Brown. Every week, without fail, a ragtag group of misfits would gather around her large oak table and share a meal. Marshals and witnesses were welcomed as equals. Ma prided herself on the tradition, though Robbie did the cooking since Ma could find a way to ruin boiled water. It was an open-door policy. You showed up and you were welcomed.

I often went to family dinner when I got to being lonely

or if the idea of another night at my house alone with my thoughts was too much. Standing at the door to the main lodge of Redemption Ranch with Effie on my arm was something else entirely.

She fussed with her hair. She'd curled it, and the waves tumbled down her back. I absently played with the ends of it as I waited for her to be ready.

"Should we knock?" she asked as her teeth sank into her full lower lip.

I laughed and pushed the door open. "This isn't a knock-on-the-door kind of gathering."

We were immediately greeted with the sounds and smells of family dinner. The large kitchen island was covered with hot dishes, salads, dessert—a family-style setup that allowed everyone to make a plate and head into the dining room and eat together.

Evan spotted us first. "Hey, man! Glad you made it."

We shook hands, and it set off a round of greetings that pulled us into the fold. Effie relaxed a bit as she and Gemma smiled at each other from across the room.

Evan's brother, Parker, and his wife, Sienna, had even made it. For the past two years they had been living near Bozeman so Sienna could go to school. While it was rare they were able to make the trip back to Redemption Ranch, it was always good to see them. Sienna and I had worked together when she'd stayed on the ranch, and she was a ball of energy and light from Chicago. I knew she and Effie would get along, and without my help, they were already in the corner talking fashion and laughing about life in Montana. Parker was a huge presence and never took his eyes off his wife except for a quick handshake. He'd softened a little since marrying Sienna, but I figured he'd always be kind of an asshole.

I set down the appetizer Effie had made as Ma rounded the island. "I was hoping to see you here tonight."

She wiped her hands on a dish towel and surveyed the eclectic mix of people with a look of satisfaction. Then she turned her attention back to me. "Word is you made some changes with the animal care and the vaccine schedule."

The urge to explain myself and pacify my friend and boss rose up, but I took a breath. "The changes needed to be made for the health and safety of the animals."

Ma gave a hard nod and the conversation was over. Though I didn't miss the small smirk that lifted the corner of her mouth.

I was trusted. In control. It was a strange and calming thing to be valued and trusted and *authentic*. I was still getting used to it, but I felt more centered than I had in my entire adult life. Even my tinnitus had softened to a dull background hum.

"You look happy." Effie flounced into the kitchen with a huge grin.

"I am." I pulled her into a hug, not caring as people moved around us, and I let my hands wander farther down her back to the top of her ass.

"That's my daughter you're pawing at." The gruff and gravelly timbre of Ray's voice had my grin widening.

"Yes, sir."

Effie winked at me as we stepped apart, and she gave him a gentle pat on the back. They were still working out the ins and outs of their newfound relationship, but overall it seemed to be going well. Ray was even slightly less of a dick when she was around, so I was going to call that a win.

"It's time," Ma called out to the growing crowd. "Grab a hand and let's do this."

The collection of Ma's misfits all gathered closer. I

watched as the group came together. Evan had Val tucked into his side. Parker had his arm wrapped around Sienna's middle, his hand protectively splayed across her stomach. Effie hooked her arm into Ray's, and her other hand slid into mine. I gave it a gentle squeeze before lifting her knuckles to my lips.

Robbie started with his nondenominational prayer, and I couldn't help but send one up of my own.

Effie and I would build a life in Tipp with Malcolm and maybe a few children of our own. I would love them for whoever they became and allow them to see me. The *real* me. I swallowed hard as the gravity of that image slammed into me. Everything I'd ever wanted in my life was wrapped up in a gorgeous little rebel.

When she sent me a flirty little wink, I was done for. Somehow she'd turned this gentleman into a rogue. So once the prayer was over, I aimed my mischievous grin directly at her. Fire danced in her eyes as I quietly backed her out of the room and out the door.

"Dinner can wait." I was breathless, searing kisses against her skin as I pressed her against the outside wall of the lodge. Dinner could go on without us for a bit longer.

She pressed a hand against her chest, aghast at how rough my voice came out. "And I thought you were a gentleman."

I looked down at her and smirked. "He's long gone, baby girl." I pulled her close and poured my heart and soul into the kiss, showing her exactly who I was.

EPILOGUE
JOSH

Two Years Later

"A little to the left, maybe. No, down. Up." Effie sighed in exasperation. "Sorry."

With my arms raised above my head, I shot Effie an annoyed look over my shoulder.

"I just want it to be perfect! Like, two and a half inches left and one inch up on the right side."

I did as I was told and suppressed a smile.

"Perfect!" Effie beamed.

I finished hanging the sign and stepped back to see how it looked.

Happy Birthday, Malcolm!

It was definitely crooked, but as Effie smiled up at it, I didn't have the heart to tell her. I pulled her into my side and kissed the top of her head just as a knock sounded at the door.

"Shit! They're here. It's time!" Effie clapped, squealed, and flounced to the door with a twirl.

I moved to the back of the house, where Malcolm was

playing a video game with his best friend. "Time's up, bud. People are starting to show."

Malcolm didn't look up from his intergalactic battle. "Okay." He tilted the controller and smashed a button a few more times. "Thanks, Dad."

My heart tumbled, as it always did, when he called me "Dad." Usually I was still "Josh," and that was fine, too, but more and more he'd been testing it out—calling me Dad in front of his friends or around the dinner table.

No matter what, Malcolm was my kid, and I was the luckiest man in the world. It took over six months to get approved to foster him and another year for his adoption to be finalized. It wasn't always easy, but we got through it.

Together.

Tonight we were celebrating Malcolm's tenth birthday—double digits.

I scrubbed a calloused hand across the back of my neck. I couldn't believe how fast time seemed to go by. I headed back toward the front door as the commotion of nearly the entire town showing up for a kid's birthday party reverberated down the hall.

Gemma popped her head out of the kitchen. "Hey, where does Effie want the cake?"

"Hell if I know." I shrugged and shot her a comfortable smile. "She'll rearrange it twenty times before she's happy with it. On the island, maybe?"

Gemma offered a jaunty salute before disappearing back into the kitchen. Over the past two years, she and Effie had become nearly inseparable. I made my way back to the front door. Effie was wrapped in a hug as Val squeezed the air from her and Evan looked on and smiled. Their son, Mateo, ran past me in a flash toward Malcolm.

"I hope you don't mind, but I brought some party crashers." Val smiled and stepped back as Sienna stepped through the doorway.

"No way!" Effie laughed and pulled Sienna into a hug. "Get in here!"

"Surprise!" Sienna giggled, and the women twirled. Parker was right behind her with their daughter, Molly, on his hip.

"I didn't realize you'd be in town," Effie said. "This is a fantastic surprise!"

I gathered their coats and snagged the guys each a beer. Sienna's smile went wider. "That's the best part. We're back for good! I am finishing up my final semester, and after graduation, we're moving home."

My eyes flew to Parker, who grinned down at his wife. They'd moved to Bozeman so Sienna could go to school to be a nurse. They were missed, and I was ecstatic they'd be coming back to Tipp.

I extended my hand to Parker. "Glad to have you back."

He shook it and suppressed a smile. He continued to look between his wife and young daughter, like he couldn't believe how great his life had turned out.

I know that feeling, man.

In a seemingly unending stream of party guests, we'd finally packed our house full. Malcolm's previous foster family came, along with several of his friends from school. Ray, Ma and Robbie Brown, Johnny. Even Al from The Rasa showed up with Irma's famous pie.

Everyone was celebrating Malcolm's day.

I grilled on the back patio while Malcolm and his friends ran around the yard. The guys shot the shit while the women circled around little Molly and Mateo as they caught up on plans for Sienna and Parker's inevitable move back to Tipp.

I walked over to Ray—now Grandpa Ray, as Malcolm called him—who was sitting comfortably in a patio chair and wearing his signature scowl. "Everything good, Ray?"

His face softened as his eyes flicked to Effie. "Couldn't be better."

I clamped a hand on the old man's shoulder and squeezed it gently.

Damn right.

After dinner and presents, the crowd had dwindled down to the usual crew—Evan, Parker, and me, our families, plus Gemma. Effie frowned as we realized the tub of ice cream had been left on the counter and had melted in a drippy pool all over. I'd made quick work of cleaning it up, but we all knew Irma's apple pie wasn't the same without a scoop or two of vanilla bean ice cream.

"What do you say we head to town for a scoop?" I suggested.

Malcolm's eyes went wide, and a grin spread across his face. It was his birthday, and I didn't mind going all out for him. I looked at Effie and she shrugged. "Let's do it."

"I can drive!" Gemma offered.

"No!" we all shouted in unison. Gemma pouted and Effie laughed as I pulled her into my embrace.

After rounding the kids up, I tugged open the front door and stopped abruptly. Standing on my porch with his hand raised, about to knock, was Scott Dunn.

Something clattered behind me, and I turned to see Gemma's face go stark white before her eyes sliced in his direction, and she pushed past him and out the door.

"Scott," I said as Gemma sailed past us. "Come on in. We're about to head to town for some ice cream, but..."

"Thanks. Sorry to interrupt. I actually need to talk with

Gemma." His large frame turned as she stomped toward her truck. The rest of us looked on in confusion.

"Gem. I need to talk to you."

"I have *nothing* to say to you." Derision dripped from her words as she jerked open the driver's-side door.

You could hear a pin drop as tension mounted between them. Parker and Evan both stood from their chairs, the bottoms scraping across the wood floor.

"Gemma." Scott's voice was cool and steady, but his expression was intense. "You've been called."

～

After the surprise arrival of US Marshal Scott Dunn and the bomb he dropped that Gemma had been called back to Chicago to testify, everyone decided that ice cream should wait. Malcolm couldn't have cared less as he devoured the pie and a piece of birthday cake before passing out on the couch.

Later that night, I lay awake with Effie tucked into my side, breathing in her clean, floral scent and holding her close.

"I'm scared for her," she whispered into the darkness.

It's like you can read my mind.

I held her close and tried to reassure her. "You should be scared for Scott. She had daggers in her eyes for him. Holy shit."

Effie laughed lightly at that, and I felt better knowing I'd eased some of her nerves. "She'll be okay. Agent Dunn is one of the best, and he'll make sure she's safe."

Effie let out a deep sigh. "Okay," she breathed. "Man, what a day."

"The party was a success. Malcolm loved the games

you'd set up in the backyard." We both laughed at the memory of Malcolm going head-to-head with Evan and Parker. The relay races were meant to be ridiculous, and everyone was a good sport about it. It even got a genuine smile and laugh out of Parker as he and Malcolm gave up on the relay race, and Parker just lifted Malcolm off his feet and carried him across the finish line. Gemma called him a cheater, but he just laughed and said, "Rules are made to be broken." Ironic words from a reformed criminal.

Effie and the women had laughed so hard they had tears streaming down their faces, and I couldn't remember a day where we were surrounded by so much laughter. Effie called it our *hodgepodge family*, and I loved that.

My fingertips trailed down her arm until it tangled with her hand. I absently played with the engagement ring that I'd given her. Effie was the glue that held me together—that I knew for damn sure. Had she not said yes when I got down on one knee, I'd have begged her anyway.

"How did I get so lucky?" I asked her this often, and usually she would smile and bat her lashes in my direction.

Effie laughed. "You just got lucky, I guess."

I bit back a laugh.

What a brat.

I pulled her under me as I shifted my weight and braced myself over her. "Wanna say that again?"

Effie sucked in her lower lip. Playful defiance flashed in her eyes. "That night at the bar, I should have seen what you were—a heartache in denim."

I clicked my tongue. "You got it all wrong, baby girl." My eyes devoured her in the dim light of our bedroom. "I won't break your heart, but if you keep being a little shit, I will make you beg."

Effie's arms looped around my neck as she pulled me closer and whispered, "Promises. Promises."

I laughed as my kiss swallowed up her groan. My hands found the familiar curves of her body and the way I reacted was unique to Effie. As my palms moved over her, worshipping her, I recounted from memory every dip and valley of her chest and neck.

Effie arched into my touch. I loved her so much it was downright painful, but nothing was as gorgeous as my woman completely undone and on the brink of falling apart. It was when I knew that I had a part of her no one else got to see.

It was those moments when my mind was truly quiet. I could think of nothing but her.

Effie. My Effie.

I moved over her, stroking and teasing until she was panting and wet. I slid into her, filling her and letting the last of my resolve drop, and I gave myself to her.

Completely.

We moved together in a dance only our bodies had learned. Deep and languid. Effie's breathing got harder as I played with her tits and ground myself against her clit, reaching the deepest parts of her.

I felt her inner walls pulse and I picked up the pace. I knew exactly what my girl needed. She clenched around me, and it took effort to not fill her right then and there.

"Fuck, Ef."

She mewled against my kisses and bucked her hips to meet my demanding rhythm. I reached down and grabbed two handfuls of her ass, tilting her hips to gain access to the exact spot I knew would have her seeing stars.

"Yes. Josh, there."

"I know, baby girl. I got you."

Effie cried out with her neck arched back and her eyes squeezed tight. Her pussy pulsed around me as I kneaded her cheeks. She pressed her lips together to muffle her pleasure, and her wet heat clamped down on me as her orgasm tore through her.

My hand wrapped around the slender column of her neck to steady myself as I drove deeper and harder. A wave of pleasure crashed over me, and I pumped myself into her. Effie's legs wrapped around me, pulling me deeper and closer as I erupted.

Neither of us could catch our breath as we came down from our postorgasmic bliss. Instead of beautiful words and poetry, I let my gentle caress show her how much I adored her.

A throaty hum broke me from my trance, and I looked down at my future bride. "Do you remember what you told me all those years ago at the hot spring?"

I smiled at her. We often reminisced about our chance encounter as children. I rolled from her, tucking her into the crook of my arm. My fingertips ran a gentle trail down her back as her leg hitched over my hip.

"You told me you wanted to run away. Be someone else. A different person in a different life," I said.

I could feel Effie smile against my chest. Her fingers tickled my stomach as she drew lazy circles across the smattering of hair. "And you told me, 'No one will ever be as perfect as who are you right now.'"

She glanced up at me from the comfort of our embrace. "How were you so wise?"

My arms squeezed tighter. "I guess I just saw what was right in front of me."

On a sigh, her head rested back on my chest, and her hand found the spot just over my heart.

"Joshua Laredo. I see you and I love you."

And that was the beginning and end of it all. Two people, willing to see each other. To love the real person beneath it all.

~

Need more Effie and Josh? Read an exclusive Bonus Scene here!

SNEAK PEEK OF THE TARGET
CHAPTER ONE

Gemma

"I still can't believe you're leaving." I lay across Kate's bed and pouted up at my best friend as she folded a shirt and stuffed it into her already-too-full suitcase. Her wavy brown hair was pulled into a low side ponytail with an enormous emerald silk scrunchie only she could pull off.

I looked at the ends of my own light-blonde hair. As a rebellious, unsupervised teen, I'd dyed it midnight black. It was getting longer now that it wasn't so overprocessed, and it was finally getting to a length just below my shoulders after I'd hacked it to a short bob in a bathroom mirror at nineteen.

"Is Trey still blowing up your phone?" I smirked at Kate. She'd been casually dating a guy from our biology class. When she'd made the decision to leave after college graduation, that had included cutting ties with the poor guy.

"We're parting as friends." She flashed her teeth in an uncomfortable smile. "I think."

"Such a heartbreaker," I teased. "At least in Michigan

you'll have your pick of some hot, sexy farmer." Kate came from a small town in Western Michigan and had told me all about the acres and acres of blueberry farms and the beaches tucked into the coast of Lake Michigan. It sounded like a dream.

"Fat chance. I'm moving from one small town to another. Only this time everyone already knows me and remembers my very unfortunate phase with bangs."

"Maybe you'll just become an old maid." I laughed at my own joke. Kate was stunning, with thick brunette hair and emerald eyes. I suspected she was the main reason we rarely had to buy our own drinks at the Tabula Rasa, the local bar in Tipp, Montana.

"Hey, kettle. It's me, pot." Kate shot me a smirk as she turned and continued packing the last of her clothes into the suitcase. She tapped a finger against her lip and looked up. "When was the last time you let someone in your pants? Hmm . . . oh, that's right. *Forever*."

I made a face at her. Sometimes having a best friend who knew all about you was a real pain in the ass. She wasn't wrong, though. It had been almost a year since I'd dated anyone, and the three sad outings Brent had taken me on had fizzled fast. There was just something unappealing about the immature, flighty guys my age, and they seemed to do *nothing* for me. I was quickly becoming bitter at only twenty-three.

The ruggedly handsome face of Scott Dunn flashed through my mind, and I hated myself for it. I hated that he was still the standard I seemed to set for any man who came after him. Truth was, no one ever came close. When I first came to Tipp, Scott was a US marshal assigned to protect my brother and me—witnesses under federal protection because of the life and choices my two older brothers had made. Scott was charming and kind and there for me when I was still healing.

He was everything. Until he wasn't.

I chastised myself for even allowing myself to think of him as anything other than who he was—a liar and a coward. Refusing to let him sour my last few minutes with my best friend, I refocused on Kate and how much I was going to miss her.

"Don't forget your granny panties," I teased as she swiped a pair of underwear off the bed. Kate paused midfold and stuck her tongue between her teeth, balled up the underwear, and tossed them in my face.

I laughed, snagging the pair midair and tossing them back to her. I rolled to my back, and a deep sigh whooshed out of me. "I'm just going to miss you so damn much."

I willed the tears away as I focused on a small water spot on her apartment ceiling.

Kate moved the suitcase to the floor and settled on the bed beside me, our shoulders touching. "It's just Michigan, not the other side of the world."

"Are you nervous?" I asked.

Kate shrugged and stared at the ceiling. Kate and I had recently graduated from the small local college a few towns over. At first I had used school as a way to get out of the daily demands of working on a cattle ranch—a cattle ranch that wasn't *really* a cattle ranch. It was all part of the facade.

The lie.

When I was nineteen, my older brother Evan and I had moved to Redemption Ranch in the middle of nowhere to hide in witness protection. To become completely different people.

I met Kate in class my first semester, and we became inseparable. She was one of the few people who knew about my double life. She never asked questions, but after one too many times of her eyes trailing down my neck and arm, taking in my scars, I'd finally let her in. She knew everything there was to know about me, and there was some comfort in that.

Now, four years later, she was leaving me behind.

"I bet your brothers are thrilled you're coming home." I clasped her hand and tucked it under my chin.

"Now that Pop is gone, and my brothers are . . ." Kate rolled her eyes.

I'd heard a thousand stories about her older brothers. Despite the fact she was the baby of the family, she took care of them, having grown up with her grandparents after her mom died and her dad got sick.

She looked down at her pile of clothes. "Nonna could use the help." A small laugh bubbled out from her. "I still can't believe I'm moving in with my grandmother. I'm such a loser."

"You are not a loser. You're taking care of your family, like you always do. You've got your whole life to figure out what's next." I couldn't help but feel a tiny pang of jealousy. While I was still under protection, my options were limited. Technically speaking, I was free to do whatever I wanted, but with two slightly overbearing brothers, my options felt stifled. Besides, tugging at the back of my mind was always the threat of someone from my old life finding me.

I was safe in Tipp, a town where everyone knew that Laurel Canyon Ranch wasn't just a working cattle ranch but a cover for witness protection. The whole town looked out for one another, and you got a no-questions-asked second chance in Tipp. That was something I tried desperately to not take for granted.

"Come visit me soon." Kate bumped my shoulder, and her serious mossy-green eyes pinned me in place.

"I will," I lied. "Maybe Sophie and I will make the trip."

Humor danced in her voice as she tried to suppress a laugh. "Just make sure she's the one driving."

I rolled to my side and propped my head on my hand. "What's that supposed to mean? I'm a fantastic driver."

Kate barked the laugh she'd been holding in. "Bullshit. Tell that to the construction sign!"

"Oh my god." I rolled my eyes. "That was *one* time!"

A fit of laughter consumed us both. I laughed so hard I nearly peed my pants thinking about that trip. I rarely left Tipp, but two years ago my friends had convinced me to drive a few hours to an outdoor music festival in Bozeman.

I was driving, and we were laughing and chatting, flying down the interstate. We all needed to pee, so I pulled off the highway onto the ramp for a rest stop. The next thing I knew, a Road Closed sign came out of *nowhere*. Of course the sign was directly in my path, and there was nothing I could do but blast through it. Wood splintered. The three of us screamed as everything moved in slow motion.

As I steered the car to the shoulder, the *whoop-whoop* of a police cruiser came up behind us. Sophie and Kate could not stop laughing.

When the officer strode up to check on us, my pulse was hammering. I speared them with a glare. I tried to tell the police officer that it was a mistake—we hadn't known that the upcoming rest stop was closed for construction. I explained where we were headed and that I hadn't seen the sign until it was too late.

He studied the three of us quietly, and when he walked back to his cruiser, I was certain I was getting arrested. I was *not* looking forward to explaining that one to Ma Brown, the woman who ran Redemption Ranch with an iron fist. She was generous and kind, but she didn't tolerate bullshit. I was also not looking forward to explaining to my brothers that I'd gotten into yet another little fender bender.

Instead of slapping handcuffs on me and throwing me in the back of his cruiser, the officer brought back a rag and wiped the orange paint that had been transferred from the construction barricade to the windshield. This, of course, sent the two idiots next to me into a fresh fit of giggles.

Relieved I wasn't getting arrested, the sympathetic officer suggested someone else take the wheel, and I had gladly sat in the back seat for the remainder of our trip.

It was one of my favorite memories.

Kate hugged me close, and we both let the fond memory settle between us. We sat quietly for a long while, and I fought tears the whole time, reluctant to leave her embrace.

If my life were my own, if I truly had a say, I probably would go visit Kate. In fact, I knew I would. But that wasn't my life. I would constantly be looking over my shoulder or have Evan and Parker hounding me via text to check in. My brothers could worry and hover unlike anyone I'd ever seen.

Finally I broke the silence between Kate and me. "I think you're right, though. I need something . . . *else*. An adventure, maybe." I added quietly, "I feel stuck."

"Well, I am the proud new owner of a giant, old-ass farmhouse. So there's a room for you whenever you're ready."

We hugged again, and I squeezed her an extra second before letting my arms fall. I left Kate to finish packing. It was too hard to see her drive away and leave me behind, so I was sure to make my exit before she pulled out.

When I stopped my old truck at the intersection at the edge of town, I paused. Left would take me down the winding country road toward Redemption Ranch, where my small, safe cottage was waiting for me. Right could take me down an entirely different path. I could drive away and start a whole new life—if I wanted to.

∼

Continue reading The Target

ACKNOWLEDGMENTS

The Rebel is the first book I finished as a full time author. To even type those words is a HUGE deal to me! I would be remiss if I didn't first thank each and every reader who gave my books a chance. I have always loved a good romance novel, and the fact that out of the endless possibilities, you're reading my stories isn't lost on me. From the bottom of my heart, THANK YOU!

To Jake for always telling me that I make you proud. I never thought that was something I needed to hear, but from you, it means the world.

To Leanne for always supporting me and helping me talk through major decisions . . . like deciding to rebrand an entire series only two weeks before a new release. You are thoughtful and kind and I trust your opinions so deeply. I am always grateful for your help in getting through all the things that being an author requires. You are a huge part of me being able to live my dream of being a full-time author! Thank you for how hard you work.

My dear, sweet friend Elsie. Poor Jake doesn't realize we're serious when we say we're eventually moving away together to live our best lives. Although, we might want to keep him and Mr. S around . . . they seem like the types who could kill a spider or chop wood when it gets too cold. Thanks for being my ride or die. I couldn't be happier that I have you in my life.

To Kandi for being, not only a true goddess, but a kind,

genuine, and supportive friend. I lucked into being a part of your circle and hope you know how much I value your humor, input, and thoughtfulness.

To Melanie for your unending generosity. Also, I appreciate you being unafraid to say the things I don't want to hear but that you know will make me better in the end. It also makes me so happy to have someone to nerd out with over craft books and podcasts!

To Nicole for unknowingly becoming an alpha reader. When I sent you the first chapters of my hot mess manuscript, I was terrified. However, your feedback and thoughts on key scenes made this novel shine. You have a gift, and I am excited to see where it takes you.

To my Vixens, this is all because of you. If it weren't for your love of my books and being unafraid to share them with the world, we wouldn't be getting these stories into the hands of new readers. Your encouragement and enthusiasm means everything. I love the supportive little community we've grown.

To Sommer for not only creating stunning covers for this series, but for being patient with me when I decided to rebrand mid-series. You elevated Redemption Ranch in a way that I could have only hoped for. I appreciate your feedback and patience as we pivoted on a dime and you're always a pleasure to work with. I am so blessed to have you on my team!

James and Laetitia, I can never thank you enough for the thorough care you give to editing and proofreading. Each book gets a special polish because of the time you spend. Your feedback is unparalleled. Also, I will never not apologize for my utter lack of mastery of the simple comma. Sorry about that.

ALSO BY LENA HENDRIX

The Chikalu Falls Series

Finding You

Keeping You

Protecting You

The Redemption Ranch Series

The Badge

The Alias

The Rebel

The Target

ABOUT THE AUTHOR

Lena Hendrix is an Amazon Top 20 bestselling contemporary romance author living in the Midwest. Her love for romance started with sneaking racy Harlequin paperbacks as a teenager and now she writes her own hot-as-sin small town romance novels. Lena has a soft spot for strong alphas with marshmallow insides, heroines who clap back, and sizzling tension. Her novels pack in small town heart with a whole lotta heat.

When she's not writing or devouring new novels, you can find her hiking, camping, fishing, and sipping a spicy margarita!

Want to hang out? Find Lena on Tiktok or IG or join her Facebook reader group!

Made in the USA
Columbia, SC
03 October 2022